KENECHI UDOGU is a Nigerian-born, London-based writer and architect. *Augmented* won the Imagined Futures Prize for young adult eco science fiction. She was Highly Commended in the FAB Prize and a runner up for the Writers and Artists Yearbook Your Next Obsession in YA Fiction Competition. Kenechi is an alumna of the HarperCollins Author Academy and the All Stories mentorship programme. She was longlisted for the Commonwealth Short Story Prize, and her sci-fi short story was published in *Dark Matter Magazine*.

'**An exciting new voice** in science fiction.'
The Bookseller

'**Brilliant** . . . Equal parts cli-fi thriller,
laugh-out-loud coming of age story and
heart-pounding action-adventure.'
Esmie Jikiemi-Pearson, author of *The Principle of Moments*

'**I cannot get the story out of my head**.'
Kathryn Evans, author of *Beauty Sleep*

'So many twi
David Fen

'I co
S. A. C

'A **great** story, with wonderful world-building.'
Kathryn Clark, author of *Things I Learned While I Was Dead*

To my family, for giving me the confidence to believe in myself and telling me it's okay to dream big.

First published in 2025
by Faber and Faber Limited
The Bindery, 51 Hatton Garden
London, EC1N 8HN
faber.co.uk

Typeset in Plantin by M Rules
Printed and bound by CPI Group (UK) Ltd, Croydon, CR0 4YY

All rights reserved
© Kenechi Udogu, 2025

The right of Kenechi Udogu to be identified as author
of this work has been asserted in accordance with Section 77
of the Copyrights, Designs and Patents Act 1988

A CIP record for this book
is available from the British Library

ISBN 978-0-571-38584-3

Printed and bound in the UK on FSC® certified paper in line with our continuing
commitment to ethical business practices, sustainability and the environment.
For further information see faber.co.uk/environmental-policy

Our authorised representative in the EU for product safety is
Easy Access System Europe, Mustamäe tee 50, 10621 Tallinn, Estonia
gpsr.requests@easproject.com

1 3 5 7 9 10 8 6 4 2

AUGMENTED

KENECHI UDOGU

faber

CHAPTER ONE

Augmentation Day
Hyde Park Biodome, London

Channel 6289X: 'What the hell is happening? How is she doing that?'

Channel 5168X: 'I don't know, but we have to stop her or there'll be nothing left to save.'

Channel 6289X: 'How exactly do we do that?'

Channel 5168X: 'We have to break the sync.'

Channel 6289X: 'No, it's too soon, it could kill her.'

Channel 5168X: 'Would you rather she brings it all down? We have to try.'

Channel 5168X: 'Are you still there?'

Channel 6289X: 'I'm thinking.'

Channel 5168X: 'While you take your time doing that, I'll go ahead and start programming the disconnection.'

Channel 6289X: 'Wait!'

Channel 5168X: 'We don't have time for this.'

Channel 6289X: 'Okay, fine! Do it. Just promise me one thing.'

Channel 5168X: 'What?'

Channel 6289X: 'If she has to die, make it quick.'

CHAPTER TWO

133 days to Augmentation Day

'How long have you been with us now, Akaego?'

Three weeks, two days, eleven hours, and if I didn't think you'd frown on me checking the seconds, I'd tell you exactly how long.

'Three weeks, Mrs Miguel?' I wasn't sure why this came out as a question.

'I told you to call me Elaine.'

'Sorry, Mrs Miguel, I mean, Elaine.'

Shifting against the hard back of the chair, I kept my focus on a lopsided stain on the wall to her right.

'We knew the adjustment wasn't going to be easy so late into the academic year.' Mrs Miguel sighed. 'Nevertheless, we expected more from you to move the transition along.'

Her pause was so long, it could only be for effect. And it worked. I wriggled again, biting back the apology on the tip of my tongue.

'You understand why your transfer was necessary? You get what this means. Not just for our academy but for the city. For your family.'

'Yes.'

'So you'll try harder?'

'Yes, Elaine,' I replied, mentally patting myself on the back for remembering.

I kept my eyes on the stain to hide my nerves. There was no telling what information the data-streaming monocle sitting over her left eye was feeding back to her about my body language.

'The good of one . . .' Mrs Miguel's voice trailed off.

'Is the good of all,' I finished the mantra.

'I won't keep you from class any longer. Hopefully, our conversation won't be along the same lines when we review things in two weeks.'

I only realised I had been holding my breath when her office door shut and I felt the air gush out of me.

'You just have to do better,' I whispered, joining the sea of noisy students flowing through the wide corridor, hoping her words would fire up the sparks I'd been trying to get going.

Because I really wanted this to work. To prove to myself that coming here was the right decision. So Dad would see I wasn't wasting everyone's time making this huge change so close to Augmentation Day.

'Hey, Engineering.'

My feet stopped before my brain could scream at them to do the opposite. Even if I hadn't recognised the voice, a waft of mint and bergamot announced its owner. Sighing, I turned around.

Joon's pearly whites flashed at me. As usual, that

3

wasn't the only thing about him that was blinging. I was still struggling to adjust to the Academy of Music's no-uniform policy after having to wear a collared blouse and pressed trousers for the last three years. Joon's bejewelled face and colourfully streaked hair always reminded me I owned far too many greys in my wardrobe and didn't have enough piercings.

Definitely nowhere near enough piercings. Was that a new hole in his brow?

'Why don't you try using my name? Just once.' I thought he'd given me the nickname because he was too lazy to remember my actual name, but after a couple of weeks, it sort of felt like he was trying to remind me I didn't belong there.

'Why? No one else answers to Engineering. It's perfect.' A hand that should have been weighed down by the metal hugging its fingers waved me off.

I had to give him a pretty big F for originality with that one. I was still trying to work out if this was some sort of caveman attempt at flirting. It wasn't like Joon Bernard-Jeong was any less of a mouthful to say than Akaego Eke.

'There's no other Akaego either. I checked.'

He closed the almost non-existent distance between us. I crossed my arms, hoping the motion would mask the annoying weakness in my knees. It was difficult not to be affected by chiselled-jaw boys who had lashes longer than mine, even when this one was confusing the hell out of me.

'Someone could turn up next week.'

He said this like there was a real chance anyone else would show up as a mid-year intake when we both knew I was the first in nearly a decade.

'Joon, what do you want?' I asked, trying not to sound impatient.

He reached into his embroidered black and amber jacket, reminding me once again I really had to go shopping soon.

'You left this at your last class. Mr Peterson said you'd need it.'

'Oh. Thanks.'

The thin black box he extended had a silver treble clef debossed on its lid with the letters A and M below it. It was the same insignia on the black metal tags strapped to my wrist and Joon's – the academy's only mandatory item of clothing.

I must have dropped the box in my rush to meet Mrs Miguel. It still didn't make up for Joon not calling me by my name.

'I would have gone back for it if—'

Joon's exaggerated tutting cut me off. 'I have no idea how things were at your old school, but here, we stop after saying thanks. We have to find a way to loosen you up.'

'Thank you,' I repeated more firmly, before taking a step away from him.

'Hey, wait.'

It was the sharp note in his voice that stopped me.

I didn't need to check my slider to know I was pushing my luck with time.

'Listen, Elaine chewed my ear off earlier about how I've not done such a great job as your integration buddy. Apparently, you should be best mates with half the year by now.' He rolled his eyes. 'Help me make things right. Will you join me and the others at Rush—'

'I have catch-up classes—'

'I know your after-school schedule is packed, so I was thinking Friday night? My band is playing. It's a small gig, but the crowd is always fun.'

He must have mistaken my non-committal shrug for a yes because his smile wattage went up a notch. Why did everything about him always look so easy and perfect?

'Great! I'll send you the deets. Bring a friend.'

I would have asked a ton of questions on any other day, but I could do that via text, so I turned and dashed down the corridor. I kept my head down, occasionally bumping into people heading in the opposite direction. Some smiled when I yelled out an apology, even though I doubted they knew who I was. Yet another thing I had to remember to do more of if I wanted to give the impression I was settling in.

'On time today, Miss Eke? Well done.'

Ignoring Mr Ericsson's tone, I scurried to the space he had set up. At our first session, I had thought one good thing about having nobody else present was

6

that I could choose where I sat. The kit my stone-faced tutor positioned right at the front of the room sank that hope.

I unwound a scrunchie from my wrist and piled my box braids on the top of my head. Mr Ericsson loved turning the thermostat up, and my neck had been covered in rashes from the intensity of the heat after our last session. I figured he couldn't tell my skin was flushed by the end of the class. He probably just assumed my cheeks were always that dark.

'Did you open it?'

I nodded and pulled out the black box, silently thanking Joon.

'Are these really organic?' I asked, lifting the lid and placing the box between us.

It was his turn to nod as he picked out one of the contents with a pair of forceps. Raising the slightly wonky oval object, he pointed out the grooves on its light green coat, his watery eyes squinting from behind his glasses.

'Anything genetically modified is never as easily affected during growth,' he explained, returning it to the box and shutting the lid. 'These came from a vault at Kew. Only the Ministry of Agriculture has access to them. In my thirty years of teaching, we've only had the honour of six students receiving ten seeds for practice. Everyone else gets five at best.'

I hadn't known that. If these were the real deal, the academy was not playing. And I had left the box lying around like it meant nothing. I hoped that little fun fact would never get back to Mr Ericsson. Or Mrs Miguel, for that matter.

'They must value your potential. Let's hope they're not mistaken.'

Before there was time for the queasy feeling in my belly to take hold, he swiped a flat screen on the table between us, tilting it to himself.

'Can you tell me where we stopped last time?'

'Mechanoreceptors?'

It was a word I'd never heard until recently.

'Is that a question or an answer?'

I resisted the urge to make a face.

'We studied how sensory receptors for plant cells differ from other organisms.'

'And did you do the extra reading?'

The next few minutes were filled with me rattling off facts about the effects of external mechanical forces on plants at molecular, cellular and organ levels.

After spending years immersed in a world of codes, I had plenty of horticultural knowledge to catch up on before Augmentation Day if I wanted to help society grow more plants quickly.

'You're fed up of all this, aren't you?' Mr Ericsson must have sensed I was waning.

I took a second to consider if admitting it would result in some form of penalty.

'I was hoping the seeds meant we were moving on.'

'I get it. We've pushed you hard, but I really want you to graduate with the rest of your year in top form.'

Knowing he was right didn't make his words any more comforting.

'But if you promise not to tell anyone, we can do things a little differently.' Mr Ericsson's voice dipped conspiratorially. 'Just for today.'

Hang on, what now? I sat up straight.

Switching off his screen, he reached under the counter and brought out a clay pot filled with earth. There was no way the seedling sprouting out of it could have survived there with no light, so he must have been planning this all along. I was actually more intrigued by the enormous smile on his face than the plant. He was usually so short with me.

'Why did the debate about plant life's ability to detect sound waves go on for so long?' he asked when he pulled out a UV lamp and switched it on over the pot.

'Because the exact frequencies that cause the reactions had not been isolated.'

'Until Dr Mwangi's fortunate discovery. And since we no longer had forty to sixty years to develop the new forests we so desperately needed, it couldn't have come at a better time.'

His smile now a full grin, he pressed his thumb to the left side of his neck, just below his jaw. After a few seconds, he repeated the action. There was no indication anything had happened, but the action was one I was familiar with. All enhanced adults did it regularly, though the contact could be anywhere on their body.

'You've seen footage, but it's time to show you the process in real life.'

I leaned in.

'Bear in mind, this plant is not organic. If we used one of those—'

My slider chose that moment to vibrate loudly in my pocket. There was only one person who would try to reach me at that hour even though he was aware of my after-school schedule. Whatever Jaden had to say, it could wait.

'Sorry.'

Mr Ericsson didn't even raise a brow, already too into the moment. The first note that left his lips was barely audible, almost like he didn't want to let it out at all.

'Keep your focus on the plant, Miss Eke, not my mouth.'

'Sorry.'

Just before he let out the second sound, my tutor tapped his neck once more. This time, the surface of his skin hardened into a thumb-shaped bulge and flashed neon blue. I felt the hair on my arms rise with the release of the deep, rumbling note.

From the videos I'd been shown after the 'incident' at my old school, I knew what would follow, yet I couldn't hold in a gasp when the tiny seedling writhed.

'Bloody he—'

My body leaned forward even more, but I didn't get the rest of the words out because the plant stopped, as if deciding on its next move, before making up its mind and shooting towards the hollow sound of Mr Ericsson's voice.

CHAPTER THREE

133 days to Augmentation Day

Jaden: Operation Readmission.
Jaden: Proposal 27.
Jaden: Start saying your goodbyes, because
I've nailed it this time.

A lump lodged in my throat at the messages flashing on my slider when I finally checked it on the Tube journey home. The memory of the day Jaden instigated my escape plan came flooding back.

'Are you having a laugh?' was my best friend's response when he found out about my transfer from Hendon to the music school in Marylebone.

My reaction would have been the same if I hadn't been stunned into silence after our head teacher, Mr Kareem, called my parents into his office to share the news that turned my life around.

All because of the footage from the skills lab.

'Mate, believe me, I wish I was,' I had sighed, twisting one of my braids around my finger as I bit into a flaky crust. Jaden always shared his mum's veggie

12

patties with me. I was probably going to miss them almost as much as I'd miss him.

'You can barely carry a tune. You don't even sing when I'm blasting Broxxie, and nobody can resist coming in at his riffs. Nobody!'

To prove his point, he hummed the grime artist's most popular tune, bobbing his head along.

I scanned the buzzing cafeteria. Jaden's voice was more elevated than I would have liked in our not-so-remote corner, but nobody seemed to be paying attention to us. Same as always.

'It's not about my singing voice,' I whispered, trying to explain a concept I was still unsure of. 'It's not really about music at all. Something to do with sound wave vibration frequencies Mechanosimulators produce to make plants grow faster.'

'Don't get me started on that mouthful of a name,' he said, pointing an accusatory finger at me as if I had invented the word.

Back then, I hadn't sat through multiple lessons on mechanoreceptors, so I just shrugged.

'At least someone had the bright idea to shorten it to Mechsims,' I offered. 'Although it sort of makes us sound like androids.'

'You sound like you need as much convincing as I do.'

I looked away. I was actually excited about training to become a fully fledged Mechsim but not sure how to say that without making it seem like I was eager to leave him at the engineering academy. There were lots of memories there I was more than happy not to relive. Memories of things that made our friendship stronger but which nearly broke me.

'You said it yourself, music has never been my thing.'

Mr Kareem had assured us that accidental discoveries weren't unusual for Mechsims, but I knew most of the kids who were found this way actually cared about music. They wouldn't all have been aspiring artists, but music had some value in their lives. It didn't have any in mine.

Ever.

Dad had made sure of that.

'Your dad must be gutted,' Jaden continued in a more sombre tone, sensing my thoughts. 'He was really chuffed when you won that coding prize last year. It's hard to believe they want you to work on enhancing a new ability so close to Augmentation Day.'

That was what swayed me the most. Kids who turned sixteen had certain abilities surgically enhanced to ensure the survival of society. It was a huge deal, yet everyone seemed willing to let me leave the engineering academy even though I'd been top of my classes. Miss Tyler had been so certain of my future, she'd shown me the location where my targeted core function enhancer would be fitted a whole term ago: on the top-left side of my skull, the same place as hers.

But now more than ever, the possibility of accelerated

plant growth trumped anything I could offer with my coding skills. If there was even the slightest chance I was a Mechsim, no one was going to waste a full academic year wondering if the incident at the skills labs had been a fluke.

Jaden came to sit beside me, engulfing my body in his long arms. I inhaled sharply. All the time he was spending with his dumbbells was beginning to show on his biceps. If I didn't need to breathe so badly, I would have slipped in a compliment.

'Don't worry, your boy is one hundred per cent not letting you get hauled out of here,' he said when I finally twisted my way out of his grasp.

I clasped his hands, widening my eyes dramatically to indulge him.

'What's our plan? Stash me away in a bunker until after Augmentation Day? Hack my chip so they don't realise it's me coming to school here?'

'Whoa, slow down. Both solid ideas, but I'll have to think. All I know is you're not leaving without a fight.'

He hugged me again, only letting go when I pretended to ruffle his overly shiny afro. It was hard to believe he towered over me. We'd come a long way from the days when, at the age of ten, I'd suddenly shot up a foot taller than everyone in our year. After an entire term of being called Ladder Legs and Stilts, and getting tripped over so I could be the right height, a skinny boy I'd never spoken to decided to grow a spine on my behalf and came to my rescue with his feistier gob.

Jaden.

Now, as the train sped silently towards my destination, I scrolled to the last three messages, gulping to dislodge the lump in my throat. I'd known I would miss seeing his face every school day, but after six years of being friends with only him, the adjustment was more difficult than I'd imagined.

Jaden: How about smuggling you to a
  Freestakers zone?
Jaden: By the time they locate you, it'll be too
  late to find your frequency.
Jaden: They'll have to let you get Augmented
  with us instead.

He hadn't stopped sending me suggestions in the three weeks since I'd left the engineering academy. None of them were vaguely plausible, but at least they were entertaining.

Akaego: Eh, someone isn't taking this seriously.
Akaego: You suggested something similar
  last week.

An image of a melting brain flashed on my slider and I chuckled.

Akaego: Want to go out on Friday?
Akaego: Kids at my school are playing at Rush.

Joon hadn't sent any details yet, but I had no doubt he would. He struck me as the sort of person who would pester me for days if I didn't show up. There was no way I'd visit somewhere so out of my comfort zone without backup.

Jaden: Noooooo!
Jaden: Who is this and what have you done with
    Akaego?
Akaego: I'm just trying to blend in. I'll explain
    later.
Jaden: Don't worry, I've got your back.
Jaden: Always.

My slider pinged, two sets of numbers flashing on the screen.

Three minutes to my stop. Fifty-four degrees Celsius at destination.

I needed to set up my hydration suit. The extra hour at school had given the temperature time to dip, but not nearly enough. I pulled my visor over my face and clicked one of the buttons on my wrist, shivering slightly as a cool mist hit my skin. By the time I arrived at my stop, the suit's internal temperature was where it needed to be.

My slider pinged again when I stepped out at West

Finchley, but I didn't look at it. I had eight minutes to get from the Underground station to my front door. To any front door, actually. Any longer and a Grade Three suit was required, and those were reserved for outdoor workers.

I power-walked home past fenced-off, parched earth, where there used to be front gardens. I would have been lucky to spot the odd bird desperately trying to find shade amongst leafless, dried-out trees. There were only a handful of suited-up people walking just as fast as I was. This was more than in winter, when temperatures dropped so low that we were forced to stay home most days.

Standing in our front porch airlock, waiting for the temperature regulator to let me in, I noticed the light on our delivery receptacle blinking green. Nothing had been scheduled for the day when I checked earlier, so I pulled out my slider.

Still nothing.

Frowning, I reached into the slot and retrieved a small blue metal case. My frown deepened when I read the label. It was for me. I wasn't expecting anything.

'Mum, is the delivery log broken?' I yelled when the airlock let me push the door open. 'This isn't listed on it.'

I inhaled deeply, a smile curling my lips. There was nothing more welcoming than the aroma of fried plantain and spicy tomato stew after a long day at school. Ever since my transfer, Mum insisted on preparing meals from a selection of my favourite dishes. She'd had no complaints from me, although plantains were becoming trickier to find. There could come a day when they would be too expensive to grow, but I preferred living in denial until then.

I peeled off my suit, hanging it in the hallway as Clifford came up to me, gazing at the door and purring.

'Not today, Clifford,' I whispered in apology, bending to stroke him.

Dad always joked that Clifford would have been happier as a street cat back when having outdoor pets wasn't equivalent to pet murder. I was pretty certain we would all have been happier outside too.

'Not that I'm aware of.' Mum's answer came from her study. She always kept the door open to hear me. 'And good afternoon to you.'

I cringed slightly. 'Sorry, Mum.'

As I approached her study to greet her, I caught the tail end of a news broadcast. The wildfire raging outside Milton Keynes was finally under control, but people were being urged to remain cautious. I once asked Mum why she had the news on in the background when it was never good, and she'd shrugged, saying something about old habits dying hard.

'How was it today?' she asked, smiling, when I gave her a hug. She slipped off her monocle, shutting off the secure data she'd been working with to give me her full attention.

I plonked myself on to her desk, ignoring her

disapproving scowl. For the first time in weeks, watching the seedling move towards Mr Ericsson's voice, I'd felt a tug of hope that maybe, just maybe, I was capable of something so breathtakingly incredible.

'I got my practice seeds.'

If Mr Ericsson hadn't locked them away at school, I would have begged him to take them after my earlier forgetfulness.

'That's good. They must think you're making progress.'

I didn't have the heart to tell her it was standard procedure; I nodded instead.

'O ga adi mma.'

Twenty-two years of living in England hadn't robbed my mother of her slightly sing-song Nigerian accent, which became even more melodic when she switched to Igbo. Dad said he was grateful she'd been let into the country just before the government stopped granting work visas to outsiders, otherwise he would never have met her.

Speaking of which . . .

'Is Dad home?'

She shook her head, leaning back to stretch her limbs.

'They extended his time in the biodome.'

'Again?'

'It could mean they are close to a breakthrough.'

I was never sure exactly what Dad was working on, but I hoped she was right.

'Do you think he'll finally tell me why he's so upset?' My voice dropped.

The last time my father had spoken to me properly was weeks ago. Outside Mr Kareem's office, to be precise.

'He's not angry with you, Akaego. Give him time.'

'He knows I didn't ask for this. What else can I do?'

Mum rubbed the side of my arm. But I wasn't prepared to let it go this time. I was tired of feeling like I was being punished for a situation I had no control over. Dad had wanted me to work as a coder at the clinical research centre with him someday, but with climate conditions far from improving, he surely knew how important it was for me to switch my enhancement speciality.

'You believe me, don't you? I may have been humming or making some other sound without thinking, but I did not sing.' Despite my conviction I was doing the right thing, I didn't want Dad to think I'd deliberately gone out of my way to get noticed.

'I believe you, but the footage says otherwise.'

'There was no audio.' My arms flailed in frustration.

'Yes, but there was one constant in all of them.'

Me.

The experts hadn't drawn their conclusion from one incident. Or two. We had been shown five videos. Videos where nothing seemed to happen as I worked alone on Miss Tyler's extra credit project in the skills lab. It was only when the footage was sped up that things became interesting.

Only then did I notice the potted plants lining the windowsills.

'Just do your best, ada m,' Mum went on. 'That's all anyone is asking.'

Hanging my head, I bit back another protest. How could I tell her I wasn't sure my best would ever be good enough? She seemed so hopeful I could tap into the frequency they claimed I unknowingly projected to grow all those plants.

'Is it okay if I go to Rush on Friday with kids from school?' I asked, changing the subject.

'Of course.' The gleam in Mum's eyes was almost blinding. 'You're finally making friends?'

'Well, Jaden is coming along.'

'Always Jaden,' Mum clucked. 'Don't you know any girls?'

That settled it. I was not telling her who invited me out in the first place.

'Come on, Mum. His dad is in your prayer group. You were happy when we first started talking.'

'You were ten then, not sixteen. Have you seen how big that boy is now?'

I held in a sigh. Even if I told her Jaden was as interested in me as he was in a box of crackers, she was convinced every teenage boy had an agenda. Jaden was good-looking and intelligent and protective of me, but I had never seen him that way. I knew he felt the same, after a girl he fancied mistook us for a couple and he'd corrected her about our pseudo-sibling relationship.

Looking for something else to latch on to, I remembered the case in my pocket and pulled it out, shaking it by my ear.

'Looks like there's a fault with the delivery log.'

There had to be, since all drone deliveries were strictly scheduled to prevent airspace clutter. This case didn't even have a code scanner on its body.

I lifted the lid.

'Is this—'

'Don't touch it!' Mum shrieked, swatting my hand before I could reach the folded paper inside.

'Ow!' I dropped the box on the desk, rubbing the back of my hand. 'How am I supposed to read what it says?'

'You'll get your fingerprints on it.'

She had every right to be concerned. I was so surprised to see the sheet that I forgot to be cautious. The sender had bypassed our security system and gone out of their way to include a message on an untrackable item. The last time I had seen paper outside of the archive collection at the school library was at the history museum a few years ago.

A knot tightened in my belly, but I couldn't tell if it was from excitement or dread.

'Do you think whoever sent something as rare as paper wouldn't wipe their prints?'

Mum didn't look convinced, so I let her grab two cooking tongs from the kitchen and watched with a mix of amusement and fascination as she used one to hold the paper in place while she lifted the fold with the other.

'What does it say?' I squinted to read the barely legible text scrawled on it.

'*Whatever happens,*' Mum read slowly, pausing to look at me, terror in her eyes, '*don't get Augmented.*'

CHAPTER FOUR

129 days to Augmentation Day

'You're the new Mechsim Joon keeps going on about,' a neon-pink-lipped girl yelled over the bass pounding out of the speakers above us.

It was unsettling having this new attention on me. Though, with only two other Mechsims in an academy of a thousand students, my ability wasn't exactly a secret. It didn't help that neither of them was in our current Augmentation year.

'Um, yeah,' I replied, bopping my head to the music, hoping it made me look as laid-back as everyone else at Rush. I prayed it was working, because relaxed was nowhere near how I felt after receiving that note.

'Does that mean you've found your frequency?' she continued.

'It's not that straightforward.' I frowned.

The skills lab footage convinced the admissions committee to take me in, but my first proper evaluation was in a month. Mr Ericsson and I had to identify my frequency first, and then I would need time to master projecting it. Most Mechsims were tested at a

25

younger age when they were discovered in their music programmes.

Although I told Jaden it didn't matter if I was musically gifted, I was totally freaked out about having zero experience with singing. What if I was deluding myself that I could get to the level I needed to be at before my evaluation?

'That's cutting it close with Augmentation Day, what, three months away?' Neon-pink-lipped girl clearly thought the same.

'Four, actually,' Jaden cut in with a lot more grit than my voice held. 'Don't worry, she's well aware.'

I squeezed his hand under the table. Getting off on the wrong foot with Joon's friends wasn't my intention, but I was glad Jaden was there for me. I was still too distracted by other recent events to engage in whatever this was with the girl. I hadn't paid too much attention to names when they were exchanged around the table.

'Are you okay?' Jaden leaned in so the others couldn't hear him. 'You seem more tense than usual.'

I hadn't told him about the note. It wasn't signed, but that didn't matter. I knew who it was from.

Freestakers.

The rebel group who made it their mission to stop pre-Augmentation Level Two kids from joining the workforce at a higher contribution status than non-specialist Level One kids. A group who believed the government's control on our lives was too restrictive.

Only a few weeks ago, we'd heard of four kids who

had been kidnapped and threatened by a faction in Liverpool. The thought sent a shudder through me. There hadn't been an explicit threat on the piece of paper, but it was worrying they knew where I lived.

Mum decided it was best not to let anyone know until we spoke to Dad.

I nodded at Jaden, throwing in a small smile to look convincing. 'I'm just a little nervous. I didn't realise it'd be this packed.'

Even with cool air pouring in through the overhead vents, a bead of sweat had formed above my upper lip. My eyes hadn't stopped darting around since we arrived at the converted warehouse in Hackney. The truth was, I'd been scanning every room I'd been in over the last few days.

Because anyone could have sent that warning.

Literally anyone.

Okay, that wasn't entirely true. Fresh paper wasn't easy to get, but with determination and the right resources, it was possible. Though I had to admit, Rush was filled with kids more likely to spend their credit on the syrupy drinks served at the bar.

I needed to relax. It was probably nothing more than a cruel prank. A cruel, expensive joke by someone bored out of their mind.

'She'll be fine with four months,' said a reassuring voice. It was the lanky blonde boy with horn-rimmed glasses sitting opposite me. We'd never spoken, but he always smiled when our eyes met during English classes. 'My cousin knows Mel Towne, the Mechsim in the year below. It only took her a few weeks to find her frequency.'

'And if she doesn't find it, she can always repeat the year, right?' the brunette beside Jaden said.

I tried not to grimace. They hadn't seen the eagerness in every adult's eyes when they heard I was potentially capable of growing a cluster of air-purifying trees in half the time it took for them to mature naturally. The unspoken expectation that failing was not an option.

Which made it even more baffling that the only person who seemed to want me to fail was Dad. He always pushed me to be the best at anything I tried my hand at. I couldn't understand what I was missing.

'I'm jealous you got to swap,' the brunette, Abigail, sighed. For some reason, hers was the only name I remembered. 'I wish I hadn't picked the piano when I decided between instruments in Year Six. I can't believe that's what I'll be stuck with after Augmentation.'

Nods were exchanged around the table.

'It would make sense if we could have two abilities enhanced,' the blonde boy agreed. 'My piano skills are almost as good as my clarinet, so why not have a little give?'

'I don't really mind having only one enhancement,' Abigail clarified. 'I just wish it didn't mean I'd be tied to that as a career path for the rest of my life.'

'I like their thinking,' Jaden whispered, turning to

me again. 'We could campaign to get you enhanced as a coder and a Mechsim. Proposal Twenty-Eight?'

With his brow scrunched up, he looked like he was seriously considering the possibility.

'But that defeats the aim of balance in the system.' The neon-pink-lipped girl shook her head. 'We each have to stick to one path.'

Abigail rolled her eyes before sipping thick blue liquid from her glass. 'Sure, Luna, I just don't see why the rest of us have to suffer because of other people's . . . inadequacies.'

'Are you serious?' Luna crossed her arms. 'You really want things to go back to how they were? When there was so much and yet never enough for everyone? When those only capable of being good at one thing were left jobless because others had multiple careers?'

The crooning of the jazz singer onstage couldn't compete with the silence that descended on our table. None of us had been born when the decision to enhance abilities was voted into law, but we had read about the skills inequality that nearly wrecked society after the climate crisis tipped over.

'Like that was the only problem with the world.'

Abigail said this so quietly it was possible only Jaden and I heard. And good thing as well, because Luna looked ready to have it out with anyone who challenged her.

Different schools of thought on how we came to be in our current societal state still got a lot of people riled up. It grew more heated if anyone brought up the mess we'd made of the climate. But one thing most of us accepted was that Augmentations ensured our survival. With limited resources, if people didn't contribute to the system in a quantifiable way, why should they expect to reap the benefits of society?

'How about you?' The blonde boy turned to Jaden, probably hoping to move things along. 'You're at the engineering academy, right? What have you decided on?'

'Software programming, like Akaego.'

Jaden's expression dared him to say I was studying anything other than that. I nudged his knee under the table. As much as I wanted to smile, these were the kids to be in with at school. It felt good to be able to hang with them.

Abigail suddenly jumped to her feet, her eyes lighting up.

'They're on!' she screeched, applauding with her hands raised above her head.

We'd arrived early to bag seats with a decent view of the stage, but I'd chosen the only one backing it. I turned to find the jazz singer swapping places with the next band, all dressed in identical shiny shell suits. A lead singer I vaguely recognised, a guitarist I only knew from the poster Joon sent, and Joon, who was settling down behind a drum kit. He trailed his fingers along a string of green beads around his neck before waving at us.

'Come on, Sky Sailors!' Abigail yelled.

'Someone's a fan,' Jaden chuckled, voicing my thoughts.

'Trust me, you'll be screaming along after you hear them play,' Abigail insisted.

Only a minute in, I could tell she wasn't wrong. They were incredible, and this was coming from someone who didn't have a single music-streaming app on her slider. I could see where Joon's annoying confidence came from if this was him playing for fun.

'Bloody hell,' Jaden said after their third electrifying pop-rock song came to an end and the entire room went wild again. 'How is that sound coming out of such a tiny body? I think I'm in love.'

I knew he was referring to the lead singer. I was glad he was enjoying himself.

'Join the queue,' Abigail laughed when the blonde boy shot a hooded glance Jaden's way. 'Matt doesn't look like the sort, but he'll cut anyone who steps in on his girl.'

Jaden looked genuinely gutted, even though I doubted Matt would hurt anyone. I was relieved to finally know his name without asking him to repeat it. I was also surprised to find that, despite all my doubts, I was enjoying myself.

But my head shot up when a deep voice came over the speakers.

'This is our last one for the night. It's a little different because it's dedicated to someone.' Joon spoke into a mic positioned over his drums. 'It's her first time here, and honestly, I wasn't sure she'd show up. Thank you for joining us, Engineering.'

He sent a wink our way, and the rest of the group cheered, aware of who he was referring to.

'Engineering?'

Jaden shared my confused expression. I hadn't told him of Joon's nickname for me, but it didn't take a genius to figure it out. After the whole Ladder Legs nightmare in primary school, he was clearly wondering why we'd come to hang out with someone who called me anything other than my name. It didn't seem like a good time to explain, so I shrugged and turned to glare at Joon, who was pulling his mic closer.

Wait, was he actually going to—

'He sings too?'

Jaden's raised brow matched mine when a baritone velvety voice poured over us in the form of a ballad. I shouldn't have been so stunned Joon could sing since most kids at the academy seemed to possess multiple talents. And since he wasn't enhanced yet, singing and drumming at the same time for a gig wasn't breaking any rules.

'Is there something you're not telling me?' Jaden didn't bother hiding his annoyance at being in the dark. 'Sounds like Drummer Boy is putting moves on you.'

'It's nothing like that.' I forced a laugh. 'He's winding me up.'

Or he was taking his integration buddy role too far. Although a song dedication wasn't the sort of thing you did for an integration buddy. It was the silly sort of thing people did when they—

Nah, that couldn't be it. Joon couldn't be flirting when he couldn't even be bothered to say my name right. Still ... Jaden had turned into a completely different person last year when he tried to get Samantha Klein to notice him and decided rapping Broxxie lyrics to her in the cafeteria was a brilliant idea.

My slider vibrated. I checked the screen, grateful for the interruption.

Mum: Your father will be home tomorrow.

A sigh escaped my lips, and I shut my eyes. We could finally make a decision about the note. Reporting it to the authorities seemed like the next logical step, but doing that hadn't stopped the Liverpool kids from being taken.

'I know he's good, but it's not eye-shutting good,' Jaden hissed in my ear, snapping me back to the performance.

He didn't like feeling left out, but he was overreacting. Couldn't he see I was as blindsided by this as he was? I ignored him and focused on the stage until the last note left Joon's lips and the audience applauded. Jaden was still scowling when the band finished backstage and joined us.

'How was it?' the lead singer, Estrella, squealed before jumping into Matt's arms. Their outfits were identical, down to their horn-rimmed glasses. Definitely a couple.

Jaden's frown deepened. It was a struggle not to snap my fingers in his face to get him to lighten up. Maybe I should have given him a heads-up about the Engineering thing. I just didn't want to make it a big deal, knowing how protective of me he was.

'You smashed it, as always,' Abigail answered, since Matt's mouth was otherwise occupied. 'That last song was so good. It's new, right?'

'Yeah,' Joon replied, grinning like she'd just said he discovered oxygen. 'I'm glad it went down well, but I'm not sure it fits with the band's style.'

'So why did you sing it?' I heard Jaden mutter under his breath.

If Joon heard him, he didn't react. All he did was raise his hands and shoot a question to the group in his usual cheery tone. 'What does everyone want? Next round is on me.'

He was barely done speaking before the others began yelling their orders.

'Oi, let's pretend to be civilised,' Joon laughed. 'Any request not sent to my slider in ten seconds will be ignored. Ten, nine . . .'

Heads dropped as everyone obeyed. Jaden and I exchanged glances but didn't join in because we had no idea how he could afford to make that offer. Unless he had been given ration-waiving rights by the venue for performing.

'Want to give me a hand?' Joon turned to me.

Seeing this as my opportunity to ask about the song

without everyone listening in, I nodded. I felt Jaden's eyes boring into our backs as we began to squeeze our way towards the bar.

'I like your look tonight,' Joon said, leaning towards me as we positioned ourselves behind a row of people waiting by the bar.

I looked down at my outfit, wondering why I cared that he noticed I'd made an effort. My white T-shirt and black bottoms weren't particularly fancy, but fist-sized hoops dangled from my ears, and my braids were held up in one of Mum's blue-and-yellow-patterned adire wraps. There were weight restrictions on flights to reduce carbon emissions, but traditional prints were one of the few luxuries she had allowed herself when she left Nigeria.

'Thanks.' I returned his smile. 'Is it weird if I compliment you back? Because I really like this.'

Joon's fingers rose to his neck and touched the pale green beaded necklace. A single black stone sat in the middle of the loop, settling just above his collarbone. It was a simple piece, which was probably why it stood out against his other shiny jewellery.

'Well, if you're only saying it to be polite, then, yeah, it is a little weird.'

'No, I really was—'

'I'm just messing with you.' He chuckled. 'My halmeoni sent it to me when I was little. I used to get very sick, and jade stones are meant to ward off illness in Korean culture. It must have worked because I'm pretty solid these days. I only wear it for luck now.'

'That's where your name is from?'

He nodded. 'South Korean on my dad's side. And your name is Igbo, right?'

I wasn't sure why I was impressed he knew this.

'Yes, although my grandmother is half Welsh. On my dad's side. We almost never get to visit her with, you know . . .'

'I guess we have that in common. Wales feels about as far away as Korea right now.'

This was the longest conversation we'd had outside of him dutifully checking in on me between classes. For some reason, I found myself not wanting the queue to move along.

'So are you glad you came?' Joon asked, his voice lifting a little.

'Actually, I am,' I admitted. 'I'm not really into music, so I wasn't sure what to expect. Definitely not a song dedication. What was that about?' I laughed.

'Wait, back up. A Mechsim who isn't into music?' Joon looked surprised. 'There has to be a story there.'

I mentally kicked myself for forgetting that detail wasn't to be shared. Someone who clearly loved music as much as he did couldn't possibly understand.

'You have an amazing voice,' I deflected.

And now I sounded like a gushing fan. It was still better than telling the truth though. It was clear from his frown that he'd sussed what I was doing, but he was polite enough not to push.

36

'Thanks, but my future is in these babies.' He wriggled his fingers. 'They'll take me all the way to sold-out shows at Hyde Park Biodome.'

I couldn't see how he thought his drumming was better than his singing. There was definitely a story behind that decision too, but there was no way I could pry after my own dodge.

'Don't you ever wish you could do both?' I asked instead, recalling the group's conversation.

He shook his head. 'We need the Estrellas of the world to shine in what they're good at. And I really love what I do.'

We had reached the front of the queue, and he scanned his slider on the counter, lighting up its screen with the list of mocktails the group had chosen. It was impossible to miss the orange circle that flashed beside the credit approval.

I wasn't sure how I managed to keep my jaw from slacking. The club's strobe lighting must have affected my eyes because, as far as I was aware, everyone living in the London bio-boroughs was assigned Level One or Two status. As children of parents in either pay grade, our spending credits reflected this: a blue square for Level One or a yellow triangle for Level Two.

There were only two other pay grades. But why would Joon have higher clearance than the rest of us? Unless the orange circle was an indication that he'd received extra credit from the venue like I thought—

A crackling sound filled the air, followed closely by loud hissing, forcing a multitude of hands to spring up to cover ears.

'Flash bomb!' a high-pitched voice yelled from our left.

And then it was too late to do anything except watch a small, rotating silver disc rise quickly above the stage before exploding into a million flickers of bright light.

CHAPTER FIVE

129 days to Augmentation Day

It's only a flash bomb.

It's only a flash—

'Are you okay?' Joon's voice slammed into me through the myriad screams surrounding us.

Fear-filled. Panicked.

Just like I felt.

I had witnessed an attack like this only once, and it had been at a Tube station with plenty of Level Two Augmented adults around. The sort of targets the enhancement frequency disrupting device was meant to affect. Not a club full of kids. My heart pounded against my chest, all my senses waiting for a crackle of static in the air to follow.

But it didn't come.

'A Class Twelve Incident has occurred,' an automated recording boomed over the speakers, confirming what we knew. 'Remain calm and in your positions until further notice.'

'It's only a flash bomb.'

'Yes, it was, thank goodness. But are you okay?'

I didn't realise I had said the words out loud until I heard Joon's reply.

Forcing my eyes open, I blinked at the contrast from the earlier blinding brightness. It took a second for my brain to register I'd dropped to the floor along with everyone around us.

'I'm fine,' I lied. My ears were still ringing, but I was distracted by the fact that my face was cradled in his palms. His hands dropped quickly when I glanced at them with a frown.

'No, you're not.'

We both looked up to find Jaden towering over us, his chest heaving, the dazed look on his face revealing just how terrified he was. He must have jumped over a few people to get to the bar so quickly.

The first twinge of pain only came when I followed his pointing finger to a bloody gash near my wrist. I must have scraped it against the bar edge when I hit the floor.

I winced when Joon reached into his pocket and pressed a soft cloth to my skin.

'Thanks.'

'Is that even clean?' Jaden crouched between us, forcing Joon to shuffle away from me.

'Would you rather she bleeds out?'

Jaden huffed. We'd joked about how I couldn't trust any of the new kids until he'd personally vetted them, but this was not the time for illogical suspicions. Joon was clearly trying to help.

'Guys, seriously, I'm fine. It's not that deep.' I raised the cloth to show them the bleeding was already stopping, even though it now stung like hell. 'I'll get it cleaned properly once they let us move.'

We couldn't rush outside without hydration suits, so the evacuation protocol in a venue like this was to stay low until a marshal confirmed there was no imminent danger. If it really was only a flash bomb, it wouldn't be long until we were released. We had been body scanned when we came in, which meant the bomb had most likely been set up under the stage before we arrived.

When Jaden gave my shoulder a gentle squeeze, there was a slight tremble to his touch. I gave him a reassuring smile. He hadn't been caught up in anything like this before, and he was probably wondering when the buzzing in his ears would stop. I knew the shock would hit him even more later.

'This is ridiculous,' Joon said, shaking his head. 'Why would Freestakers set off a flash bomb in a place like this? There are hardly any enhanced people here.'

He wasn't alone in thinking this. Rush didn't seem like the kind of place the limelight-seeking anti-enhancement group targeted with their signature move. The purpose of the bombs wasn't to create panic, even though they did a great job of it. They set off an electromagnetic signal which temporarily shorted all enhancements in a fifty-metre radius.

'Maybe this wasn't about enhancements,' Jaden reasoned.

'Wait, you mean our sliders?'

No one was surprised to see red bars flashing across our screens. The other side effect of flash bombs was scrambling signals to electronic devices. Never for more than a few minutes; only enough time to make sure codes used to activate bombs were destroyed before they could be traced by the authorities.

'How are the others?' Joon asked, suddenly remembering his friends.

Jaden's cringe was one of someone who hadn't bothered to check on anyone before he dashed our way.

'I think they're fine,' he muttered unconvincingly.

He was probably right, unless someone had also bashed a limb against a table and needed Joon's hanky.

'Class Twelve Incident clearance confirmed,' another recorded message came through the speakers. 'Please approach the airlock in an orderly manner.'

On cue, Joon's slider buzzed.

'Signal's back.' He smiled with relief, swiping his screen. 'Hey, Matt, you okay?'

He hung up after confirming the others were fine. The band had already started packing up, and the bar lights were off to indicate service was over. It was unlikely there would be another attack, but most places shut down as a precaution after a security breach.

'I'm guessing that's all we're going to get,' I said.

'Above our information grade,' Joon snorted, offering me a hand up.

The orange circle flashed in my mind. Whatever

42

pay grade his parents were on didn't give him access to any knowledge they may have. The secrecy around Dad's work made that clear to me.

'I should get this cleaned.' I pointed towards the loos.

'I'll come with—'

'I'll take it from here.' Jaden didn't let Joon finish, jumping to his feet and steering me along by the elbow before I could protest.

'Hey,' I hissed at Jaden, freeing myself from his grip once we were out of Joon's line of sight. 'Why are you being like this?'

Surprise flashed on his face, like he hadn't realised how he'd been acting.

'Are you forgetting the flash bomb?'

'You were being territorial even before that.'

His exasperated huff matched his frown. 'You're letting him call you Engineering like it doesn't bother you. I know how triggering names are for you.'

'I don't think he means it that way,' I protested, even though I wasn't sure how Joon meant it. I didn't want to be the person who always crawled into a shell at what could easily be innocent banter. I shook my head when Joon's song pushed its way into my mind, making me wonder if there was more to all this.

'Come on, you asked me to look out for you. You're the one acting strange. I mean, what the hell are we doing here?' Jaden gestured around the room. 'This isn't you. So who are you trying to impress? Him?'

'I told you, I'm trying to blend in.' I said this slowly, as if it would make him understand better. 'I thought you were having fun, seeing as you were gushing over Estrella. Is this because she's with Matt?'

Jaden slapped a palm to his face. 'Sure, let's just say it's that, Akaego. I'll see you when you're done.'

With that, he took off towards the booth.

Someone fell in behind me, and I instinctively turned. I had to drop my gaze a few inches to meet the top of the girl's head, which was unusual for me since I was only five foot four. But that wasn't why I frowned.

Like all thermal-vacuum-controlled venues, Rush was kept at a constantly cooled temperature, but the chill didn't explain the girl's oversized black fedora and high-collared jacket. Unless her outfit was intended as some sort of artistic statement, like the boy I'd spotted earlier with a heavy stole draped across his shoulders.

'Why is he trying so hard? What's so special about her anyway?'

'Could be the Mechsim thing?'

I turned back sharply when the words echoed towards me from further up the line. I couldn't see the speakers, but I recognised the voices. Abigail and Luna.

'I like her,' a third voice added. Estrella.

'Yeah, she doesn't say a lot, but she seems all right.'

'Dedicating a song to her was a bit much.'

'He didn't even do that for Kasia when they dated,' Luna sighed.

'Aww, are you jealous?'

'Whatever. She's just a tad bit interesting because she's a Mechsim. Once he's done with this whole integration nonsense, we won't have to hang out with her any more.'

'Did he say that?' Abigail asked.

'Why else would he ask us to be nice to her? He probably has to report back to Mrs Miguel that she now has at least one friend.'

'It can't be easy changing schools mid-year,' Abigail said.

'It's not our problem she can't make friends on her own.'

Tears stung my eyes, and I held my breath to stop any sound escaping.

'What about that Jaden though? He's lush!' The voice that was possibly Estrella's purred, and they all laughed.

The queue moved forward, saving me from whatever else they had to share. I stared at the gap between me and the boy ahead. Jaden was right. What was I doing there? These weren't my people.

I glanced at my wrist. It wasn't bleeding, and I was sure I could hold my pee. I spun around, intending to grab Jaden and leave before the girls returned to the booth. The last thing I expected was for fedora girl to step in my way, raising her head to reveal dark brown eyes and high cheekbones set in a long, pale face.

'Excuse me, I need to—'

'Speak to your father.'

45

'I'm sorry, what?'

Her voice was deep and so low it was possible I'd misheard.

She glanced behind her, aware people were waiting for us to move on. Her words came out faster and even lower.

'Ask him about Deathsims.'

About what now?

'When he gets back tomorrow, ask him to tell you the truth.'

She backed away, and I reached out to stop her, but she disappeared behind a group of chattering boys heading to the main seating area.

What the actual—

My slider vibrated. Pulling it out was an automatic motion.

Mum: Why in Jesus's sweet name are you still
there?

Crap! She must have received the flash bomb alert. My location would have shown on her device after our signals returned.

Mum: Get home now!

CHAPTER SIX

128 days to Augmentation Day

D-E-A-T-H-S-I-M-S

I was supposed to be working on vocal warm-ups, but twelve hours after meeting fedora girl, I was entering the word into my search engine for what felt like the hundredth time. My fingers typed it out slowly.

There are no results for this entry.

Search results for Mechsims are displayed below.

If the girl's intention was to freak me out, it had worked. Nothing with the word *death* in it could be any good. Especially when it was clearly a play on the ability I was hoping to get enhanced. An enhancement I had just been warned to abandon.

But why warn me off something that had so many benefits?

I'd initially thought the value of Mechsims was in growing food crops. But in fact, food production had been one of the easier issues to tackle after plant life depleted. The authorities moved farming into thermally controlled biodomes, approving nearly all GM crops. Crops were needed for so much more than what came to our plates. Creating medicines, improving air quality and cooling the urban microclimate by pumping filtered air out of the oxygen-rich domes. There was still some hope the wider ecosystem could be slowly revived.

I tried again, this time separating the words. My screen filled with a few thousand entries.

Most of the topics were on either death, game simulations or both. Nothing that linked to Mechsims. Nothing that felt like it needed Dad to specifically spell out its meaning. Nothing that explained the urgency in the girl's eyes. I was going to have to wait for Dad to come home, or let it go. The girl could simply have been out in the heat for too long.

Except she had known when Dad was coming home.

How? The only explanation was a hack. Our delivery system had clearly been accessed to get the note to me. I couldn't rule out the chances of her being connected when both incidents seemed related to my ability.

Part of me wondered if I should tell Mum about her, but she was worried enough as it was, with the note and the bomb scare. If this was really nothing, I wanted to spare her the additional stress.

And yet, in spite of everything that happened at Rush, one thing in particular had rocked me: the moment I heard Joon's friends talking about me.

It felt worse knowing the reason they thought Joon was being so nice to me, the reason I was supposedly of any interest at all, was for something I had no control over.

48

Talking to Joon at the bar had been so easy, I'd thought we'd had a real connection, and now I wasn't sure.

Sighing, I closed the search page and checked my messages. My two-word apology to Jaden remained unanswered. He hadn't said much on our journey home, but he had given me a quick hug when he'd hopped off the train at Highgate. I had been too upset, and I guess too ashamed, to say anything in between.

Maybe I deserved his silence. I'd called him out for something he'd been right about.

Mum poked her head through my bedroom door. The smile on her face was all the information I needed.

'Dad's home?'

I raced out of the room. Dad stood by the hallway's airlock door, holding Clifford in his arms. If any of us could stake claim over our household feline, it would be Dad. He'd heard the marbled tabby's desperate meows as he walked past an abandoned house four years ago, then insisted on keeping him despite Mum's objections that we couldn't afford to feed a pet.

I didn't pause for a moment, forgetting all the awkwardness of the past few weeks and throwing myself at him, squashing the ball of fur between us.

'Whoa, Ego, let's not lose Clifford today,' Dad laughed, but he didn't let go until Clifford protested by clawing at our chests.

I was so happy to hear his laugh. Maybe, like Mum said, all he needed was time and he was over whatever it was that had been bothering him.

49

When I pulled back, the first thing I noticed was how exhausted Dad looked. He had a tendency to forget to eat when he got caught up in a new project. The light behind his hazel eyes was dim, and patches of dryness dotted his usually shiny brown skin. Mum never commented on his diet at the biodome, but I noticed she always cut down on her food portions to bump his up for the first few days after his return.

Maybe this wasn't the day to bombard him with questions.

'How is my Ego?' he asked, placing a hand on my cheek. Unlike Mum, he was Hendon born and bred, and his North London accent was as thick as mine. The only difference being that every breath he took had to pass through an electronic voice box in his throat, making his words come out with a slightly synthesised undertone.

I nodded, unable to find my words. He was acting . . . normal. There was so much I wanted to say, yet I didn't want anything to shatter this vibe.

'You should have dinner, Eloka,' Mum interrupted, probably sensing my struggle.

She always made moi-moi using red beans for his return day despite Dad not being a huge fan. I was pretty sure he hated all types of beans, but they were one of the highest protein sources grown in the agro-biodome at Richmond Park. He definitely needed that to get his strength back. His lab technician work wasn't particularly labour intensive, but it used up plenty of brainpower.

50

'Not yet,' he said, turning to me. 'Your mother told me about the delivery.'

I glanced at Mum. That was fast.

'It's okay, you need to eat first.' I forced a smile, even though I wanted to get the discussion over and done with.

He must really have been hungry because he nodded and headed for the kitchen. 'I won't be long.'

True to his word, half an hour later, we were sitting in our small living room with the blue metal case and offending piece of paper on the table between us.

'If the note was sent by Freestakers,' Mum said, 'the flash bomb last night could have been their next warning.'

Dad frowned. 'It sounds like something they'd do, although following up with an attack so soon seems off. We've barely had time to process the note.'

'What's a Deathsim?' I asked, seeing no point in easing into it.

'A what?'

'A girl approached me last night.' I glanced at Mum, hoping she would see the apology in my eyes for keeping it from her. Then I faced Dad. 'She said you would know what it meant.'

For a fraction of a second, something close to horror flashed in Dad's eyes. It vanished before I could be sure I'd not imagined it.

'Deathsim?' Mum turned to him too. 'Eloka, what's this about?'

51

'I have no idea.'

I could have sworn I heard a quiver in Dad's voice synthesiser. I was certain he knew more than he was letting on.

'Why would she say you had an explanation if you don't?'

Dad shook his head. 'Who knows? These people deal in terror. They are probably trying to frighten you by throwing the word *death* around. I don't think we should do anything for now.'

'So, you're saying we ignore this.' I pointed at the paper like they wouldn't know what I was referring to.

Dad looked pained, but he nodded.

'Reporting the note could aggravate the Freestakers. You haven't been tested. This will go away if it turns out you can't find your frequency.'

The frown on my face didn't shift. If the threat was real, it was possible I could still get kidnapped if I went back to coding. After all, stopping any type of enhancements was the rebel group's goal. But Dad's wait-and-see suggestion suited me.

As scary as the thought of being taken by Freestakers was, with only seventy-two active Mechsims in the country, there was too much at stake for me to stop before I had the evaluation to confirm I was one. I also had a feeling the authorities wouldn't let me back away, even if the choice was meant to be mine.

'You're going through a lot of changes as it is,' Dad continued. 'If anything else happens, I know someone in the Met we can speak to. But to be safe, I think you should limit your outings to school only.'

My jaw dropped.

'You're grounding me?' I heard my voice rise by a full octave.

'You make it sound like I'm punishing you.' Dad sighed.

'That's what it feels like.'

'Akaego, calm down.' Mum's hand settled on my arm. 'Your father is trying to protect you. I should have done the same after we got the note. This time it was a flash bomb; next time it could be something much worse.'

'But we don't even know if they're related.'

I wasn't sure why I was protesting so hard. It wasn't like I had a social life outside of occasional meetups with Jaden, and I wasn't exactly in his good books at the moment.

'We can't know for sure.'

'So the solution is grounding me until Augmentation Day? Great!' I crossed my arms before the rational side of my brain could stop me from reacting.

'Watch your tone, young lady,' Dad clucked. 'If nothing happens over the next few days, we can review the situation when I return.'

'You're going back already?' Mum beat me to it, heavy disappointment in her tone.

Dad generally worked from home for three weeks, then spent a week at the biodome tinkering away with his projects. It made sense for him to stay there instead of wasting time shuttling back and forth. He was rarely gone for over five days, although his last stint had been nearly ten.

His eyes shut. 'There's a test result I can't access remotely. I leave on Tuesday.'

Maybe it was good he was going away so soon. I was pretty sure I'd be furious with him for the next few days.

I went to my room and turned on the vocal slides video I should have tackled earlier. I couldn't shake the feeling Dad knew what a Deathsim was, and just wasn't saying. But I didn't have the luxury of time to dwell on it. My test was in a month, and I still wasn't comfortable as I aaayed and ooohed my way across the music scale. If I didn't try my best, I would never forgive myself if the test outcome was less than expected.

A few minutes into feeling rather silly and wondering if the noise I was producing sounded remotely human, a message popped up on my screen, pausing the video.

Jaden: Why exactly are you sorry?

I don't think I'd ever been happier to see his name. We didn't fight often, and when we did, I hated the way it made me feel. Especially when it was my fault.

Akaego: Because I should have listened to you.
Jaden: Something happened in the loos,
        didn't it?

54

Akaego: Maybe.

Jaden: Maybe?

Akaego: I don't really want to talk about it.

I watched the screen, wondering if Jaden had logged off.

Jaden: Proposal 29.

Akaego: I thought we were on 28.

Jaden: Are you forgetting what I said at Rush?

Akaego: Ah, of course. Go on.

Jaden: We make a special plea to the
chancellor.

Jaden: Once she sees your potential as a coder,
she has to let you come back to us.

That would actually not have been a terrible idea if I wanted to swap back to coding. Chancellor McKenzie was the highest-ranking official in the country, presiding over all the bio-boroughs. If anyone could overrule the decision, it would be her – though we knew there was little chance anyone would sacrifice the potential of a Mechsim for yet another coder.

But when our chat ended and the vocal slides sequence started up again, I had a small smile on my face as I opened my mouth and let out the sweetest sounding aaay of the day.

CHAPTER SEVEN

123 days to Augmentation Day

After a month at the Academy of Music, I thought I'd discovered all the things I liked about the place. The wash of daylight that poured through its amphitheatre's aerogel glass dome, the fact that it only took a minute to get to the airlock from the Tube station, and finding their cafeteria food wasn't half as bad as my last school's.

Now another item was added to the list.

Empty rehearsal rooms.

I could rush into a class seconds before the teacher arrived, then dash out the second the bell went to lurk in one of the unused rooms dotted around the building. Joon's friends didn't know I'd overheard them, but maintaining a poker face wasn't something I'd ever been good at. I wasn't sure how I'd react if one of them flashed me a fake smile and tried to make conversation. So I did what I did best and avoided them, including Joon. If he was only sticking around out of a sense of duty, I didn't want his pity. I didn't need a fake friendship with a timer on it.

The problem with all that scurrying was that I

was constantly glancing backwards to make sure they weren't around. So I shouldn't have been surprised when I walked right into Mrs Miguel on Thursday afternoon.

'Where are you rushing to?' she asked.

Crap!

'I'm sorry, Elaine, I was just heading to ... er ... English.'

Why was I so flustered? I hadn't told a lie.

She nodded, her expression softening. 'It's good I ran into you, or you into me. I was going to call you to my office later.'

That didn't sound good. It was still a week before our next fortnightly check-in. I racked my brain for what trouble I could possibly have landed myself in.

'Why?' I snapped, forgetting who I was speaking to.

'We're putting you in the Augmentation Day Pageant.' She was so excited, she appeared not to have noticed my rudeness.

It took a few seconds for her meaning to sink in. My heart began pounding. She was referring to the broadcasted showcase of top graduating students from all the bio-boroughs. Every Level Two worker had equal status, so having this display of talents was a chance for schools to attract future students to their programmes by celebrating their best.

'But I've still not been tested,' I heard myself say.

'Ericsson has confidence you'll be ready,' she carried on. 'And we can always withdraw you if things don't go as planned. But if your testing is successful, we must have you in the pageant.'

I stared at her, feeling naive for not realising they'd want to show me off. The thought of having so many eyes on me made me queasy. The last graduating Mechsim had left the academy over five years ago. My arrival had probably sent their marketing department into a frenzy of delight.

'We'll have you ready,' she repeated, perhaps more to reassure herself. 'There's a small reception for London-based participants at the mayor's residence this weekend where candidates for her summer internship will be announced. You've been put on the guest list. Other students will perform; you just need to show up and talk to the mayor about your progress.'

'Mayor Bernard?'

'I wasn't aware there was another,' she said, like I was being ridiculous. 'I hear she's taken an interest in your discovery. It should be an easy outing for you since you're already friends with her son.'

Wait. What—

My eyes widened as the penny dropped.

'Joon is the mayor's son?'

The clue was right there in his double-barrelled surname. And just like that, the orange circle made sense.

'Flying under the radar has always been one of his strengths.' Mrs Miguel smiled. 'I'll send details to your parents. I'm sure you'll do us all proud, Akaego. The good of one . . .'

I could tell her I was grounded, but I had a feeling attending the event trumped Dad's caution, so I responded like I was supposed to. 'Is the good of all.'

Everyone else in the corridor had melted away in the time we spoke, but once Mrs Miguel carried on past me, nodding at students who greeted her, the previously muted ambient noise cascaded over me.

What. Just. Happened?

'Engineering.'

My luck was clearly on holiday. How else was Joon standing in front of me after three days of successfully avoiding him? Weirdly, I felt a lightness in my chest as I took in his familiar easy grin.

The orange circle popped into my mind again. If I recalled correctly, Mayor Bernard was in the middle of her third five-year tenure, which meant Joon had lived most of his life on Level Four status. The air of nonchalance about him was probably because he truly didn't have as many cares in the world as the rest of us.

'Hi, Joon.'

His smile wavered a little at my unenthusiastic response.

'Look, I know you've been avoiding me.' He paused, sounding unsure when he went on. 'Something happened on Friday night, didn't it? Did someone say something?'

Wait, did he know what the girls had said?

My chest tightened when I spotted Matt and Estrella waiting to the side. Luckily, no Abigail or Luna in sight.

59

I didn't think I could handle a polite conversation with them around. I could tell Joon what had happened, but would he admit he felt sorry for me?

'I did what you asked, and Mrs Miguel seems happy I've settled in.' So happy, she'd added me to a showcase. 'Let's just go back to saying hi to each other and nothing more.'

Now he looked really confused. 'I thought we ... I don't know, connected the other night. Is this because of the flash bomb? Because I promise that wasn't me.' He laughed, even though I could see he was hurt.

I felt bad for leaving him hanging, but it was easier to cut ties now and not spend the rest of term wondering if he was being sincere.

'I have to get to class.'

'How about after school?'

'Extra classes.' I used my well-worn excuse.

'Haven't you heard? After-school activities have been cancelled.'

'What? Why?'

He showed me a yellow weather warning on his slider.

'Tonight's thunderstorm could hit early.'

I frowned. I needed every single lesson with Mr Ericsson now I'd found out I had to up my game. Yellow weather warnings were fairly predictable, but they sometimes escalated to amber status, which meant nobody took them lightly.

'I'd really like to clear up whatever this is,' Joon said,

'so if you change your mind, I'll hang around here after school. No pressure though.'

The smile he sent my way was small as he turned and walked off. Not that it would have made any difference, since I still planned on doing my best to avoid him. Now I was being forced to attend the reception at the weekend, I'd also have to figure out how not to bump into him in his own house.

I made my way towards the rear of the building once the last bell went. Using the gym exit gave me a better chance of leaving unseen. I wasn't expecting anyone to be there now that the weather warning had been pulled forward, but it looked like a session was coming to an end.

No one was allowed to enter when the gym was in use, but the group of kids and their coach weren't paying attention. There wasn't a single black metal wrist tag in sight, so I knew they must be outsiders. This wasn't unusual. As the only school in the area with an indoor multi-use games area, the academy opened its facilities to nearby Level One–status kids with non-specialist skills in lower-funded schools.

All I had to do was hide in a corner by the stands and slip out after they left. I pulled on my hydration suit as I waited for them to get going.

'Oi, Rosita, don't forget your bag,' someone called out.

I have no idea what made me look up at that moment, but when I did, I blinked twice. Was I seeing things? I had to be, because there was no way fedora girl was standing a few metres away from me, reaching down to grab the bag in question.

No bloody way!

But I could never forget that face. Not after she'd dropped a word I still hadn't been able to find the meaning of. Dad refused to say any more about it. Mr Ericsson's response when I'd asked about Deathsims had been a frown and a head shake, and I couldn't think of who else to go to.

Until now.

If anyone knew what the word meant, it would be this girl.

She pulled her helmet over her cropped black hair and moved away before I could catch what she said to her friends.

Once the group was suited up and the coach took a final headcount, the doors to the airlock opened. Another thought occurred to me: what if her being at my school wasn't a coincidence? What if she had been sent to spy on me? She must have watched me at Rush, and I'd had no idea. There was no way I was letting fedora girl just walk out now.

No, not fedora girl. Her name was Rosita.

Knowing that simple detail made me crave more.

Fastening my visor, I raced behind the stands and slid in beside the kids, keeping my head down. Setting suit temperatures was the distraction I needed to go unnoticed. I locked my eyes on Rosita's suit. I had already identified a marker on her left shoulder, a fraying patch of fabric. It wasn't much, but it was better than following the group blindly.

My next moment of panic was getting to the station and watching the group split up. As Rosita walked towards the southbound platforms, the ludicrousness of what I was doing hit me. I had no business heading in the opposite direction to home when there was a weather warning.

But Dad was holding out on me. Something in my gut couldn't let that go. If this was my chance to get the truth, I had to take it.

I hopped into her carriage just before the doors closed, placing a few bodies between us. Her group had slimmed to six, but they were as loud as twice that number. My stomach contracted when she lifted her visor; it meant we weren't getting off soon. I didn't dare take mine off, in case she turned towards me.

Her friends said goodbye over the next few stops, yet she sat back, flicking through her slider. Kids in Level One schools usually lived near their homes because those types of schools didn't vet people based on special skills, so where was she headed?

At last, she secured her visor. It was a lot harder not to be obvious when she jumped off at Clapham Common. I had never been this far south on my own, but there was no going back. I followed as closely as I could.

I always felt a twinge of sadness whenever I walked

past places which used to be parks. The common hadn't been included in the spaces to save under the Biodome Creation Scheme decades ago. The only survivors were a handful of bare, ancient trees which somehow still withstood frozen winters, oversaturated springs and scorching summers. I sometimes imagined what spaces like this would be like if I could help rejuvenate them. If the ability everyone believed I had would be able to provide more enclosed green leisure spaces for people to enjoy. But there was no time to think about that today.

Rosita was making her way down a narrow street with boarded-up brick houses now. There was no one else heading in that direction, so I stayed as far back as I could.

Ten minutes later, I was convinced she must be wearing a Grade Three suit. There was no other explanation for her quick pace when I had started to flag minutes earlier. Where the hell was she going amongst the never-ending rows of abandoned buildings?

I looked up when the first drop of water hit my visor. Damn. I had forgotten about the thunderstorm, but the darkened skies hadn't, suddenly letting loose a steady stream of rain. There were no flashes of light or rumbling sounds, which was good, at least. Shutting my eyes for a second, I welcomed the coolness the moisture brought with it.

They flew open when the first rock slammed against my helmet.

Hailstones?

And not just any hail. Fist-sized clumps of ice hit the ground around me. I had to get inside fast, but I looked ahead first.

Rosita was gone.

The hailstones were coming down hard now. Great, I was probably going to get crushed to death, and it had all been for nothing. I glanced around for signs of an open door and found none. And then someone grabbed the back of my suit, pulling me down with such force that I smacked my head against the wet pavement and everything went dark.

CHAPTER EIGHT

123 days to Augmentation Day

I was sure of two things before I opened my eyes: it was cooler, and I was dry. For a blissful moment, that was all that mattered, until a pair of hands began to feel their way up and down my torso. I threw my arms up to protect myself, opening my eyes.

'Not too fast; you hit your head.'

Rosita's voice was barely audible against the backdrop of rain hitting the walls. She was sitting next to me on the warped timber floor. Despite her warning, I shuffled away from her, turning my head around to take in our shelter as I wondered why the hell I'd thought it was a good idea to follow her.

My visor off, I could tell it was too warm to be a sealed space. Unsealed houses were usually fine for short periods of time; they just weren't habitable. I used to wonder why abandoned buildings hadn't all been knocked down, but Mum said the cost wasn't justifiable. This gave me hope we wouldn't be staying here for long.

'Carl said to apologise,' Rosita continued. 'He didn't mean to knock you out.'

I opened my mouth to ask who Carl was, but then I saw Rosita was holding my slider. She was swiping the screen and typing, which made no sense since it was locked.

'What are you doing?' I tried to grab the device, and she pulled away.

'Setting your location to the academy. I'm telling your mother you're stuck at school.' She carried on typing. 'Think she'll buy it?'

My shoulders tensed. She wouldn't be switching my location if she had nothing to hide. I hadn't told Mum my extra classes were cancelled. Someone needed to know where I was before Rosita and Carl, whoever he was, decided to do more than knock me out. And yet I found myself nodding. If I played along, maybe she'd be caught off guard when I made a dash for the door.

'I'll also let your boyfriend know you can't meet him. He sent a text.'

It took a moment for my brain to clock that she was referring to Joon. There was no point telling her we weren't even friends.

'Are you a coder?'

Based on her presence at our gym, Rosita was in a non-specialist school, but she'd unlocked my slider and altered my location at a speed that suggested she knew her way around tech. Most kids at my Level Two engineering academy wouldn't have been able to do that.

She snorted. 'Not everyone needs a label. I'm good at many things.'

But she was wrong. Labels gave every individual in society value and a sense of ownership over their ability. Ever since I'd taken the Level Two aptitude test before entering secondary school, I knew how I was going to contribute to society. I knew who I was going to become.

Until the video footage surfaced.

'We can stay here for another half an hour.' Rosita handed my slider to me. 'Hopefully, the hail will have stopped by then.'

I glanced at the slider and back at her. If she was returning it, did this mean I wasn't being held hostage?

She smirked. 'Don't worry, I'm not going to hurt you.' My fear must have been written all over my face.

I wasn't sure whether to believe her, but the sound of ice balls hitting the boarded-up windows wasn't easing, so it wasn't like I could run outside. My suit also needed time to cool because it had switched to power-saving mode after I passed out and Rosita lifted my visor.

We sat quietly, listening to the hail. If it came down long enough, our home rainwater-harvesting tanks would fill, giving the local atmospheric water generators a break. We needed as much water as we could get with the stretches of drought summer brought with it, although it was a different story when the rain carried on for days in spring and autumn. The flood barriers around the Thames hadn't done a great job of holding up in recent years.

Glancing at Rosita, I wondered why I didn't feel as panicked as before.

'You knew I followed you.'

Rosita grinned and nodded. 'I noticed you a while back and figured this was a great place to get rid of bodies.'

She threw her head back with laughter when my eyes flitted to the door.

'Calm down, I'm kidding.'

If she wasn't kidding, she was so small that I could probably take her. The issue was the mysterious Carl.

'So you weren't spying on me at school?' I had to be sure.

'We were never supposed to meet again. I only called for backup when I realised you weren't going to turn round.'

'I'm confused.' I sighed. 'A warning was sent to my house just before you gave me a cryptic message last Friday, and you expect me to believe all of this is purely coincidence?'

Rosita shrugged. 'My school uses your gym weekly, and we never see anyone because they don't let us out. If I'd known you'd be there, trust me, I would have made an effort to go unnoticed.'

She hadn't admitted to sending the note, but she hadn't asked what warning I was referring to, so maybe the incidents really were linked.

'Seeing as we're stuck here, are you going to tell me what a Deathsim is?' I wiped a line of sweat from my forehead, feeling my braids sticking to my neck. Hailstorm or not, we couldn't stay there much longer, and I needed answers.

'You still don't know?' Rosita frowned.

'Obviously. You're wrong about my dad knowing what it means.'

Her shoulders sagged. 'I can't be the one who speaks to you about this.'

'Why? You know what it means, right?'

Rosita glanced towards the door.

'It doesn't work that way. I'm just a messenger.'

'For Freestakers?'

When she raised her brow and looked at the door again, I understood. Someone was listening in. To my surprise, she shuffled closer and dropped her voice.

'I do what I'm told, and I move on. I'm not that high up the ladder.'

I looked at her. How could someone so young be involved with such a radical group? She looked about the same age as me.

'You can't drop a word like that on me and expect me to believe you don't know what it means,' I whispered back.

'All I can tell you is things could get worse if you get Augmented as a Mechsim.'

The emphasis she put on that last word made me ask my next question.

'But not if I'm enhanced as a coder?' The quiver in my voice only expressed a fraction of the panic I had been suppressing ever since Rosita approached me at Rush.

She hesitated before nodding.

Whatever this Deathsim thing was had to be pretty bad if Freestakers were trying to stop the enhancement of an ability with so much potential for good.

'And I'm just expected to believe you.'

'You're expected to believe your father. That's what I've been saying all along.'

'I could report you, you know. I have your name, and I could find out your school. You may call yourselves rebels, but what you guys do is basically terrorism. The authorities will get you to explain what this is about.'

I crossed my arms and gave her my fiercest glare. She pulled out her slider. She scrolled past dozens of files until she came to a video.

'What's this?' I asked as she turned the screen to me.

'Just watch.'

There was no sound to the footage, but I quickly realised it wasn't needed. The shot was from a camera positioned high up in a glass-walled room filled with rows of pots which had frail-looking sprouts of green emerging from dirt. A group of masked people came into view with tanks strapped to their backs and nozzles directed towards the pots.

Rosita swiped the screen and the same room showed up again. Not a single speck of green was in sight. The timestamp was two hours after the first video.

'When we set up greenhouses outside of their domes, they destroy them,' she said. 'Last week alone, we lost six plots just outside Milton Keynes. Not that you'll see the real reason in the media.'

I remembered the news about the recent fires in that area.

'By they, you mean . . .'

The look she cast my way made me feel silly. But she couldn't be right. Everyone knew Freestakers bad-mouthed the authorities. The masked crew hadn't even been wearing anything to identify them as government workers. This was taking it too far.

'How do you know these aren't doctored?'

'I've seen razed plots with my own eyes. It's the most heartbreaking thing you could imagine.'

'But why would anyone deliberately destroy plants? There aren't enough as it is.'

'It's simple – if you control the food supply, you control the people.'

I closed my eyes and shook my head. This sounded like Freestakers' propaganda. It made absolutely no sense for someone like me to train to grow food quickly if the authorities were going around destroying other people's efforts at doing the same, rebels or not.

'You still haven't said why.'

She sighed. 'Because we refuse to let them dictate how we live our lives.'

I'd never had cause to question the way the system worked. My household was Level Two, and I had been

72

earmarked for a Level Two future with my coding ability from an early age. I knew I would never go hungry or have to worry about where I would live. As cliché as it was, the good of one really was the good of all.

There were obviously people who didn't agree with this. People who didn't think it was fair to be stuck in Level One because their abilities didn't qualify for enhancements. Gym instructors, waiters, barbers and so many others. All worthy in their own way, just not on the list policymakers set up when the skills level system came into place. But there was sound logic behind the rules.

'We can create thermally controlled greenhouses using renewable energy off the grid,' Rosita explained when I remained silent, 'but no one gets licensed to set up farms outside of the domes without being Augmented. There are a whole lot of people who want to be self-sufficient and legally can't do anything about it.'

'You can't just go around doing whatever you want—'

She cut me off. 'What about our right to choose? People should still have that.'

'We destroyed the climate with that kind of thinking.'

I said this with certainty – not because it was what we were taught at school, but because there was no denying it. Letting everyone get on with their own agenda, not minding how their activities affected the natural environment, had caused the chaos that forced all the controlled measures that had brought us to this point.

'It still doesn't give them the right to stop people from trying to create equally sustainable societies which can function outside of theirs.'

The empty pots flashed into my mind. If the government really was responsible for that type of destruction, why wasn't it more widely known?

'Look, we aren't old enough to fully understand how these things work.'

Rosita scoffed. 'Justice doesn't care about age. My da—' She caught herself. 'Just know that the good of one is not always the good of all. You'd understand this if you'd seen some of the things I have.'

I wanted to ask what these things were that had convinced her to sign up with a group who thought it was okay to threaten and kidnap kids, but there was a tap on the door. I realised I could only hear the whoosh of wind outside. The hail must have stopped, or it had at least reduced to a level where we could make a dash for the station.

Rosita grabbed her slider off me and scrambled to her feet.

'Don't try following us. Carl may not be so lenient next time.' Before she walked out, she turned and added, 'And don't tell anyone about today.'

I wasn't sure why, but I had already decided I wasn't going to. What surprised me was Rosita seemed like a regular kid, not some violence-crazed fanatic I'd imagined Freestakers would be. She seemed sure Dad knew what a Deathsim was, and with my own doubts about his response, I couldn't help believing he did.

Pulling my visor on, I waited quietly with a hundred questions racing through my head before I set my suit to chill.

CHAPTER NINE

121 days to Augmentation Day

'Is that a robin?'

A dozen heads turned in the direction of the voice as a small redbreast sailed over our heads and perched on a leafy branch a few metres away.

'Squirrel!'

Our heads turned again in a synchronised motion.

'If you're going to point out every creature you see, we'll never go in,' Mrs Miguel said shortly, but she must have expected this reaction.

I'd never been in a biodome for anything other than a field trip, and I doubted others in our group had either. People who went on a regular basis were mostly workers who dealt with crop growth and any advancements to this: horticulturists, engineers, scientists, ground workers and security staff. The exception to this was the few who got to live in the domes, Level Four officials who had convinced everyone that those in high positions of authority needed to stay in the most secure locations.

All London biodomes were fully agricultural or

economically operational, except for Regent's Park, where we were now. The dome installers there had preserved as much plant and animal life as they could when they erected the climate-controlled enclosure over the expanse of the four hundred and ten acres. Most of its historic buildings had been converted to housing. They even managed to keep a good chunk of the zoo operational, although it wasn't open to the public.

We didn't need suits in the comfort-controlled space, so the first thing I noticed once I got past the airlock was the noise. Beautiful sounds we almost never heard outside the dome. A symphony of bird calls, bees buzzing, dogs barking. I wished Mum was here to experience it with me. If I could make a difference with my ability, it gave me joy knowing I could one day keep amazing spaces like this thriving. And, maybe, even bring abandoned spaces like Clapham Common back to what they used to be.

Someone sneezed, and I mumbled an automatic, 'Bless you.' Dad sometimes joked that we would have had to deal with millions of hay fever sufferers if there was enough plant life to sustain pollen in the air outside. He wasn't wrong, but a few sneezes wasn't a bad trade-off for sweet-smelling, clean air.

'Remember, we are here to make a good impression.' Mrs Miguel gestured towards the three-storey white stone mansion we stood outside. 'Feel free to let loose a little, but don't forget: your academy's reputation depends on you.'

'Yes, Elaine,' we chimed before following her towards the double doors.

At today's reception, other than performances, we were going to find out who had been selected to be part of the mayor's summer internship, a programme which gave students the opportunity to shadow the city's top official for a week. Only six people were chosen across all academies, which made it even more competitive.

Anyone who got through had the opportunity to advocate for schemes they were passionate about to be considered for implementation by the mayor. It also looked great on the record of those who had future political aspirations. I knew I couldn't be in the running because I was untested, but being here for the announcement was thrilling.

'Nice suit,' a familiar voice came from behind me when I crossed the threshold.

Luna stepped into view, a smile on her face as she looked me up and down. This was our first interaction since Rush, other than the nod we'd given each other at the biodome's airlock. My heart sank.

I couldn't tell if Luna was being sincere. With few options at such short notice, I had borrowed Mum's mauve ankara pantsuit, which was a little tight in the chest and hips but mostly fit. Luna wore a tailored green jumpsuit that made her look way more stylish than I felt.

I didn't get a chance to respond because we were moved further into the large foyer by another group behind us. A tingle of excitement ran through my body when I scanned the high-ceilinged space lit by a large glass chandelier hanging between a grand double staircase. I managed to stop my jaw from dropping at how stunning the space was. And this was just the lobby. I couldn't believe Joon got to live here.

We were ushered into a larger room with dozens of works of art hanging on the walls. Most were paintings, but there were also vibrant prints and what looked like an old coin collection. People from other schools were already mingling. I spotted two girls from the engineering academy. It was weird how that chapter of my life felt like it happened forever ago.

The event kicked off with a musical performance by a quartet from last year's Augmentation class. There were going to be displays by other academies, but from the smile on Mrs Miguel's face when the audience applauded, the reception could have ended that moment and she would have been content.

I snuck to a corner of the room, glancing around until my eyes stopped on a tall, red-haired woman, the only person who'd had the luxury of putting on a dress for the event. Having to wear hydration suits meant the only way anyone could get away with non-trouser attire was by changing into it at our destination.

Draped in a floor-sweeping, off-the-shoulder fuchsia number, Mayor Bernard stood in the middle of a cluster of eager faces, smiling and nodding with quiet confidence. I was aware I was staring, yet I couldn't take my eyes off her. Her face was familiar from the telly and articles I'd read about her for school, but it felt different being in the same room as the person who'd pretty much run the city for over a decade.

If I hadn't been told earlier, I wouldn't have clocked that Joon was related to the mayor because he mostly took after his Korean father. It was only when I watched her for a little longer that I noticed similarities in Joon's and his mother's bottom-heavy lips and square jawlines. There was also an unmissable warmth to their wide smiles.

'Is it okay if I join you?'

Joon appeared beside me as if he knew he was on my mind. The question lacked his usual burst of energy. In contrast to my ridiculously formal outfit, he was wearing a white T-shirt, navy jogging bottoms and mustard trainers. The only thing that made it look like he'd made an effort for the reception was his perfectly coiffed black hair.

'Looking for some luck tonight?'

I wanted to kick myself the second the words left my lips. Humour had seemed like a good way to avoid things feeling weird after ending our possibly fake friendship on Thursday. But why did it come out sounding a lot like flirting?

Joon's expression switched to one of confusion until he followed my gaze and settled on the jade beads around his neck. When he looked back up, his face lit. Probably because I hadn't told him to bugger off.

'Maybe.' He positioned himself so he was facing the room like I was.

'From what I can see, you don't need any more luck,' I carried on, unable to stop my mouth from running off.

'Don't get weird about it,' Joon clucked. 'Living here is the only way I could have been invited to this party. I'm not exactly the best drummer in the academy.'

At least he wasn't trying to pretend about his status. I still wasn't sure if I liked knowing the truth about who he was. It made me feel like I was meant to act differently.

'So what do you think?' he asked, crinkling his nose.

'It feels like I took a wrong turn and ended up in the twentieth century,' I admitted. 'I can't believe you actually get to live here.'

He shrugged and said nothing for a few seconds.

'Are you going to have this?' he asked, poking at the plate I was clutching to my chest.

I'd been so nervous about the reception, I'd barely eaten all day. I'd grabbed a canape off a waitress and hadn't got round to eating it.

'Not now you've touched it.'

Joon ignored my scowl and popped the grilled bread and tomatoes into his mouth.

'Don't worry, there's plenty more over there.'

I looked at the queue snaking its way around the food displayed on the other side of the room, and my tummy grumbled. I was contemplating if I should join the line or wait for another server to make their way to our corner when Joon pushed himself off the wall.

'Wait here, I have an idea.'

He disappeared into the crowd, and for no good reason I could think of, I waited until he returned and handed me a balled-up napkin. I eyed the cloth before unfolding it to reveal three croquettes. I would have asked what was in them, but the pain in my tummy tightened at the smell of the fried treat.

I wasn't expecting the explosion of flavours that hit me when I took a bite out of one and its gooey filling hit my tongue.

'What the hell is this?'

'Cheese,' Joon whispered like he'd just revealed it was liquid gold.

'I know what cheese tastes like. This isn't it. This is ...'

Moreish was probably the word I was looking for, but it didn't sound enough.

Panic flashed on his face. 'You're not lactose intolerant, are you?'

If I was, I wouldn't know. But if he was asking whether I could digest dairy, it could only mean one thing. My hand shot to my mouth.

'I know what you're thinking,' he continued in a low voice, 'but it's legal.'

It couldn't be. Animals weren't kept for food consumption any more. Not since a ban came into place to reduce carbon emissions long before I was

82

born. Growing food for livestock within the domes was classified as unsustainable. Anyone who wanted the taste of animal products had to opt for expensive cultured stuff.

'From cows at the zoo,' Joon explained. 'Technically, they aren't being kept for food, but we're sent fresh milk and cheese for events like this. My mother likes to serve special dishes to her friends.'

I glanced Mayor Bernard's way again as I finished off another croquette. It was worth finding out if I was lactose intolerant later for the goodness erupting in my mouth. It was also surprisingly easy to ignore the part of my brain that told me I shouldn't be okay with them getting away with this perk only because they were Level Four.

'What about your dad?' I looked around, trying to spot anyone who bore more of a resemblance to Joon than his mother. 'Is he here?'

'He's dead.'

Joon had to pat my back to help me cough out the piece of croquette that went down the wrong way. I had expected him to point at someone in the room, not hit me with that.

'I'm sorry,' was all I could offer when his hand returned to his side. I felt worse now, because everyone knew of the death of the mayor's husband in a Freestakers' attack a few years before she came into office. My brain still hadn't reconciled the fact that the same person was Joon's father.

'It's okay, it was a while back. I'm mostly over it.'

There was something in his voice that suggested he wasn't as okay with the loss as he wanted me to believe. So when his face twisted into a frown, my guard went up.

'What's wrong?' I asked, my expression mirroring his.

'You've got something on your—'

'There you are!' Mrs Miguel's squeal cut across the room, causing us to turn in her direction as she rushed over to us. 'I've been searching everywhere for you. Didn't I tell you the mayor would like to meet you?'

I remembered her mentioning the mayor's interest in my ability, but I'd forgotten the bit about talking to her.

'What am I supposed to say?' My voice carried the uncertainty I felt.

'Wipe your mouth,' she said with a note of irritation, 'we don't have much time before the other displays begin.'

She turned and made a beeline for the mayor, not waiting to see if I followed. I dusted crumbs from my lips, receiving a thumbs-up sign from Joon. I found myself hoping I'd run into him again before the event ended.

Mrs Miguel and I had to squeeze our way past dozens of people to reach the inside of the circle surrounding the mayor, where she appeared to be in the thick of a heated discussion. Mrs Miguel gave me a look that told me to stay quiet, as if I'd planned on doing otherwise.

Mayor Bernard was smiling at an elderly man who stood with his arms crossed. 'I didn't make the rules,' she said, 'but they were put in place to preserve our society, and they've done just that.'

'Not everything works as well as you keep suggesting, Patrice,' the man challenged. 'For one thing, if we truly live in a democratic state, you could start by looking into improving the appalling rights of non-status citizens.'

Mayor Bernard's smile remained, although it was no longer relaxed. I wasn't sure why, but that slight shift made me feel a little more nervous about meeting her.

'What choice was there after immigration was curbed and the two-child policy was implemented? Population growth was cut to stabilise the strain on our resources, but we still need the right skills to sustain the economy.'

The man shook his head. 'Yes, we've made many sacrifices as a collective; however, these people are paying a bitter price for their beliefs in individualism.'

He was only saying what people sometimes debated on telly, yet the air was charged as we waited for the mayor's response. I wouldn't have thought much of this exchange if my encounter with Rosita wasn't so recent. Was it possible he was referring to the crop destruction she'd shown me? Or were there other prices non-stats paid that were worse?

'Everyone has value, and everyone must contribute

85

as much as the next to gain from the system,' the mayor insisted. 'Wouldn't you agree, Akaego?'

She turned to me and I took a step backwards. I hadn't realised she'd seen me, or that she even knew who I was. It was only then I noticed the monocle perched over her left eye, which was probably sending her high-level information she needed to know about everyone in the room.

'I ... er ... I think ... yes. The good of one is the good of all.'

It wasn't my proudest moment, but Mayor Bernard's expression softened before she faced the man again.

'This isn't the time or place for this discussion. We are here to appreciate the achievement of these children. Kids like Akaego who sacrificed years of training as a coder to become enhanced as a Mechsim instead.'

All eyes turned to me. I wrung my hands behind my back, suddenly unsure what to do with them.

'She knows the value of her ability, and she is willing to contribute to society in the right way. That is the kind of selfless attitude we should expect when what is offered in return is a chance for all of us to survive this tragedy we inherited from past generations.'

The thing was, although I was honoured to accept my new role, it wasn't entirely selfless. Knowing everyone expected me to make this super-important switch meant I'd felt pressured into making my choice. I didn't think voicing that fact was going to change the effect her story had on her audience.

I was spared saying anything else because the lights dimmed, signalling the start of the next display. Everyone's attention shifted to the lit stage where three dancers had already started thrusting and pulling their bodies to the hypnotic sound of rain music.

A few seconds in, I felt a light tap on my shoulder and turned to find Joon with a finger placed to his lips. He motioned for me to follow. I was eager to escape before the performance ended, so I obeyed without question. We made our way out of the room, only stopping when we entered a courtyard garden. Domes were watered by overhead sprinklers synced to match seasons, so every plant was lush and green. I wasn't surprised to find others enjoying the rare chance to appreciate so many exquisite flowers in bloom, but my face fell.

Luna was out there laughing with some kids from school. I wished I hadn't come.

'Sorry about my mother,' Joon said. 'She shouldn't have put you on the spot like that. It's kind of what she does.'

'It's all so beautiful.' I pointed at the plants, hoping my cover sounded genuine since it wasn't completely a lie.

Joon beamed. 'I thought you might like it, especially with your area of expertise.'

If only he knew.

'And it's the perfect place to test your ability, isn't it?' Luna had crossed the courtyard to join us. Her smile could have been mistaken for innocent if I didn't know how she felt.

Joon waved her off with a laugh. 'Let's not get ahead of ourselves; you know Akaego hasn't been tested.'

'But you must be close to ready, right?' Luna frowned. 'Why not give us a taste?'

The others had started to draw in on us, having overheard her loud request.

'Luna . . .' Joon's voice took on a steely note.

'What? I don't think anyone here's seen a Mechsim in action, and since this is a night of displays . . .' Her voice trailed off suggestively.

It was the smugness in her voice that made me take a step towards her. It had only been a few days since she'd asked if I had found my frequency. This felt like a challenge. Despite all the logic running through my head, begging me to think clearly about my next move, I puffed out my chest.

'It's okay, Joon.' I couldn't tell if the eyes that turned to me were filled with disbelief or delight, because my focus was only on her. 'I'll do it.'

CHAPTER TEN

121 days to Augmentation Day

'Are you sure?' Joon asked, his brow arched. 'You don't have to.'

'Go on, do it,' someone else called.

Luna was right; they all wanted to witness something they'd never seen before. The truth was, even Mr Ericsson didn't think I was ready to channel my voice towards plants. He kept insisting I master techniques first. But the irrationality of my acceptance was worth it just for the look of surprise on Luna's face. I had studied the basics and more, and I had watched Mr Ericsson grow a seedling. I knew what was required. I was willing to give it a shot.

I glanced around the garden before walking to a bushy shrub.

'That's an antique rose.' Joon's voice held a note of warning. 'It only flowers once a year. You might want to try something easier.'

I had a feeling if I looked over at Luna, she would be expecting me to back away, but there was one advantage of sticking with the rose: I could fall back on Joon's explanation if this failed.

89

'It's okay,' I repeated, sending a small smile of gratitude his way.

Closing my eyes, I silently offered up a plea to the heavens and tried to recall all I'd been studying. As well as working on finding my frequency, I'd learnt about different plant species. Until recently, I would never have thought conifers and citrus responded differently to stimuli or that mature plants reacted slower than seedlings.

I felt someone come up behind me.

'Breathe,' Joon whispered.

I turned to him with a raised brow. I shut my eyes again and shook out my limbs, letting my mind search for the four frequencies Mr Ericsson's spectrum analyser identified as most likely to be effective for me. Someone sniggered when I blew a raspberry to loosen my lips, but I ignored them.

The first note came out louder than I'd expected. A flat sound, much like the rumble Mr Ericsson emitted when he'd shown me his skill. Straight away, I knew it wasn't right, although I couldn't tell why. I hadn't felt any particular way when Mr Ericsson marked it as noteworthy, but that had been weeks ago, before I'd learnt more ways to project my voice.

The second also felt off. Like it was catching in my throat, reluctant to escape into the world. I abandoned it without hesitation.

My head tilted backwards with the next note. This one had more of a melody to it, and I latched on to it.

Unlike the others, it felt light, like it wanted to roam free, like it wanted to be more than just air trapped within my body. The longer I let the sound wobble out of me, the more confident I felt that it was the one I needed to stabilise, so I did just that, turning it into a low hum. A hum that carried clear until there was nothing left in me to give.

'What was supposed to happen?' an unfamiliar voice asked after I had been silent for a few seconds.

When I opened my eyes, I wasn't surprised to see everyone crowded around. The frowns on their faces echoed the question.

Nothing had happened. Not even the tiniest change in the direction of a sprig.

'There's usually only meant to be a little movement,' Joon took it upon himself to explain. 'We probably didn't see anything because she isn't enhanced yet.'

I blinked back tears. I was grateful for his second attempt at saving me from embarrassment, but I was curious how he knew so much about Mechsims. Most students who weren't identified as one weren't burdened with learning about it as part of their curriculum.

'Of course.' Luna's smile edged towards a sneer.

I wanted to be upset with her, but I couldn't be. Her reservations were valid. I hadn't tried the fourth frequency, but that third one had felt so right, I didn't want to try another and risk disappointing myself even more. Because somewhere in the last few minutes, I'd realised I was doing this for myself. Not Luna or Joon or any of the strangers in the garden.

And I was worried this would prove what I'd feared all along. That the skills lab incident had been a massive fluke. That I was wasting everybody's time.

Applause erupted from inside the house, and everyone's attention moved in that direction. I stifled a sigh of relief when someone reminded Luna and some others that they had to prepare for their performance. Soon Joon and I were standing alone.

'Luna doesn't know when to stop sometimes,' he said. 'You didn't have to try to impress her.'

'She wasn't wrong.' I took a deep breath. 'I should be better at this by now, but how am I supposed to know what my frequency feels like when it's different for everyone? What if they've wasted all these resources trying to prove I'm something I'm not?'

I wasn't sure why I was saying this now, and to the mayor's son of all people, but I was glad the words were finally out. I must have looked pretty miserable because Joon shuffled so close to me, our arms nearly touched.

'One thing I know for sure is you're not going to find it if you stress about it,' he said quietly. 'You just have to let it come when it's ready to be found. You know it's in there, somewhere. That's all that matters.'

I smiled and mouthed a thank you, feeling a little less silly about my confession. Maybe that was why I'd voiced my doubts to him. Because I needed to be reassured by someone who wasn't relying on me to get the process right.

We might have stood staring at the flowerless plant for longer if my stomach hadn't chosen that moment to let out the loudest of gurgles. Joon snorted a laugh.

'Sounds like you are lactose intolerant after all.'

'Hey.' I cringed and punched his shoulder lightly before I could think not to. I probably shouldn't have eaten all three croquettes. 'You're the one who fed me real cheese. This is on you.'

I couldn't meet Joon's eye when he told me the way to the closest toilet. He did a good job of pretending not to hear the loud sounds my stomach continued to make. I was still so embarrassed when I came out of the toilet, I felt the need to keep my head down as I brushed past people. Which was why I completely missed the small waitress as she swung into the corridor. She was fast on her feet, managing to save her entire tray from spilling, except for one glass which tipped its red liquid contents over the front of my suit jacket.

'I'm so sorry, I—'

The words froze on my lips when I looked up at the person I was apologising to.

'Rosita?'

The name tag on her chest claimed she was Stacey, and an ash-blonde bob framed her face. A thick layer of make-up made her look older, and her nose seemed a little longer, but it was definitely her.

If I needed any more proof, the waitress quickly scanned the mostly empty corridor before grabbing my wrist and dragging me into an alcove.

'How is it you're everywhere I go?' I whispered fiercely. For someone I'd only met a week ago, I'd sure as hell bumped into her more times than I cared for. And now I knew she was working with Freestakers, her presence at the mayor's house, dressed in disguise, did nothing to ease my still-queasy stomach.

Rosita balanced the tray on her arm and handed me one of the napkins on it. 'Maybe the universe is trying to tell us something.'

She made a good point, but there was nothing comforting about the universe trying to get me caught talking to a rebel.

'You weren't on the guest list.'

'I was a late addition.' I didn't bother asking how she had access to the list. 'Why are you here?' I wasn't sure I really wanted an answer, but I had to ask.

Rosita popped her head into the corridor before turning back to me. She pursed her lips as if she was weighing up something, and then she reached into her jacket pocket.

'You know what? I'm going to listen to the universe, and I think you should too.' She held out a black disc that fit in the palm of her hand. 'We were down one person, I prayed for help and you were delivered. Here, take this.'

When she thrust the device into my hand, the griping in my stomach was replaced by a hollow fear.

Flat and shiny, with a keypad made up of tiny buttons, it was like nothing I'd ever seen. I tapped a random button, and the entire surface lit up.

'Careful,' Rosita chided. 'You're meant to be good at coding, right?'

'Yes, but—'

'I need you to hold this when you're back in the reception room. The coding bit is in case you need to deactivate it.'

'Are you having a laugh?'

'Don't worry, it won't hurt anyone.' Rosita waved me off like she'd just handed me a glass from her tray. 'Think of this as a peaceful protest. I'll be in there with you. This just means I don't have to hand this over to . . . actually, the less you know, the better.'

It wasn't the answer I was looking for, but it told me she wasn't alone. I wasn't sure whether to be in awe of Rosita's activist spirit or to find a security guard and report her.

But there was no way I was going to get muddled in whatever this was.

I pushed the device back at her, shaking my head.

'No. You have to stop whatever this is before you get caught.'

Rosita huffed and held it out to me again, like I was the one being unreasonable.

'All you need to do is hold it until the end. You'll know when to get rid of it.' She was barely done winking at me before her expression switched to one of annoyance. 'Damn it, your boyfriend's here. Don't say anything to him about this, okay?'

Rosita stepped forward, making a show of mopping up my jacket before she shoved the disc into my pocket. I didn't have to look into the corridor to know who she meant. Joon drew closer with a frown. I hoped I imagined his eyes dropping to my pocket. I didn't think he could have seen what Rosita did from that angle.

'What happened?' Joon asked, his gaze flitting between me and Rosita, who was doing a good job of turning her face away from him.

This was my chance to show him the disc and call security on all the Freestakers who had found their way in there.

'It's my fault,' I heard myself say. 'I wasn't looking where I was going.'

As much as I wanted to rat her out, what if he didn't believe I wasn't a willing part of the mission? If there were cameras in the corridor, security would see that instead of raising the alarm right away, I'd had a few minutes of conversation with the rebel I was reporting. That would be suspicious enough.

No, I would find somewhere without a camera to lose the device before whatever Rosita hoped would happen took place.

Joon's frown deepened as he took in the dark blotch setting into the mauve fabric.

'Come with me. I'll get you one of Mum's tops to change into.'

'You don't have to do that,' I objected, watching Rosita head towards the reception room. I didn't know what the deactivation code was or what the device did, and I had missed my moment to find out. I was bricking it, but I had to trust she was true to her word and no one would get hurt.

'Would you rather walk around like that? The laundry room is just round the corner.'

I looked down at myself. The stain was pretty bad.

'Don't worry, you can give it back on Monday,' Joon said, taking my silence as an answer.

The laundry was as massive as every other room in the house, and I waited by the door while Joon rummaged around. I settled on a black T-shirt because everything else was much too heavily patterned to go with my ankara trousers. It was clear where Joon got his fashion sense from.

'I'll get your jacket cleaned for you,' Joon said before stepping outside. 'Mum likes to get her internship announcement in at the middle of these events before people get bored, so you'll have to hurry or we'll miss it.'

I swapped tops quickly, moving the disc from my pocket and sliding it between a stack of clothes to the side. Joon came back in, and I handed him my jacket.

I froze when he moved towards the section where I'd hidden the device. Of course I had to have chosen the dirty pile. Why didn't I think of placing it in a cupboard or anywhere else? He plunked the jacket on top of the

97

clothes, and I watched in horror as the disc fell out, clanking noisily to the floor.

'Is this yours?' Joon bent to pick it up, turning it around.

I should have said no. If the room had no cameras in it, I would be scot-free. He would hand it over to security and they'd take it from there. But I panicked.

My hand shot out and snatched the device.

'Must have fallen out of my jacket.'

Transferring the disc to my trouser pocket, I heaved a silent sigh when he didn't ask what it was. Joon made a beeline for the reception room. I had no choice but to rush after him, my heart pounding as we entered.

I paused by the door, wondering if there were any blind spots I could position myself in to discard the disc. There had to be cameras dotted around a place like this.

'Coming?' Joon turned when he realised I wasn't behind him.

I nodded and caught up with him just as the mayor walked on to the stage, taking in our applause. The irony was I had spent all week avoiding Joon and now spent all evening glued to his side for one reason or another.

'First of all, I'd like to thank everyone for joining us in celebrating our incredibly talented youth.' Mayor Bernard didn't need a microphone for her voice to carry. 'The high standard we have seen tonight gives me confidence that they will excel after their enhancements, helping us maintain our strong and sustainable economy.'

As she spoke, I kept my eyes peeled for Rosita. When I spotted her, I was surprised at how at ease she looked, posing with her empty tray in a corner when my heart felt like it was beating out of my chest.

'And now, for the names you've all been waiting for.' Mayor Bernard's hand rose to adjust her monocle. 'Mar—'

A rattling sound cut her off at the same instant I felt a vibration in my pocket. Unlike the familiar tremor of my slider, this was like an electrical current passing through me.

What happened next left our mouths hanging open. Every single metal item of cutlery on the serving table floated into the air in unison before swooping across the room to hover over the stage. In a flash, they split into smaller groups, then divided again, organising themselves into what was beginning to look like letters.

M
U
R
D
E
R
E
R
S

'Murderers!' Someone shouted the word as if we couldn't all see it.

The pulsing in my pocket stopped, and all the cutlery fell to the ground. Which wouldn't have been an issue if the mayor hadn't been standing right beneath it.

'Mum,' Joon yelled, diving forward.

We were so far into the crowd, he would have been too late to reach her in time. Fortunately, someone else sensed the danger and dragged the mayor off the stage just before the first fork prong dug into the raised floor.

The intensity of screams that followed was the same as at Rush. As my body was forced towards the exit, all that kept running through my mind was Rosita's promise that no one would get hurt. Was the mayor no one to her?

I looked for Rosita, but she was gone. Of course.

I pulled the disc out and wiped it with the mayor's shirt, praying all my prints rubbed off. Then I let it fall to the floor, making sure not to look down as I crushed it with my heel.

I couldn't see Joon, and I hoped he had been bundled away to safety. If anything bad happened to him, I would never forgive myself for holding on to the device that made this possible.

We were finally let out of the biodome in batches over an hour later, after a thorough body scan and manual check of every device everyone had. I didn't stop looking over my shoulder. I must have been out of my mind to keep quiet about Rosita. If the mayor was hurt, it was going to be even harder to untangle myself from this mess. What if someone had seen me?

I jumped when my slider vibrated in my pocket, the sensation of the detonator still too recent a memory.

Joon: I know what you did.

CHAPTER ELEVEN

119 days to Augmentation Day

'You look rough.'

Joon stood across from me in the empty practice room we'd arranged to meet in at lunchtime on Monday. Mum's jacket lay on the desk beside the mayor's shirt, a not-so-subtle reminder of why we were there.

I couldn't take offence. In the time since I'd received his message, bags and dark circles had been fighting for space under my eyes. My guilty conscience hadn't been helped by Pastor Ayo's Sunday sermon on the consequences of dishonesty. Every time Mum nodded at each damning point he made during the virtual church service, I felt my soul cave in a little.

I didn't know if Joon had really sussed the situation or if he was just fishing. Still, I'd waited all weekend for a security team to bang on my door and drag me away to wherever they held rebels. The irrationally bold type who had the audacity to attack the mayor in her own house. Surely they'd suffer a worse fate than others. And I would be lumped in with them. To be fair, what I'd done had also been pretty illogical. I just hadn't known how else to react in the moment.

The attack was all over the news.

Jaden: I heard things got exciting.
Jaden: Hope you're okay.

Seeing those words on Saturday, I suddenly knew I had to tell him everything. Dad's weirdness, the note, Rosita. This burden was too much to bear alone. Jaden always gave good advice when I was stuck. I should have talked to him earlier. But this wasn't the kind of thing to be revealed in a text or on a call. I had to convince Mum to unground me.

Being grounded was also the reason I couldn't meet Joon sooner to find out what he thought he knew. When no one showed up at the house by Monday, I allowed myself to hope he didn't have enough to go on.

'What do you think I did?' I asked now, shoving the jacket into my bag and trying to appear nonchalant. He hadn't exactly spelt it out, and if he knew what had happened, why hadn't he reported me?

Joon raised a brow. 'You wouldn't be here if you didn't believe I know something.'

I silently stared him down. He sighed and placed an object on the table. A fragment of something flat, black and shiny.

'We were standing together during the attack. Is this what I felt vibrating?'

I couldn't stop the gasp that slipped out. I thought I'd covered the moment when Joon saw the detonator in the laundry room. But if he was only basing his suspicions on finding the smashed device, maybe I still had a way out of this.

'Oh, you found it,' I said, praying I sounded more relieved than panicked.

When I reached for it, he held the bent disc over his head. I sighed and crossed my arms.

'What are you doing?'

Joon mirrored my stance. 'What is it?'

'It's a frequency synchroniser.'

I used to think I was bad at lying, but I had been outdoing myself lately.

'A what?'

Good, he didn't know what it meant. Although that bonus didn't stop my heart from hammering away.

'Something I was working on with Jaden. I was hoping it'd help me find my frequency faster. We've been trying a few things on our own to speed up the process.'

He frowned. 'And you brought it to the reception?'

This time, I rolled my eyes so it would seem I was getting fed up with the questioning. 'I was going to meet him later on. What did you think it was?'

He looked long and hard at what was left of the disc before shaking his head.

'I don't know. I saw you with that waitress, and something felt off. After the attack, I couldn't stop thinking about the vibration I'd felt.'

He was right on point, but I did my best to look offended. 'Wait, you thought I had something to do with the attack? You think I'm a *rebel*? I'm just a kid. And why would I be training so hard to get Augmented? And if you believed I was involved, why haven't you reported me?'

I really hoped he hadn't, or even mentioned it to one of his friends.

'I wanted to give you a chance to explain.'

'And now?'

Joon said nothing, his eyes searching my face.

'I believe you,' he said at last.

Swallowing a sigh of relief, I nodded. 'Thank you.'

'No, thank you.' Joon slumped on to a chair. 'I spent the last two days worried you were tied up in Freestakers nonsense. I'm relieved I was wrong.'

The desperation on Rosita's face when she showed me the video of the destroyed greenhouse was fresh in my memory. She certainly didn't believe what they fought for was nonsense.

But right now I was just grateful he'd bought my story.

'Can I have that back?' I pointed at the disc. I couldn't risk him changing his mind and handing it over to security.

'You don't mind if I hold on to it for a little longer, do you?'

'Actually, I do. It's the only prototype we built. We can salvage bits of it.'

He handed it to me and I quickly stuffed it in my bag. It was going in a bin the second I came across any.

I was about to head out to find one when Joon's face lit up.

'Oh, before I forget . . .' He found something on his slider and turned it to me.

A rose shrub in full bloom stared back at me. I frowned at the image for a second longer before it clicked.

'Bloody hell! Did I do that?'

'You must have.' Joon's excitement matched mine.

Open red petals looked ready to burst out of the screen, begging to be touched. I couldn't take my eyes off them.

Whoa! I had made something grow!

And the best part was, I remembered the exact tone that escaped my lips. Somewhere within that sound was my growth-activating frequency. The doubts gnawing away at me melted away in seconds.

I was going to be Augmented as a Mechsim. I was going to be able to make a difference to society in such an incredible way. But then I realised something.

'Hey, what's wrong?' Joon asked when my smile faded.

'It shouldn't have . . .'

I stopped, unwilling to voice the fact that something wasn't right. Once I left the garden, the plant's cells should have continued to be affected, but the most I would have expected would have been extra leaf or stem

106

growth. I wasn't Augmented, so even with organic roses, it should have taken a few weeks before anything so fully formed appeared.

'Shouldn't have what?' Joon urged.

'Nothing.' I wasn't sure if it was that much of an anomaly or if the plant's specific make-up could explain it. I would ask Mr Ericsson. 'It's pretty amazing.'

'Mum thinks so.' Joon grinned. 'She's buzzing.'

'She is?' For some reason, it hadn't clicked that anyone else would have seen the roses.

'She discovered it today before I left for school. I had to explain what happened on Saturday. It never flowers more than once a year. And even then, not this much.'

Knowing the mayor was impressed brought the smile back to my face. Maybe it was because of the way she'd spoken about me when she pulled me into her discussion. I didn't have to worry about not living up to what she'd said.

'Actually, this reminds me of something else,' I said, pulling out my slider and taking a shot of his screen. 'How come you know so much about Mechsims? Don't get me wrong, I was grateful for your help in the garden, but I am curious.'

'When I was younger, Mum tried checking if I could be like you. A lot of parents have the same idea once they find out their child is musical. The rarer the ability, the prouder they are, obviously.'

Joon wrinkled his nose, not doing much to hide his

resentment. I had never seen him with his mother, so I didn't know what kind of relationship they had. I kept quiet and let him carry on.

'I wasted a few months enrolled in evening classes. Sometimes I wonder if that's why I moved away from singing and got into drumming instead. I wasn't surprised when Mum suggested I volunteer to be your integration buddy.'

My eyes narrowed. 'She made you volunteer?'

'She always meets new Mechsims when they are discovered, before they even join the academy. I figured this was her way of checking in until she does the same with you.'

Mrs Miguel hadn't been kidding. The mayor really was interested in Mechsims. There was part of me that wanted to believe that Joon and I could be friends after all, but if his mum was counting on him to report back on the shiny new Mechsim, it didn't make me feel better about his attention.

Though I couldn't pretend I didn't like the way his light, minty scent lingered even after he walked away. And I didn't really mind the way he was looking at me now, intently, like I was—

'You've got a lash on your cheek.' Joon's head tilted.

I was thrown by the change of subject. When he raised his hand, a silent request for permission to touch me, I leaned in, holding my breath.

The door swung open behind us just as the tip of his finger met my skin.

My head jerked around to find Abigail standing by the door.

'Am I interrupting something?'

'Hey, Abs,' Joon called out, barely glancing her way.

I sprang up. Then checked myself. Why did I care what she thought? I hadn't done anything wrong.

'Hi, Abigail,' I said, ignoring her question and grabbing my bag. 'Bye, Joon.'

I rushed out before either of them could say anything more, praying Joon would come up with a good excuse to explain why we had been there. If he mentioned my jacket, what if he ended up blurting out something about the detonator?

I spent the rest of the school day waiting for it to end so I could ask Mr Ericsson about the roses. As one of few active Mechsims, he also had duties to carry out in the biodomes. This meant he wasn't at school unless he was teaching the younger Mechsims or for my after-school sessions.

I was ecstatic I'd found my frequency. As silly as it was, some of my happiness was in knowing I could use my voice to grow as many plantain trees as I could convince my future team to agree to. There was no way I was going to let my favourite food die out. Yet that joy was dampened by knowing the roses bloomed too fast. I hadn't come across that speed of growth in any of my readings. It didn't feel like something I should ignore.

'Akaego Eke, please report to my office.'

I glanced up when Mrs Miguel's voice resonated

through the corridor. School was over, and I was heading to see Mr Ericsson. I couldn't think of what would prompt a summons from the head teacher. Had Joon backtracked and said something to her?

No, I was sure he wouldn't. He'd looked sincere when he said he'd let it go. I turned and made my way to her office, determined to keep calm no matter what this was about.

When I walked in, Mrs Miguel's smile was the widest I had ever seen it.

She jumped up. 'There you are. How are you feeling?'

'Fine,' I said with a slight frown. Students who attended the reception had received multiple calls from her and the school counsellor to make sure we were okay. 'I'm sure everyone is still a little shocked by it all, but I'm all right.'

'Oh, I don't mean the attack.' She moved back to her desk and flipped her large screen around.

I didn't need to lean in to read the small text because the article's headline said it all.

Candidates for Mayor Bernard's summer internship programme, including new Mechsim, have been announced.

Below this were seven portraits, one of which was the unflattering shot taken of me the day I arrived at the Academy of Music.

'I'm on the programme?' I asked. I stared at my image, the news sinking in.

Mrs Miguel couldn't stop beaming. 'I received a

call from the mayor's office this morning. None of our students were on the original list of six, but the mayor requested your inclusion today. You must have made an impression.'

Not in the way Mrs Miguel was thinking. The roses did this. The thought made me giddy with delight for a second. I wasn't sure if they'd mentioned the roses to Mrs Miguel. She looked ready to explode with pride; the news that I'd found my frequency would probably push her over the edge. I decided to leave that moment for someone else to deal with.

'Since you're still catching up on your academics, we can't have you missing classes or your after-school sessions,' Mrs Miguel carried on, returning to her chair, 'so you'll be split from the rest of the group, who will attend the programme next week. We've agreed your days are to be scheduled for Saturdays over the next month instead.'

I tried to hide my frown. Unlike other candidates who'd known for months they were on a list of possibles, I'd had no time to consider being selected. With everything that happened at the weekend, I had almost forgotten about the warning note, but it pulsed in my mind now.

'What if I say no?'

The look Mrs Miguel gave me was incredulous. 'Why on earth would you turn this down?'

I couldn't tell her what I was afraid of. If I accepted my place on the programme, it was a clear show of defiance to the warning. If I joined the programme, what would the Freestakers do?

Mrs Miguel was waiting for my answer, so I put on a smile. I couldn't turn this down.

'I attend prayer group sessions on Saturdays with my mum, but I can miss a few. This is important.' As lame as it sounded, it was the only excuse I could think of as a cover for my question.

'Brilliant! Now let's get these consent forms sent over to your parents. The good of one . . .'

I shook her outstretched hand. 'Is the good of all.'

CHAPTER TWELVE

114 days to Augmentation Day

Regent's Park felt different. Or maybe it was me.

I sat in an automated electric cart on my own, heading for my first internship day with the mayor, my stomach in the tightest of knots. I hadn't been told what to expect from today, which made it all the more unnerving.

With my face plastered across television and slider screens, there was no way the Freestakers hadn't heard of this position. Mum was as concerned as me, but once again, she'd waited to hear what Dad thought of this new development.

'When you're there, don't say anything to draw attention to yourself,' he'd said after he rang and I told him why I thought I'd been selected. His time in the biodome had been extended until Saturday evening, and he wasn't keen on discussing things over a network that could be hacked.

'But it's just me at the session, Daddy.' I tried not to laugh at the ridiculousness of the request. 'I can't see how that will be possible.'

'Just make sure you say as little as you can,' he insisted. 'I'll explain why when I return. Please, don't mention the roses to anyone else.'

That ship had sailed. I'd asked Mr Ericsson about them after my meeting with Mrs Miguel. When I showed him the image, I expected him to share my fascination, but he looked confused.

'You're saying you did this?'

'I think so?' It came out as a question because, despite being confident it was me, I knew Mr Ericsson relied on properly documented information. One photo was not that.

His frown deepened. 'I can't take this as fact until we can measure the results in a controlled environment on your test day with approved Ministry of Agriculture equipment. This changes nothing with your training. We'll continue as scheduled and start channelling your voice next week.'

'Have you seen anything grow this quickly before?'

He shook his head. 'There may be records of working Mechsims achieving something this ... aggressive. I'll do some investigating.'

My attention was pulled back to the present when the cart took a turn into a familiar-looking driveway.

'It's at the house?' I inanely asked the empty vehicle when it became clear it was following the route we'd come through on Saturday. I'd assumed I would be at an office building within the park.

A straight-faced man with a monocle waited for me.

114

'Change of plan,' he explained, leading me to the door. 'There was a scheduling clash for refurbishment works at the office. Your sessions will take place here.'

Taking a deep breath, I forced myself to focus on the reason I was there. I was training as a Mechsim because it was for the good of all. I hadn't known it would lead to me attending the reception or being selected for this programme. I wasn't going to let Rosita and her friends' crimes stop me enjoying this moment.

I stepped in. With no horde of people as a buffer, the lobby seemed even larger than I remembered.

'Hey, Akaego.'

I was surprised to see Joon, and even more surprised that he'd actually used my name.

'You're here,' I said.

He came closer, his brow slightly raised. 'I live here, remember?'

I had given up on avoiding Joon at school. If he still held any suspicions about my involvement with Freestakers, evading him would only make it seem like I had something to hide. Which, to be fair, I did. But he didn't have to know that.

'I meant, you're not out and about doing something fun on a Saturday?'

Dressed in shorts, a T-shirt and house slippers, he didn't look like he was going anywhere outside the park.

'I'll let you in on a secret.' He leaned in to whisper with a small smile. 'I'm actually a slacker on weekends.'

115

'I know she's your friend, but you shouldn't be hogging my intern, Ki-Joon.'

We jumped at the mayor's voice, turning to find her standing by a side door with the monocle man behind her. Her tone had been stern, but her smile was warm. It matched the burnt-orange sundress she had on, paired with kitten heels. Although I'd been told to dress up for a promo shoot to be used for future programmes, my plain black collared blouse and trousers didn't measure up.

'It's only eight fifty-eight.' Joon smiled stiffly. 'I was saying hello before she gets sucked into the vortex.'

When his mother's eyes narrowed, Joon's sigh was low and heavy before he mouthed 'Good luck' to me and disappeared through another door.

'It's an honour to have someone with your talent on this programme.' Mayor Bernard motioned for me to join her at the bottom of the staircase for the photographs. 'Unfortunately, I only have four hours to spare today, but I'm sure we'll make good use of the time.'

Standing rigidly beside her, I couldn't stop thinking of how an untested Mechsim came to be interning with the most powerful person in London. If Luna hadn't goaded me that night, the mayor wouldn't have seen the product of my effort. Perhaps Luna deserved my thanks the next time I saw her. The thought lifted my lips.

'Is what I'm saying amusing?'

I cringed, realising I hadn't caught whatever the mayor had just said.

'I'm sorry, Mayor Bernard, I'm a little overwhelmed. Thank you for letting me take part.'

We had walked down a corridor and reached her study, and she opened the door with a chuckle.

'Trust me, the pleasure is all mine. The point of this internship is not only for students to get a glimpse into the running of my office. I benefit by keeping a finger on the pulse of our youths' interests. We have to work together to create a better future. This starts with understanding the talents of each graduating Augmentation year.'

She sat behind a wide desk and gestured for me to take the chair opposite her.

'Humour me for a second, Akaego. Shut your eyes.'

It seemed a little odd sitting in front of her with my eyes closed, but I obeyed.

'Picture the future.' Her words were slow and soothing. 'What do you want to accomplish with this amazing gift you've been given? It can be anything. The smallest of dreams, the most ambitious reach.'

No one had asked me about that before – what I wanted to achieve, not what I thought I was meant to achieve – yet it was easy to bring the vision into focus. Because I'd sometimes imagined it when I watched movies from the days before things began to die. Back when I'd never thought I could be a part of bringing it to life.

Green, lush spaces stretching for miles. Bees collecting nectar from a dizzying selection of flowers in bloom. Dogs barking as they jumped to catch thrown balls or Frisbees. Flocks of ducks waddling towards clear blue ponds to cool off. Squirrels scurrying up trees to gather nuts to hide. And butterflies. Lots and lots of butterflies.

Healthy domed places for everyone to enjoy all the time, not just those on Level Four.

Me and Mum and Dad having a picnic, Clifford able to run outside like he always wanted to. Well, not quite outside, but close enough.

When I opened my eyes, the mayor was grinning.

'Whatever you saw, we can make a reality. It will take time, but your ability will make huge changes possible. We are privileged to live in a society with so much talent to develop when other countries are still trying to figure out how to make their systems function half as well.'

She spoke with such confidence I returned her smile with a nod, certain I could accomplish anything I put my mind to with her at the helm. I felt myself relax.

'Are there any . . .' I couldn't think of the right word for a second, 'negative sides to this? To my ability?'

I didn't want to use the word *Deathsim*. If she was as interested in Mechsims as Joon said she was, the mayor might have heard the term. Though how would I explain how I'd heard it without revealing my conversation with Rosita?

'Negative?' She looked puzzled at the suggestion. 'What could be negative about an ability to grow plants quickly in this world we live in?'

'Nothing,' I agreed hurriedly. 'I just want to know if there could be any limitations to what we can achieve. I haven't come across anything in what I've studied so far.'

My enthusiasm was clearly the right response because her smile returned.

'Most countries would give up entire GDPs to find more people like you. Like anything in life, there will be challenges which I'm sure you'll discover and resolve along the way. That's what your more experienced counterparts will be there for.'

She leaned against her desk and tapped something into the screen on it.

'Now I'm interested in this vision of yours. What is it you want to deliver for society's advancement?'

She nodded as I told her my idea for creating dedicated health parks, interjecting with suggestions. Her encouragement filled me with so much hope, I was bursting to tell Mr Ericsson. With food and medicinal crop growth taking centre stage, I'd thought my plans would be seen as trivial. But with the mayor's endorsement, I was less worried they'd be brushed aside.

After that, monocle man entered the room and her real work for the day began. I sat quietly, making notes as she had rounds of on-screen meetings with different departments about policies I had no chance of understanding. It was impossible not to stifle a yawn or two, and I was relieved when she stood and stretched her limbs.

'I know that wasn't particularly thrilling,' she said as we took the final round of promo photos standing in front of her desk.

'It sounded very important.' I hoped she hadn't said that because she noticed my yawns.

'It's been a pleasure meeting you properly, Akaego.' She took my hand in hers, pressing it firmly. 'I look forward to hearing more about you over the next few weeks. You must have lunch before you leave. I'll have Joon grab you something from the kitchen.'

I hadn't thought I'd get to see Joon again, and I was surprised by the twitch in my stomach. More so because the feeling wasn't unpleasant. Not even a little bit.

'Can I see the roses?'

The request tumbled out when Joon met me in the lobby, after the mayor left for her appointment. I had been hoping to see the reason I'd been chosen, but asking the mayor didn't feel like the right use of our time together.

'The courtyard's been closed off all week.' Seeing the disappointment on my face, he added, 'But there's a window in the family room we may be able to get a view from.'

He motioned for me to follow, and we made our way to a section of the house that guests hadn't been allowed into for the reception.

'You know, I wasn't sure how to feel about having you here every weekend.'

I stopped walking, forcing him to do the same. 'Why?'

'You made it pretty clear you didn't want to hang around me after Rush.'

I had, but with everything that had happened, it felt like aeons ago. 'That was before the reception. And we've spoken since then.'

He resumed walking, shaking his head. 'Yeah, I just don't want to make assumptions about where things stand between us.'

I agreed. If I was going to see him at home over the next few weekends, it was probably not a bad thing to clear the air. 'I didn't want you spending time with me because your mum told you to.'

Joon frowned, like I was being absurd. 'Okay, fine, we probably wouldn't have spoken at all if I hadn't been assigned to you, but you know you're interesting enough on your own, right? No one is making me want to be friends with you.'

He stopped, opened a door and went in. The room we entered was smaller than most I'd been in, but it was clear where it got its name from.

Digital frames dotted almost every surface, displaying sequences of photos, many of which showed a younger Mayor Bernard and a grinning man with his arms around her. A few had a baby in them who slowly morphed into a toddler. In older photos of the child, the only parent present was the mayor. With so many intimate memories surrounding us, it felt like I wasn't supposed to be in there.

Joon moved to stand behind me when I stopped in front of a frame dedicated to his father.

'You look a lot like him,' I said.

He shrugged. 'I wish I remembered him, even a little.'

I kept quiet, not sure what to say.

'He was one of the scientists on shift that day at Crintex.' Joon's voice was so small, I barely heard him. 'Just someone doing his job. Nothing to do with the government that Freestakers keep claiming are oppressing them.'

There were no survivors from the chemical explosion at the aerogel manufacturing plant in Croydon thirteen years ago, the single largest loss of life in the bio-boroughs in sixty years. Nobody had been charged because the surveillance footage had been deleted remotely, yet it was widely accepted that the incident was an attack by Freestakers. They had sent threats to the company, which allegedly made inferior insulation for Level One-status buildings.

'I'm sorry, Joon,' I said, resisting an urge to place my arms around him. Remembering the part I'd played in last weekend's attack, one orchestrated by the group who took his father from him, words didn't feel like enough of an apology.

'It's okay.' He shrugged again. 'Mum went through

the worst of it. She said running for office after that was what held her together. Sometimes, I think being in this position is what still does.'

Now I thought of it, Mayor Bernard's re-election campaign a couple of years ago had been quite heavy on its policies to crack down on Freestakers. Her sentiments towards them made a lot of sense.

Joon shook his head. 'Anyway, you can see why I was concerned when I thought you were part of what happened the other day.'

I forced a smile, nodding.

'What do you have planned for the rest of the day?'

The switch caught me off guard, but I was grateful for it. He must have really wanted to move on from the subject, and I could understand why.

'I'm meeting up with Jaden.'

I'd fired off a message to him after the mayor said she was leaving early. If Mum thought I was at the park, I could get around my grounding and meet him before she got back from her prayer group.

'You two seem close.' There was a lift to Joon's voice that made me look at him. Was that his way of asking if there was more between me and Jaden?

'We are.' Even if it wasn't his intention, I found myself wanting to make things clear. 'He's like a brother.'

I would have liked a brother. One of the moves brought in to manage population growth was the sterilisation of every adult who reached their two-child quota. This could be hit with one or more partners or exceeded with one multiple birth, but that was it. People with no interest in kids were offered early procedures, and if someone decided to apply for a third, they could get a non-parent to sign off their allocation at no extra cost to the system.

My parents had tried for a second child. It wasn't something they'd talked to me about, but I'd grasped snippets from calls Mum had with her parents. I suspected they'd been hoping for a boy to pass on the Eke name because Dad's father made him promise not to have his legacy end as the first half of a hyphenated surname. It sounded medieval, but some traditions never die.

That was one of the reasons I wanted to make Mum and Dad proud. I was all they had. It felt like a lot sometimes.

'Ah, so that's why he's so protective.' Joon nodded, his lips curling up.

'Well, since you've stopped calling me Engineering, you won't have to find out how much more protective he can get.' Even though I was serious, I smiled, hoping to make my words sound less accusatory. I didn't want to ruin the good mood entirely.

'You really don't like it?' His look turned earnest.

I could have told him about the bullying that made me hate nicknames so much, but I didn't want to get into it. He didn't need to know what happened to stop being so unreasonable about it. I nodded.

124

'Okay.'

It was suddenly that easy? 'Okay?'

'I didn't realise it was that big a deal. Henceforth, you shall be known as Akaego of the house of Eke.'

I laughed when he pretended to read this declaration off an imaginary slider, and he grinned.

'Look at us.' He turned towards a window. 'We haven't checked for the roses.'

How had I forgotten about them? We went to the windows, but the area we'd stood at last Saturday was a little too far to the left for us to see. Not being able to see the flowers didn't dampen my spirits. I knew I had three more weekends ahead of me.

I left the biodome feeling much lighter than when I'd arrived. Meeting the mayor was meant to have been the highlight of my day. Yet, somehow, my brief time with Joon took that shine. There had been no one to pretend for in the family room. After last Saturday and today, if this was what he was really like, I decided to trust my gut about the boy I was warming to.

The thought of meeting Jaden to talk about the events of the past week made my mood even better as my train sped towards West Finchley. I got to the station early and went to some vending machines lining a side of the concourse, close enough to the escalators to see people coming up but not so exposed that I could be spotted by Mum if she came back. Meeting elsewhere would have been smarter, but changing my slider's location wasn't something I wanted to make a habit of.

125

After a couple of minutes, I sensed someone stop a few paces away, and looked up.

'Akaego.'

For a second, I wondered how this boy could possibly know who I was, and then I remembered all those internship articles. Great! I was now famous enough to be recognised by complete strangers. I wasn't entirely sure how I felt about that.

'I'm Carl.'

He carried on looking at me like his name should mean something. I frowned. And then it clicked.

'Carl? Carl from Clapham?'

He nodded. This was who had slammed me to the ground? This boy, who was probably only an inch taller than Rosita, and just as slender. I remembered how scared I had been during the storm, and nearly laughed.

'We have to talk.' His voice was as small as his build. 'Privately.'

There was a plea in his chestnut-brown eyes. Eyes that looked familiar even through his visor.

'You're Rosita's brother.'

He didn't respond.

'Wait, did she send you?' I glanced around, wondering what this would look like to anyone passing by. 'Do you know how much trouble I nearly got into last time?'

He frowned.

'I need your help,' he said instead of answering me.

I shook my head, starting to walk away. 'Nope, not happening.'

'Please,' he whispered, grabbing my suit sleeve. 'Just give me a minute, and then you can decide if you still want to leave.'

Carl had a strong grip for someone his size. I glanced towards the escalators for Jaden.

'You have ten seconds.'

He didn't waste any time. 'I need you to help me find my frequency.'

His frequency? That could only mean one thing.

Mechsims were so rare, it would be an amazing thing if he was one of us. But why ask for my help when there was a programme dedicated to doing exactly what he needed?

'What do you mean?'

'I think I'm a Mechsim, and I need your help to confirm it, but nobody else must know. Not even Rosita.' His voice dropped lower. 'Especially not Rosita.'

CHAPTER THIRTEEN

114 days to Augmentation Day

Following Carl down the escalator, I wondered what the hell I was doing. But every time he looked back to make sure I hadn't disappeared on him, I knew I couldn't have made any other decision. Mayor Bernard's words rang in my ears. Our ability could make huge changes possible. Why did he want to hide his?

The best place I could think of to talk was by the tracks. No one was going to pay attention to two kids chatting on a tunnel platform, and I didn't plan on staying long enough to look suspicious.

I texted Jaden an apology. I didn't know how long this would take, and meeting him later would clash with Mum's return. I hoped he hadn't reached the station. It would be hard to explain why I'd bumped him for a stranger.

'How did you know I'd be here?' I asked when the first train raced through the tunnel in front of us.

'I tapped into the tracker on your slider.'

I glared at him. Hearing that my data was easily accessible to someone who looked so young didn't do my nerves any good.

'What are you, ten?' Rosita's involvement with Freestakers didn't feel so impressive any more if they were letting people that age in.

Carl sighed, resting his head against the wall. 'I know what you're thinking, but ten isn't too young to be involved in this. I'm thirteen, anyway.'

I stared. Maybe he would look older with his helmet off, but I'd been generous thinking he was ten.

'You really think you're a Mechsim?' Another train came through, so I cut to the chase.

He nodded.

'And Rosita doesn't know?'

'Actually, she's the one who joked about it a few months ago because my mum's hydrangea keeps flowering out of season. She just doesn't know I took it seriously.'

'So why do you need me? Your school should be able to get you on a frequency testing programme.'

From the look he gave me, I could have said he should jump in front of the next train. 'They can't know about this. My family would never let me attend a Level Two academy.'

What was wrong with these people? Rosita definitely had the skills to become enhanced, and her brother likely did too. I couldn't understand what was so awful about achieving Level Two status. They could contribute so much more if they stopped trying to fight the system and worked with it.

'Your parents don't want you getting Augmented?' I tried making sense of it.

Carl stared at his hands. 'Staying on Level One exposes us to less risk of discovery. I won't be able to get tested officially, but if I can make things grow quickly, maybe the government won't be fast enough to destroy the greenhouses before we get a chance to harvest.'

It didn't sound like a bad idea. If his instincts were right, even without Augmentation, making a little difference to the crops rebels were able to grow was better than nothing. I could also see why, if his parents were Freestakers like Rosita, they wouldn't want to draw attention to themselves.

But something didn't add up.

'There's little risk of anyone forcing you to get Augmented if none of your lot tell on you,' I reasoned. 'Why not ask your parents for help? Or Rosita?'

He frowned. 'Dad's not keen on Mechsims at all. He'll flip if I ask about it. But if I show him my potential, he won't be able to ignore me. He'll have to let me do something with it. Rosita will always go along with him.'

I had to wonder if his father's concerns had anything to do with Rosita's warning about Deathsims. Without knowing what the word meant, it was impossible to tell.

'I can't help you, Carl.'

'You have to!' His voice rose. 'You helped Rosita, right? I don't know any other Mechsim siding with us to ask.'

Had Rosita told them I'd helped them willingly? Was that the reason I'd had no further threats or approaches?

'I'm still learning. I'm not qualified to teach anyone anything.'

'I just need a few pointers.' The desperation in Carl's voice was growing. 'I'm smart, I'll figure out the rest on my own.'

But I couldn't do it. I couldn't make these people believe I was with them any more than they already imagined I was.

Unless . . .

What if I was able to convince him to get tested? Mechsims were rare and important. If his family could see how the mayor hoped to do so much more for society, maybe they would realise the government wasn't the destructive monster they thought it was. They just had to give the system a chance.

'If you decide to get tested, I'll be there for you, okay? I'll help you learn all the techniques I know.'

'They won't let me,' Carl huffed, his shoulders sagging. 'I have to do this alone.'

We sat a little longer, his disappointment hanging thick between us.

'Thanks for hearing me out,' he said as the next train pulled noisily alongside the platform. 'If you change your mind, find me on Roulette. My handle is xcarlitox. All you have to say is yes, and I'll know what you mean.'

I nodded, knowing I would never be posting anything on the encrypted message board he was referring to.

'Good luck, Carl,' I said, standing.

He rose with me, and we waited until the passengers began leaving the train.

'Ego?'

I froze. Only one person shortened my name in that way.

'Dad?'

I couldn't hide the panic in my voice. He wasn't due back until tonight. If I had known he'd be early, there was no way I would have come down here with Carl.

The expression on Dad's face was a mix of delight and confusion. 'Aren't you meant to be at your internship?'

I was still thinking up an excuse when his head turned to the figure beside me. Dad's smile fell off his face in an almost comical wave of recognition and alarm.

'We need to go.' He reached for my wrist, spinning me away from Carl.

'Wait, Dad!' I turned to see what Carl was doing, but Dad pulled harder.

'What are you doing with him?'

'We were talking.' I tried slowing down again. 'Dad, you can't—'

'I can't what?'

He stopped, and his glare was so intense that I took a step back. I'd never seen him this furious before. His go-to move in anger was usually elongated silence. I didn't know what to do with this.

132

'Do you know who he is?' I doubted the words even as they came out. Because why would Dad know this boy I'd only just met under the weirdest circumstances?

'We'll talk about this at home,' Dad snapped.

The walk home was silent, but the racket in my head was deafening.

'This is my fault,' Dad barked, dropping his bag on the floor when we were released from the airlock, just missing Clifford, who came to attempt his usual dash for the outside world. 'I should have been firmer with them after they sent that bloody note.'

I picked up Clifford, needing a buffer between me and Dad. He still hadn't explained how he knew Carl, but there was no denying he knew who the boy was involved with. If he was implying he knew Freestakers and hadn't admitted it when Mum and I told him about the note, I was now more convinced than ever about one other thing.

'Why did you lie?' I asked, barely able to keep the anger from my voice. 'When I asked about Deathsims, you pretended not to know what it meant.'

Dad pinched the bridge of his nose and sighed.

'It's a good thing your mother is out,' he said, leading the way into the kitchen and opening the fridge. 'She can't know you've been talking to them. Nobody can.'

I put Clifford down, even more annoyed now. What could be so terrible about that word that was worth lying to us?

I watched Dad gulp a glass of water before he perched on a stool by the breakfast counter. He patted the one beside him, and I slipped on to it, waiting for whatever he was struggling to share. Dad pulled out his slider and found something.

The object on the screen was short and cylindrical. Its core had been hollowed out, and in that space, a network of fine lines crossed each other.

'What's this?'

'It's a disruptor. It's what I've been working on in secret for the past month. Why I haven't been home so much.'

When I continued looking at him, he sighed as if it pained him to carry on.

'It will neutralise certain sounds your vocal cords produce.'

Now I was really confused. 'But ... why?'

'I haven't been able to complete it because you're still untested,' Dad went on like he hadn't heard me. 'The best solution was to have the academy train you up, and once you'd isolated your frequency, target it to make sure it never gets heard again.'

I shook my head. He wasn't making sense. I knew he hadn't been thrilled when my abilities came to light, but he couldn't seriously be suggesting I mess with the thing that made it possible for me to be a Mechsim.

'But, Dad—'

'I can't let you become like me.'

Seconds ticked by. My brain couldn't form the

words to send to my lips. When they finally did, they came out in a whisper.

'You're . . . you're a Mechsim?'

I silently willed him not to confirm it, my fingers curled tightly into my palms. But it was much worse when he finally spoke.

'No, Ego.' He shook his head. 'I'm a Deathsim.'

CHAPTER FOURTEEN

114 days to Augmentation Day

I don't think I'd ever truly been gobsmacked in my life until that moment. I'd known being a Deathsim was never going to be anything good, but the look of anguish on Dad's face solidified it.

'You're going to have to take this back for me.' I stood up, starting an aimless walk up and down the length of the kitchen.

'You may want to sit down,' he suggested quietly.

'I'm good.'

I couldn't look at him. What the hell was this death-tinged word that he'd thought it better to lie to us about it when he actually was one? Had he really believed ignoring Rosita's message would keep whatever danger it held away? And if he hadn't seen me with Carl, would he have lied instead of giving me a real explanation like he'd promised?

'I was younger than you when my parents had me tested,' Dad began.

I stopped pacing. If he was going all the way back to his childhood, this was going to take a while. The idea

136

of him going through anything I was experiencing had never occurred to me. The anxiety I felt over finding my frequency was something he would have struggled through, yet he hadn't tried to calm my fears. Fury bubbled away in my chest.

'I loved singing as a child, and we had a conservatory garden where I spent a lot of time with my mother. She was the one who realised something had to be making her tomatoes ripen early, and her primroses flower out of season.'

Carl's reason for thinking he was a Mechsim had been similar. The coincidence wasn't lost on me.

'That's why we never had music at home,' I cut in, irritation creeping into my voice. 'You didn't want to risk me doing the same. All this time I thought it was because it was difficult for you to bear the sound of it with your condition.' I pointed at his neck.

Dad's head dropped. 'I couldn't explain it to you without revealing the darker side. I hated taking the joy of music from you. That your mother couldn't sing to you when you were a baby like my mother had done with me. But I hoped we would never need to find out what you could be.'

'Dad—'

His hand flew up, silencing me. 'Just let me get this out, okay?'

I swallowed the comeback on the tip of my tongue and nodded.

'Frequencies had only been isolated for a few

years, and scientists were still experimenting. I got tested and did exceptionally well. I was happy. We all were. My father was an immigrant whose citizenship only got approved after he married my mother. They were both Level Ones, so you can imagine how he felt learning his son was not just Level Two material, but could be a vital contributor to society as a rare Mechsim.'

I never met my grandfather. From what I'd heard, he was the sort of person for whom class and privilege mattered, having come from neither.

'That was why it was difficult to voice my concerns when I began noticing things weren't quite as I was taught. But I didn't want to let anyone down.'

'What kinds of things?' I asked.

'We were all still learning how this whole Mechsim thing worked. My tutor made notes and carried on. With practice, the intensity of the sound I emitted was meant to strengthen, so she was excited when plants started skipping days of growth instead of hours.'

I held my breath.

'When things started to skip weeks, she began to worry. I was only fourteen and growing fruit-producing apple trees from seeds within a year.'

A few weeks ago, the gravity of what he said wouldn't have struck me. But now I knew apple trees took anything from two to ten years to start producing fruit, I found this hard to digest. He wouldn't have been enhanced by that age, so it would have all been him.

138

'It got stranger when I was taken to see a special advisory team of scientists to the chancellor—'

'The chancellor?' I gasped.

Dad nodded.

That was bigger than I had imagined.

'I suspected something was up because I was told not to disclose details to my parents. The team was invited to review my test results after my tutor filed her reports to the Ministry of Agriculture. They worked out that at the rate I was going, if my ability was Augmented, I could make trees grow so quickly, the trees would die within weeks.'

I staggered over to the seat I had vacated. Dad was right; I needed to sit down. All I could see were the full red roses on Joon's slider. Roses I knew had bloomed too quickly.

'I thought the word *Deathsim* was rather dramatic when it was coined,' Dad snorted, 'but that's exactly what it is. A death simulation. The effect of the frequency carries on much longer than it is supposed to. If I was enhanced, I could have wiped out expanses of land, thinking I was helping.'

This was the reason Rosita said he should be the one to explain. I would have laughed if anyone else had tried to sell me the story.

'But you could keep on growing plants safely as long as you didn't go through with the surgery, right?' That sounded like a simple enough solution.

Dad's smile was sad, a memory stirring something

in him. 'Chancellor Stevens was one of the first leaders who had to deal with Freestakers. There was a fair amount of public support for them back then. The nation's views on Augmentation were still wavering, and referendums had been proposed in Wales and Scotland.'

We had been taught about the referendums in school. Most people ended up voting to stay in the system when they realised it worked as well as it could under the circumstances.

'Freestakers had set up small but fast-growing anti-enhancement communes around the country which were beginning to cause unbalance in the system. Stevens was a visionary who didn't believe in violence in the face of a rebellion. He didn't want to create sympathisers and more unrest. At least, that was what we were led to believe.'

Dad paused, contemplating his next words. 'When the scientists told me I was to be Augmented as planned, I was told they'd found a way to dampen the effects so I could do more good than harm. My parents weren't clued up on how Level Two training worked and accepted I was part of an advanced programme which met outside of school.

'There were so few communes back then, the chancellor believed starving them by quietly destroying their food at source could force rebels back into the workforce. Weaponising me was part of his wider plans to curb their progress.'

Rosita's words came back to me. *If you control the*

food supply, you control the people. Chancellor Stevens's time in office was long over, but if the videos Rosita had showed me weren't doctored, it appeared his legacy remained.

'Please say you didn't go through with it?' I didn't want to believe he'd agreed to destroy precious resources even if it was to stop rebel groups expanding.

'Freestakers were breaking the law.' Dad wouldn't look at me. 'I was supposed to keep everything a secret since the new process was untested. They rigged me up to a temporary enhancer and I let loose on enclosed fields of crops, only discovering later these were illegal farms they'd found. That was when I understood how destructive it could be.'

He ran a hand along his throat.

'I was told it was to help them understand how to curb the effects of my ability. It was much later that I realised the other ways they hoped to harness my frequency. Months later, when the experiments took a shift towards a different angle, tests channelled towards other biological molecular make-ups.'

He waited a moment for this to sit with me.

My eyes widened. 'You can't mean . . .'

I didn't complete the statement because it didn't make sense. The growth-affecting frequencies Mechsims emitted worked only on plants. It was the first thing I'd learnt. I hadn't come across anything that said otherwise, but I knew the human body had multiple skin and joint mechanoreceptors responsible for pain reception, balance and a host of other sensations. Had they thought Dad's frequency was different enough to affect the growth of animal tissue in some way?

'I couldn't believe it either, until the test samples scaled up from petri dishes to mice in cages.'

Bile shot up to my throat.

'I didn't see the impact of what I was doing, but the team was keen to ramp up testing from the results. Alongside those experiments, I continued to witness the devastation my voice caused to plants. I told myself it was for the good of all, but I would lie awake with images of starving people seared in my mind. I couldn't bring myself to think of the effect something that aggressive could have on animal life if they were able to channel it that way.

'When I went to the chief scientist with my concerns, he said the chancellor would have my father deported if I didn't comply. I was fourteen. I didn't know he would need more than just his word to have it done. I thought I had no choice.'

He would have needed a lot of psyching up for what was to come, because becoming Augmented was only the beginning. After graduation, students moved to specialist colleges for four years before being released into the workforce. That was where we were pushed to our limits, although it didn't sound like Dad's abilities needed any more push.

'With time, I realised I had some control.' There was a sudden lift to his voice. 'You know the sound quality of our frequencies isn't as effective when recorded, right? I had to be physically present for any missions.'

Dread rammed into me again. I forced myself to remain quiet.

'I read up on ways to change the pitch of my voice and came up with a solution. If I scarred my larynx a little, the effect could be enough to alter my frequency. But the mixture I took ended up burning my throat so badly, I was hospitalised for weeks.'

I stared with my mouth open, horrified. I'd known Dad's condition was the result of an accident, but he had done this to himself. No, he had been *forced* to do this to himself.

'I'm so sorry, Daddy, I'm so sorry.' My throat closed up as I imagined the agony he went through when he realised his plan had gone so terribly wrong.

Dad reached out and placed a hand on mine where it rested on the counter. I looked down at it, surprised to see I was trembling.

'My Ego, don't cry. I don't regret my decision.' He stood and wrapped his arms around me, remaining silent as I sobbed.

The fact that he'd had to go through so much pain. The burden he'd had to bear all this while. The unfairness of it all.

Dad didn't let go even after my wailing subsided. I didn't want him to either.

'I couldn't spread the word about what happened because I didn't want people knowing such a dangerous ability existed.' Dad's voice was woolly as I hugged him. 'I transferred to the engineering academy, but kept an eye on my old school. My fear was that they would continue looking for other people like me.'

'They let you change careers without a fuss?' I frowned when I raised my head. I was surprised they didn't force him down to Level One status or worse.

'My hospitalisation was picked up by the media. They didn't want to draw any extra attention by punishing me. Stevens was eventually replaced, but I kept tabs on members of his team who had bought into his ethos.'

Dad cupped my face with his hands. 'The chief scientist was a man called Jonathan Bernard.'

My brow rose. That surname again.

'You can imagine my thoughts when his daughter became London's mayor on a strong anti-Freestakers manifesto. Someone who has taken an active interest in Mechsims.'

I could see where he was going. Did he think the mayor could have her own vendetta?

Joon.

My chest tightened. Could his mother really be linked to something this horrible? He hadn't hidden the fact that she'd told him to be friends with me, but was there more to it?

'That's a bit of a leap, Dad. You don't even know if she's aware Deathsims exist.'

'For all our sakes, I wanted to believe the same,

until a few years ago. I was accidentally copied into a message at work with a heavily redacted dossier called the EE-code.'

He waited again for me to pick up on what he meant.

'EE for Eloka Eke?' I asked. 'That could have stood for a million things.' It felt like he was reaching.

'I know; however, I was referred to as EE when I worked with the scientists. What I read made me worry someone at the mayor's office was digging up old bones. The file disappeared before I found a way to copy it.'

'You can't know for certain she's involved.' My words were barely audible. The woman I'd met had been kind and enthusiastic about the good I could do. She didn't seem like the sort of person who would be okay with experimenting on children.

'No. That's why I started work on the disruptor. I didn't want to take any chances. I stopped developing it when I thought it was safe to assume you wouldn't be discovered. You would have to hold the perfect pitch for a period of time, and with so few green spaces, I couldn't think of a place you would stay in long enough to trigger any noticeable growth.'

I couldn't think of one either, but that hadn't stopped fate from intervening. The plants in the skills lab were introduced as part of a wellness scheme after complaints were made about the bleakness of learning spaces. I had even signed the petition when it came around.

I sighed deeply. The problem with all this was, even

if Dad turned out to be right, I didn't want my frequency altered. The ecosystem present in biodomes was possible on a wider scale if we could make vast amounts of plants grow quickly enough within new enclosures. We could create new domes dedicated not just to farming and oxygen production but to social healthy living.

I couldn't lose something with so much potential because of a danger we weren't even sure was real.

I asked another question that had been nudging at me.

'But how can you possibly know Carl? He's just a kid.'

The discomfort on Dad's face was different from before.

'I know his parents. I had to strike up relationships with Freestakers to monitor government officials. I don't agree with how they go about fighting for their rights,' he continued, 'but it became clear they were the best source of information. And to gain their trust, I had to share some things about my past.'

From the look on Dad's face, it wasn't an association he particularly cherished.

'That's how they know about Deathsims?'

'Only the London-based faction I aligned myself with. They agree more people shouldn't become aware of this kind of power. But lately, we haven't seen eye to eye—'

The front door slammed, causing Dad and me to jump.

'Not a word,' Dad whispered when we heard Mum say something inaudible to Clifford.

'I can't lie to her, Dad,' I whispered back. As it was, I was struggling under the weight of all the lies I had already told.

'It won't be for much longer.' His eyes pleaded with me. 'I promise I'll tell her everything once the disruptor is installed and we know you can't be used. For now, she doesn't need this burden.'

'Eloka? Akaego? You're home.' Mum frowned when she entered the kitchen.

Although I didn't have a chance to give Dad an answer, the forced smile I shot Mum was enough.

'The mayor had an appointment, so we finished early. I bumped into Daddy on the train.'

'Eloka, you didn't tell me you'd be back so soon.' She planted a peck on Dad's cheek.

'I wanted to surprise you.' Dad hugged her, his demeanour a contrast to the solemnness of the last half hour. 'In fact, I was hoping to cook dinner tonight, Ifeatu. It's been a while since I made my courgette lasagne.'

Dad was responsible for preparing most of the non-Nigerian meals we had at home. Despite not having the exact ingredients to make the meals she grew up with, Mum was innovative with her substitutions when it was her turn to cook. Spinach for ugu leaves, sweet potatoes for yam, oat flour for garri. I suspected I ate more Igbo-influenced dishes than some people who lived in Nigeria.

'I won't argue with that.' Mum beamed.

While they busied themselves in the kitchen, I edged towards the door, hoping to escape to my room. Dad caught my eye.

'Later,' he mouthed.

I nodded. Carl had given me plenty to think about, but my talk with Dad was far from over. The roses were a clear sign I was a Mechsim, but I didn't want to jump to conclusions about my ability being anything like what Dad described. Things weren't the same as they were thirty years ago. And if it turned out they were, there was no way I was going to agree to being Augmented. This time, I was not alone. There had to be another way.

First, I had to gather more information. I went to my room, opened my slider and typed:

Effects of sound frequencies on mechanoreceptors in humans.

The screen lit up with results. I clicked on the first entry and began to read.

CHAPTER FIFTEEN

113 days to Augmentation Day

'Son of a—' Jaden howled, jumping and grabbing his toes.

'Are you kids okay in there?' a voice called from outside the room.

Jaden poked his head through the door. 'Sorry, Mum,' he called. 'I dropped something.'

'Don't go breaking anything you can't replace, young man,' Mrs Clarke threw back.

Jaden winced, picking up the VR headset. Compared to the gaming monocles we used for battling each other at weekends, the head-hugging contraption was humongous. It had found its way into Jaden's hands in the three-year phase where he'd fancied himself a collector of historic objects. A lot of the credits his parents made in their Level One jobs as fruit pickers at Hampstead Heath Biodome had gone to the very inessential items in his room.

He carefully placed the headset on the table beside a set of equally oversized and never-used walkie-talkies. When he turned to me, his eyes were narrowed.

'Nah, mate, that's not on,' he said, shaking his head. 'I knew that bloke was dodgy. Something about him just didn't sit well with me.'

'I don't think he has anything to do with it,' I said defensively, shifting on the bed where I sat cross-legged. Out of everyone I mentioned, Joon was the person Jaden chose to latch on to. 'It's his mother.'

It was the only explanation I could come up with to explain why Joon so easily told me his mother's suggestion for him to be my integration buddy. But also, however bad the rebels were, I wanted to believe the mayor wouldn't go so far as trying to turn a teenager into a weapon. The hours of research I'd done last night hadn't unearthed anything about Mechsim sounds having any effect on humans. Dad had to be mistaken.

'Same difference.' Jaden was having none of it. 'He's doing her dirty work by keeping tabs on you. How is that not being involved?'

'Come on, Jaden. Look how clueless *I* was about everything Dad's been hiding.'

'Fair point,' Jaden mumbled. 'Just don't be conned by him. I bet he gets away with a lot with that face.'

I smiled. Other than the odd expletive, Jaden had taken it all fairly well. After yesterday's failed meetup, the only way I was allowed to come to his house was under the pretext of helping him study. We'd gone as far as getting his mum to ask mine to make it look real.

'I don't get how your dad intends to fit the disruptor.' Jaden leaned back in his chair. 'Aren't you

150

going to need surgery for something like that? Someone will figure something out for sure if you suddenly end up in hospital and lose your ability.'

I hadn't yet told Dad I wasn't keen on his plan. He'd had years to think about this and other problems we would face if it turned out I was like him. The disruptor was designed so the procedure could be carried out at home with the right equipment. A few small items he said he could sneak out of a lab at work.

'Why can't I just refuse Augmentation?' I'd asked, stacking the baking tray in the steam cleaner after we'd finished off Dad's lasagne and Mum took over the sofa to watch the finale of a matchmaking show. 'Isn't this supposed to be my choice?'

'You don't really believe that, do you?' Dad handed me a plate, keeping his voice low. 'Once your ability was made public, we lost any hope of choice. This is the only way they'll let you get enhanced in coding like you've always wanted.'

'You mean, like *you've* always wanted.'

I wasn't sure where that came from. I knew he was trying to protect me, but I was struggling to accept the destruction of this part of me I'd just discovered. My testing was only weeks away, so we would find out soon enough if I had Deathsim potential. But even if I was one and the mayor really did have a dark scheme brewing, there had to be some other way to deal with my ability, not kill it entirely. There just had to be.

Dad placed both arms on my shoulders.

'I understand how you feel, Ego, but you'll come to realise this has to be done. The only other option is going off-grid like non-stats. If we do that, it won't just affect us. Everyone in our family will be hounded when the government tries to find us.'

I thought of Grandma in Wrexham. She'd moved back to Wales when Grandpa passed away. We only saw her at Christmas because she hated coming to London, and tickets for three on a bullet train to a place that far away cost a full month's credits. But that didn't mean I wanted her affected by any of this. Dad also had a few cousins dotted around the country. They wouldn't know what hit them.

'I've heard what life is like outside the tempered zones,' Dad carried on. 'I could never subject you and your mother to something like that.'

I didn't know what else to say, so I nodded.

Dad released my shoulders. 'I was going to ask you about that boy. What did he want?'

'He wanted me to ask you about Deathsims.'

The lie slipped out easily. I should have told him about Carl's tutoring request and Rosita pulling me into the attack at the weekend. I couldn't understand why the words refused to come out.

Dad's frown said he didn't believe me, but he didn't push.

'Ego, stay away from these people. I'm going to let them know we have spoken so they can leave you alone. You tell me if they approach you again.'

'Your dad is right,' Jaden said now. 'You don't owe these people anything. He's taking measures to make sure you're not pulled into their schemes.'

'I've still been sucked in. Asking me to make a choice is asking me to be involved.'

Jaden reached for one of the fritters on the plate Mrs Clarke had forced into my hands before I came upstairs.

'You haven't seen the girl since the reception, have you?' he asked.

'Rosita? No.'

I had stayed away from the gym in case she showed up with her school again.

'Good. If you do, run the other way.'

'Jaden,' I said, my voice dropping. I had been considering how to bring this up. Mum often said the best way to get over a difficult task was to get on with it. 'What if I help him?'

Jaden's hand stopped midway to the plate. 'The boy? Are you having a laugh?'

'Hear me out.'

There had been a desperation in Carl's eyes that I couldn't forget.

'What if I can convince him to get Augmented?'

'You want to convince a rebel to get Augmented?' Jaden said this slowly, like he wasn't sure he'd heard right.

'Think about it. There are less than eighty active Mechsims in the country who are meant to support far too many people by growing food in not enough biodomes. The worst that could happen is he finds his frequency and helps Freestakers like he wants. The best result would be he sees reason and decides to get Augmented and helps everyone.'

I'd also realised I was a little in awe of Carl's bravery. I don't think I'd have been so bold to risk being reported as a rebel just to try and find out if I was capable of doing something like this. It made me want to be courageous enough to do equally big things and take risks for my own beliefs. Something I could be proud to tell someone as powerful as the mayor. If I succeeded.

'So you're going to help them?' Jaden's tone wasn't as shocked as before.

'Not them. *Carl*. Besides, if I sway him, it could be a way to make it clear I'm not with the Freestakers if it ever comes out I sort of helped them during that attack.'

He stared at me for a few long seconds before coming over to the bed and placing the back of his hand on my forehead.

'What are you doing?'

'Checking if you have a fever.' He looked dead serious. 'Doesn't feel like you do. Did you hit your head? Is that what this is?'

'You should have seen him, Jaden.' I sighed, swatting his hand away. 'He's just a kid, and he hasn't got the type of support I have from the academy. I can only imagine how disjointed everything feels. He may end up never discovering his frequency, but we can try.'

'I'm trying to think of something to say to change your mind.' Jaden sat back down. 'But I have a feeling you'll just bat back everything.'

When I remained silent, he nodded.

'Fine.'

'What does that mean?' I realised I was frowning.

Jaden exhaled loudly. 'I'll help you. You know, be your sidekick and all. I'm not letting you fall into a rebel trap just because you've decided to grow wings.'

I laughed when he sat up and flapped imaginary wings. That was what I loved about Jaden. He could joke about something this serious. Leaping off the bed, I threw my arms around him.

'Thank you, thank you, thank you!' I squealed. 'I promise, if it starts to feel shady, I'll back out.' I didn't exactly need his help; it wasn't like he knew anything about frequency finding, but it felt good knowing I could rely on him for emotional support.

'You won't get that far,' Jaden said as I sat back on the bed. 'I'll drag you out before then. Just don't tell your dad I knew what you were up to if he ever finds out.'

I knew he was right. I would have to make sure that never happened.

'There's no time like the present,' I said, getting out my slider.

Logging on to the Roulette app, I tried to remember Carl's handle. I searched for scarlitos.

The account's avatar was a pouting doll-like blonde. From the dozens of threads scarlitos participated in,

I could send a few credits to get them to forward any photos I wanted. Not this one.

I tried xcarlitox next. This avatar came up blank, and its chat action was hidden. There was no way of knowing if it was him, but I couldn't think of anything else the name could be. I set up a private chat and typed *yes* before tucking my slider away.

'That's it?' Jaden asked.

'That's it. We wait.'

'Well ... I actually really do have a test next Wednesday,' Jaden said with a grin, picking up his tablet.

'Do you need any help with it?'

He plunked himself beside me.

'You know I could never say no to you.'

CHAPTER SIXTEEN

107 days to Augmentation Day

'This isn't going to work.'

'Why?'

I scanned the room and looked at Carl like it was too obvious for a response.

'It's too loud, too crowded,' I said when he continued to stare at me.

'That's why it's perfect.' He signalled for me to keep walking.

I couldn't tell if he was joking. He hadn't stopped grinning since we'd met. Actually, if he hadn't come up to me, waving, I probably would have missed him in the mass of people waiting to be let in at the scanners past the airlock.

Carl looked younger without the helmet. The only word to describe him was *cute*. Shoulder-length dark brown hair that curled at the tips, wide eyes that took in everything like they'd just seen it for the first time, and a small gap between his two front teeth. Not at all what a rebel would have looked like if I had to pick one out of a line-up.

Looking around, I had to admit he might be right about this place. That is, if we could find a spot we could hear each other clearly without yelling. Rammed with brightly lit devices that pinged thrilling music when someone pressed play, knocked out an opponent or won a game, nobody took any notice of anyone else in the arcade. I had been with Jaden a couple of times and always found it a bit too intense.

'Over here.' Carl looked back to make sure I was following.

He led us to a two-seater booth, far away enough for the machines and crowd sounds to be an acceptable level of background noise. Most people in that section looked quite cosy, holding hands or squeezed in together on one seat. Definitely no one was paying attention to us.

'Okay, you're right,' I said, sliding in opposite him, 'this is perfect.'

'What changed your mind?' He asked the question I knew was coming.

'Honestly? You.'

Carl's puzzled expression was understandable, but I didn't elaborate. It wasn't like I could tell him I had a conversion plan going. It had been a week since I agreed to meet him, and this was the first chance I'd found to make good on it.

After finding the mayor could only spare three hours this Saturday, it felt safe tagging our meeting on to the end of it without telling Mum and Dad I wouldn't be coming home right after. Although I was

158

eager to continue discussing my health park plans with Mayor Bernard, I was relieved at the brief session. It was impossible to sit across from her without wondering if she was truly capable of anything Dad suggested. I couldn't feel her out about Deathsims because monocle man, whose name I learnt was Darren, never left us alone.

'Did you study the clips I sent?' I asked Carl.

'Yes,' Carl said, making a face. 'Are you sure some aren't just a piss-take?'

'Don't worry,' I laughed. 'I felt the same at first. They do actually help after a while. Just don't warm up in front of anyone if you don't want them to catch on.'

'Trust me, I won't be making that mistake even if I wasn't trying to hide this.'

I tried not to smile when my mind popped up an image of Carl burrowed under layers of bedcovers, trying to warble at low volume.

'You have to remember, all I can share is what I've learnt over the past couple of months. I can't promise you'll get the result you want.'

Carl nodded. 'It's better than nothing. I keep singing to my mum's herbs, waiting for something to happen.'

'If you find your frequency,' I went on cautiously, 'the effect will be different from mine. No two Mechsims can grow plants in the same way. Can you get your hands on seeds? Preferably something that would usually sprout in a day or two like beans?'

159

Seeds weren't cheap, and his parents would notice if a few went missing from the free home-growing quota households received seasonally to supplement the food we got from the biodomes. My mum certainly would. The seeds would be GM, but they would have to do.

His response was quick. 'Chives?'

'Perfect. Those grow really fast. You'll need them when we eventually start to—'

Someone stood directly behind me, casting a shadow on the table. But that wasn't what cut me off. It was the look of dismay on Carl's face.

'One of you had better start explaining what's going on here.'

A scowling Rosita walked into view, positioning herself at the end of the table and blocking our path of escape. My stomach plummeted.

'What the hell, Rosita!' Carl found his voice before me, but he didn't stand up like I did. 'Did you track me?'

'Of course.' She crossed her hands, fully focused on him. 'What else was I supposed to do when you've been acting shifty all week, hiding in toilets, making weird noises? I thought you were on drugs or something.'

Carl buried his face in his palms.

'Well, I wasn't wrong. Next time you're going to lie about who you're out with, don't use Lewis as an alibi. He can't pull it off. And you . . .'

When she turned to fix me with a glare, I actually flinched.

'What do you think you're doing?'

'Hold on, Carl came to me.'

'But why would he need *you*? The only thing you could possibly help with is—'

Her eyes widened with realisation at what Carl intended to do.

'You can't be serious!'

'I'm helping.' I lowered my voice. 'Isn't that what you people want?'

'Look at him.' She reached across and tilted Carl's head up towards me. 'Does he look like he could be involved in anything in the realm of what you've seen me do?'

Wait, did she mean he wasn't part of the Freestakers? I raised my eyebrows at him, but I knew guilt when I saw it.

'If you don't want me involved, why ask for my help when she followed you?' Carl reasoned.

Rosita's sigh was long. 'You think I wanted you there? I didn't have anyone else to call at such short notice. I definitely regret that now.'

'But I'm ready to do what needs to be done,' Carl snapped, banging his fists on the table. 'Why won't you believe me?'

I glanced around the room. Rosita did the same, looking nervous. A few people were taking in the spectacle.

'I thought the whole point of meeting here was to be discreet.' Jaden appeared beside Rosita, gesturing for us to keep it down.

I wasn't sure whether to smile at him or yell. True to his word, Jaden had volunteered to be my lookout for the day and arrived at the arcade a minute after me.

If Rosita's expression had been one of annoyance before, now she was livid. I was grateful we were in clear view of a few dozen eyes.

'You told him?' she hissed, somehow managing to keep her voice down.

'I don't think that's the issue here,' I said, realising I could spin this in my favour. 'If anyone has anything to answer for, it's you for lying.'

Rosita frowned.

'You said nobody would get hurt that day.'

Her brow unknitted when she realised what I was referring to. 'Don't be ridiculous. Someone was bound to pull her off the stage before anything bad happened. If not, she really should consider changing her security team.'

'What if things hadn't turned out well? Innocent people could have been hurt.'

'They weren't.'

I stared, exasperated. If anyone was to blame for Carl seeking me out, it was her. He was clearly trying to follow in his sister's footsteps. Thankfully, since our voices were no longer raised, people seemed to lose interest in us.

Facing Carl again, I shook my head. 'Are you really thirteen?'

162

'He told you he was thirteen?' Rosita couldn't resist a snort.

I shut my eyes. Of course he wasn't thirteen. I should have trusted my gut on that one.

Jaden leaned in and whispered, 'He does look young.'

'I'll be thirteen very soon,' Carl explained, like it made any difference.

And then I realised it really didn't matter. Carl would have been tutored and tested as young as the age of ten if he had been from a regular family who weren't sceptical of the authorities. I was disappointed he'd lied to me, but that didn't change anything.

'That's old enough for me to carry on.'

'Really?'

The simultaneous responses came from Rosita and Carl; one with surprise and delight, and the other not so much. I sensed even Jaden wanted to chip in, but he kept quiet and let me handle it like he'd promised.

'If you're not really a you-know-what,' I said to Carl, 'are you sure you want to do this for them? There are other options.'

'Wait a minute—'

'Yes.' Carl cut off Rosita's protest without hesitation. 'I want to carry on.'

'But why, Carl?' Rosita looked confused. 'You know how Dad feels. There are so many other ways you can help when you're a little older.'

I understood why their father would have reservations

about his child being tested and monitored. Rosita probably knew too, but they evidently hadn't told Carl.

'Guilt.'

'Guilt?'

He nodded, looking at me like this explanation was for me, not her.

'I'd never considered the reality for non-stats. Not Level Ones like us who still get to live in the system. And not the people who live off-grid by choice. I'm talking about the ones who secretly make their way into the country even though they know they'll get deported if they get found by the authorities.'

He was at the age when we'd been taught the dangers of immigration and overpopulation at school. Despite the restrictions imposed on us, other countries were much worse off. Places that hadn't implemented social changes fast enough to curb population growth. Countries without the wealth to build the number of domes we constructed when it became clear the world's feeble attempts at carbon emission reduction weren't going to temper the extreme heat and long freezes.

It was unbelievable that anyone would attempt to cross treacherous waters to get to a place where they would be marginalised, but they never stopped coming. These were people who had nothing other than what they made for themselves. Any 'good' they had to offer couldn't be accepted by the government because it would encourage others to come.

The idea that anyone would destroy the facilities

164

they were able to cobble together was hard for me to take now. I could see how someone with a lot of will and passion, like Carl, with strong ties to Freestakers, would want to do something about the situation if he could.

'Flash bombs and protests won't benefit them directly, but this could,' Carl continued.

Rosita remained quiet for a little longer before she answered. 'Did you speak to your father?'

I wasn't expecting her to address me, but I kept a straight face. 'Yes.'

'And?'

'It's nothing we can't deal with.' She didn't need to know about Dad's device if he hadn't discussed it. And I wasn't going to tell her that my grand plan so far was to figure out a way to avoid being Augmented if my testing showed I was a Deathsim.

'You're sure?'

'What are you two going on about?' Carl asked, glancing between the both of us.

'We can handle it,' I insisted, staring Rosita down.

She sighed. 'I hope you know what you're doing.' Then, grabbing Carl's hand, she said, 'And you're wrong. I'm not letting him do this.'

What? That was it?

Carl didn't make it easy for her when she pulled him up, but she succeeded.

'Hold on,' Jaden said, stepping in her way before she could make her exit. 'Aren't you being a bit of a hypocrite?'

'Excuse me?' Rosita's voice went up an octave.

Jaden didn't look bothered. 'How is it okay for you to drag Akaego into dangerous situations, but she can't teach the kid something that could actually be useful? He's told you what he wants to use this for.'

'Well . . . yes . . . but . . .' Rosita stammered, looking flustered for the first time, 'it's not that simple.'

'Why?' Jaden pressed on. 'Because you're afraid he'll get into trouble? He'll draw attention to himself? He's clearly capable of doing that all by himself. Did you know he followed Akaego all the way to West Finchley and approached her in public?'

'I'm worried because he's a child, you ignoramus!' Rosita spat back. 'What part of that can't you understand?'

A thought occurred to me.

'How old were you when you got involved in all this?' I knew I would have to back down if it didn't work.

Rosita looked uncomfortable again, and when she didn't answer, we knew her response would blow her argument away. She was too stealthy to have only joined the rebels recently.

'What does that have to do with anything?' she finally said. 'This is not about me.'

'Please, Roz.' Carl covered the hand that held his with his free one. 'I can do this. What do we have to lose?'

His last plea was heartfelt enough to make her let go of him. She pulled him in for a hug, holding his head against her shoulder before tugging at his cheek.

'You'll kill me one day, you know that, Carl.' Her attention returned to me. 'Tell me one thing.' She took a step closer. 'Why are you doing this?'

It was the same question Jaden had posed, but I couldn't tell her the truth.

'I won't lie and say I've bought into your thinking,' I admitted, 'but whatever side he's on, one more Mechsim in the world has got to be a good thing, right? Besides, do you want him tracking down any other Mechsims to beg them for help? I haven't reported you, so at least you know I'm safe.'

Rosita considered my words. She looked at Carl and back at me. 'All right.'

I was surprised. 'All right?'

'I'll think about it.'

Not quite a victory, but it wasn't a shutdown. There was nothing left to say, so Jaden stepped aside. As we watched them disappear into the crowd, he nudged me.

'You never said she was cute.'

'Seriously, Jaden?'

'Just saying.' He patted his low afro to make sure it was in shape. 'I could have prepared myself. Worn a nicer shirt.'

It was my turn to jab him in the side.

'I'm glad that's over,' he said with a chuckle. 'Seeing as we're here, how about I teach you a game or two? Your treat. I'm saving my credits for Broxxie's concert. Those tickets aren't cheap.'

I rolled my eyes but I didn't object when he took my hand and led me towards the machines. There was still hope this could work. I was going to hold on to that.

CHAPTER SEVENTEEN

100 days to Augmentation Day

'How is this our third week already, Akaego? It feels like we've only just started.'

I nodded at Mayor Bernard, feeling the same. Choosing Saturdays might have made sense to fit around my classes, but with the rushed arrangement, no one seemed to have factored in her other social commitments. Again, today, we had only four hours, most of which had been spent in meetings. If I had to describe a day in the work life of the mayor, the resounding word would be *boring*. How many documents did one person need to read and sign?

Darren had stepped out. Wiping sweaty palms on my trousers, I sat up straight. After days of holding on to so much information, I finally had a chance to test the waters with the mayor. But if she had ulterior motives, I couldn't outright quiz her about the things Dad had said without setting off alarm bells.

'What are your thoughts so far?' she asked with her usual wide-eyed look of interest. The one that made me feel she genuinely wanted to know what I thought.

'Has any of this made you consider a future in office? I know that's not what the programme is about, but people with your tenacity and vision are what our nation needs.'

Me? Tenacious? I had never thought of myself that way. If that was the vibe I was giving off, maybe some of Jaden's go-getter attitude had rubbed off on me. But I knew I had been passionate every time we discussed health parks. Maybe that was it.

'I'm not sure I could do what you do,' I admitted. 'It sounds like you have to make a lot of difficult decisions. Aren't you ever afraid you'll make the wrong ones?'

Her smile widened with her nod. 'All the time. Anyone in a position of power who claims not to be afraid of the impact of their decisions is either lying or a bad leader.'

She stood and perched beside me on her desk.

'We all choose to give up or take up something at every level. Although some choices seem bigger than others, even the tiniest consideration is a sacrifice of something. Like you, I chose to step up by changing course. The work I did as a physician was important, but what I do now changes lives in ways I could never have accomplished back then.'

She had given me a way in. 'Even though you're no longer one, you'll still stand by that oath doctors take, right? Do no harm? That would apply to non-stats and rebels.'

She frowned. 'Lawbreakers must be dealt with accordingly. We have policies in place to tackle dissenters humanely.'

'I know, but . . .' I paused to choose my words. 'We would never jeopardise resources just to punish them, right? We would never actually break the law even if it felt justified.'

When her brow remained knitted, I wondered if I'd come too close to spilling what I'd been told.

'I don't think I—'

Darren barged in then. I was so nervous about carrying on the conversation, I was relieved for the interruption.

'You have a call.' He glanced at me before leaning in and whispering in her ear.

The mayor's eyes narrowed. 'You'll have to step out for a few minutes, Akaego,' she said, returning to her chair. 'This is confidential.'

I was disappointed at the interruption, but when I stood outside the room, I looked around, wondering if I might see Joon. Saying hello at school felt different from meeting at his house. Like I was a part of his life in a way the others weren't. Which was a silly thought, since his friends probably visited all the time.

I strolled down the corridor. There was no one to stop me wandering, so I carried on into another wing until I got to the door that led to the courtyard. A *Do Not Enter* sign hung across the handle. Joon had said it had been closed off two weekends ago, but he hadn't said

171

why. Seeing the roses on his slider had been exciting, but I wanted to see them in real life.

I would be out before anyone noticed.

A minute later, my mouth hung open as my brain tried to process why there was a patch of earth where the rose bush had stood.

'What are you doing?'

I jumped at the proximity of the voice. Darren stood behind me.

'It's gone.' I stated the obvious as his gaze followed my finger to the barren spot.

'And?'

'The roses,' I said, my voice squeaky. 'What happened?' I wasn't just talking about the rose bush. There had been other plants surrounding it. Now anything about a square metre around it was gone.

'You shouldn't be snooping.'

'I wasn't. I only came to—'

'She's only being curious, Darren.' I hadn't noticed Mayor Bernard enter the courtyard. She came up beside me, nudging her head towards the door for him to leave.

'What happened?' I repeated when we were alone, unable to calm my pounding heart. 'Did it—' I bit my tongue before the word *die* came out.

She stepped closer to the empty space. 'I should have known you'd come here. You're obviously aware the growth you facilitated got you on to this internship.' She turned to me with a sad smile. 'I would have shown you the roses that first week, but there was an accident with the cleaning crew shortly after the reception. The plants in this area were moved to a nursery nearby for rehabilitation.'

'Everything?'

She placed a hand on my shoulder and steered me away. 'I'm not a horticulturist, I just listen to what they decide. It's too late today, but I can ask the team to take you to the nursery next time you're here. The flowers will still be in bloom.'

The easy way she offered this dispelled my initial fear the plant was dead. If she was hiding something, would she be so relaxed? Two weeks ago, I wouldn't have thought twice about her explanation. The reason I was suspicious at all was because of Dad.

I nodded.

'I'd like that. Thank you.'

The rest of the afternoon was uneventful. It was only as I made my way to the front door to head home that Joon appeared, looking like he'd just fallen out of bed, all ruffled hair and rumple-clothed. It was past noon, so I doubted he had. Even with that, as always, it felt like he was seconds away from stepping on to a photo shoot.

'Leaving without lunch?' He waved a half-eaten pear at me.

I faked a cringe and clutched my stomach. 'I don't think I should take anything off you after last time.'

His exaggerated laugh made me smile. 'I promise this won't make you sick.'

I wasn't hungry, but I found myself nodding before I followed him to the dining room, where a tray of muffins was laid out. He picked one for himself, and I did the same. Blueberry. I shut my eyes for a moment. It tasted so good, it was gone in no time.

'Delicious, huh?' Joon asked when I turned and saw a smile tugging at his lips.

'I could eat these all day.'

'Have as many as you want.' Joon pushed the tray towards me. 'They'll go stale otherwise. If you want something a bit healthier, I'll ask someone to make you a sandwich.'

I frowned, wondering why the muffins were baked if no one else was going to eat them. Probably one of the many privileges of being on Level Four. It felt weird to have so much when people at other levels had their rations capped. Joon didn't seem to think anything of it though. He had lived most of his life in this cocoon.

'Who doesn't make their own sandwiches?' I asked instead, picking up another muffin.

'That's what I keep saying.' He raised his hands like he'd had this discussion many times. 'But I was banned from the kitchen after I tried following my halmeoni's kimchi recipe and somehow ended up getting the paste on every countertop. Don't ask.'

I kind of wanted to, but I moved on to something else. 'It's a shame about the roses. I really want to see them.'

'Yeah, it was weird how the rose bush died like that.

The cleaning crew must have spilled some toxic as hell chemicals when they went in.'

I froze in the middle of reaching for a third muffin. 'Died?'

He nodded, not noticing how still I'd gone. 'I'm pretty sure it was dead when I saw it a few days ago. All dried up and limp.'

'Your mum just said it got moved.' I managed to keep a quiver from my voice.

He stared at me like I was being obtuse. 'Yeah, because it died. Along with a few plants around it. I saw them being carried out.'

No, he couldn't be right. The mayor wouldn't have invited me to the nursery if there was nothing to see. But why would Joon lie?

'Hey, Akaego, are you okay?' He came closer.

'I'm fine. I think I probably ate the muffin too quickly,' I lied. 'Thanks for the treat. I'll skip the sandwich. Got to hurry home.'

Concern was etched on his face when I said goodbye at the door and hopped on the cart waiting outside. It was entirely possible he was wrong and it hadn't died. But the knots in my stomach didn't loosen.

I desperately wanted Joon to be wrong.

The house was empty when I got home. Rushing to my bedroom, I took down the small pots I'd stashed on the highest shelf closest to my window.

Two basil seedlings sprouted from the earth, looking frail but doing their best for plants that had grown in the shaded light that entered my room. I'd nicked them from Mum's stash and sown them a week after Dad made his revelation. They needed at least two weeks to grow to a certain stage before I could experiment on them.

They weren't there yet.

My first seedling practice with Mr Ericsson would be on Monday. My testing was only days away, so the week ahead would be filled with sessions of voice projections and stalk measurements. If I let the sound I believed was my frequency loose on those organic seedlings, it was possible I'd have an answer about my abilities before testing day.

A Deathsim or just a regular Mechsim. My stomach filled with dread at the thought of the dead roses. Whatever happened, I would know what I was soon.

CHAPTER EIGHTEEN

93 days to Augmentation Day
The Test

'Are you sure you're okay?' Mr Ericsson crouched beside me, concern on his face. 'You look a bit peaky.'

A stiff nod was all I could offer.

'Don't worry so much, it'll go well. This is all just for show.'

Knowing it was didn't stop the nerves from creeping in and solidifying.

I'd held back during our session with the first organic seedling a few days ago, trying different sounds as Mr Ericsson watched, only moving to the one I'd used in the mayor's courtyard at the last moment, and then letting it out for just a few seconds. I'd tossed and turned that night, waking in cold sweats from dreams filled with three-metre beanstalks. In one, masked guards grabbed me the moment I stepped into school. I'd finally given up on sleep, passing the time until morning watching shows instead.

But when I came into class the next day and he showed me the seedling, Mr Ericsson's excitement had been contagious. I'd turned the pot around in my hand with a smile, staring at the stalk, which had shot up a couple of inches in height, still amazed I was capable of such a miracle.

The overnight growth was nowhere near as advanced as the roses. And nothing had come of my work on the not-quite-ready basil plants at home. Maybe I wasn't a Deathsim after all. Maybe I was a high-functioning Mechsim who could make plants grow even quicker than a regular Mechsim. The thought filled me with hope.

A week of focused work on that seedling and three fresh ones still didn't bring the results I feared would come. I wondered if it was because I wasn't giving it my all. Mr Ericsson urged me to relax now it looked like we'd found my frequency. But as much as I wanted to let go, the anxiety still tugged at me.

And today was the moment of truth.

'You're sure you don't need that adjusted?' Mr Ericsson asked one last time.

My hand reached for the stiff band around my neck. The dark grey metal collar was a one-size-fits-all contraption that replicated an enhancement effect, but since it was mostly used to test younger children, it ran small. Even expanded to its widest fit, I felt choked when Mr Ericsson clipped it around my neck.

'I'll be okay.' I managed a smile, trying to ignore my stomach gripes.

'Good.' He returned my smile with a less rigid one. 'Everyone's waiting. We'd better head out.'

My test was scheduled for noon in the smallest recital room at the academy. I was glad it was a Saturday so I didn't have to encounter any chirpy students. Entering the room through a side door, I walked to the front, where a table stood with three clay pots.

A linear lamp hung over two of the plants, providing the UV light needed for this stint of accelerated photosynthesis. This time there weren't just seedlings. My frequency had to be tested on different stages of growth. It was only after I took in the set-up that I had the courage to lift my head to face my audience.

My heart stopped.

Sitting in the front row were Mrs Miguel, Mum, Dad, two music teachers and a rep from the Ministry of Agriculture. Two faces I hadn't expected sat in a row behind.

My eyes darted from Joon to his mother, and then to Dad, who looked uncomfortable. Considering she'd brought me on to her internship, it wasn't too surprising the mayor was there. Our session today had been postponed to accommodate my evaluation. I wished we'd been told she would attend so Dad could have prepared himself.

Mr Ericsson made a quick introduction, describing what was about to happen.

As I listened, I pictured Dad in front of a table similar to this. He would have been younger than I was, but I bet his confidence was sky-high. I always wondered what he sounded like before his accident. Now, knowing he had loved singing, I imagined he wouldn't just have pushed out sounds. He would have found a melody to work with his frequency like I'd heard some kids did.

'Whenever you're ready.' Mr Ericsson faced me, gesturing to the pots. 'Activate the device and begin with specimen A.'

I nodded, the pulsing in my ears almost deafening. This was meant to be the most exciting point in this process, yet I couldn't enjoy it. Not until I was sure Dad's fears were unwarranted. And if he was right, having the mayor witness this moment was even more unsettling.

I'd warmed up earlier, so all I had to do was depress the small tab on the collar. Its signal was the same one permanent attachments gave off after Augmentation, meaning evaluations could happen in one sitting instead of everyone waiting a day or two to see the effects.

Specimen A was a tried and tested bean seedling. I had projected my frequency enough times that week that the sound came easily, filling my chest with its lightness before pouring out of me. I knew exactly what to expect, yet I sprang back when the plant jumped towards the sound of my voice. With the collar on, hiding behind my smallest effort was impossible. The stalk stopped growing after about two inches.

I moved to the next pot without looking up. A marigold plant with three vibrant orange buds. They'd chosen a quick-flowering species for obvious reasons, and it took only a moment for the petals to unfurl after I did my bit.

It was becoming difficult to ignore the thunderous sound of my heartbeat.

The last pot held a tomato plant with plump green fruits hanging from its branches. It was the only one not under the bright light because it had been grown until its fruits were close enough to ripening for this display. My voice filled the room again, and I watched as a sheen of red spread across the skin of the tomatoes.

And then I looked up at Dad.

His expression was blank, but I could imagine the turmoil inside him. It would probably match the conflict raging inside me.

'That was exceptional.' Mrs Miguel was the first to rise and approach me, applauding with so much pride, you would have thought she grew the plants herself. 'I don't think we've seen a response so strong before, have we, Chris?'

Mr Ericsson's smile was in close competition with hers for widest of the moment, and for good reason. I had only been training for a few months, yet each result had been achieved in seconds, not minutes. Responses quicker than he could produce after many years as a Mechsim. Of course he saw this as a success.

'I knew you were holding back on me.' He patted my shoulder, using his other hand to touch one of the marigold petals lightly, like he couldn't believe it was real. Even as he released me from the collar, he couldn't take his eyes off the flowers.

I had to stop myself from shrinking away when the

elderly man from the Ministry also stepped forward to congratulate me. All the attention was making my head spin. How would I cope when I had to repeat this at the Augmentation Day Pageant, with hundreds in attendance and millions viewing at home?

My parents finally made it to the table. It wasn't a surprise Mum was the one smiling.

'Ada m,' she cried, throwing her arms around me, 'imela o. I knew you could do it.'

I felt myself well up when her voice cracked, heavy with relief. I hadn't realised she felt any anxiety about this whole process. The pressure for me to succeed must have been weighing on her all along.

'You must be very proud of your daughter.'

The mayor's expression was a flawless depiction of gratitude. Dressed in a cobalt jumpsuit and with her auburn hair swept across one shoulder, she could easily have been at a campaign rally addressing supporters. Joon was close behind, but he looked less cheery. If anything, the way he rubbed his neck and avoided my eyes, I would have said he was nervous.

'Yes, we are, Mayor Bernard.' Mum beamed, answering for the both of them. 'We knew she was special from the moment she was born. Her name in its full form is Nwakaego. A child who has more value than wealth.'

I just about stopped myself from leaping forward to cover Mum's mouth.

'Very special indeed,' the mayor concurred with a

nod, unbothered by Mum's mushiness. 'You must call me Patrice. None of this Mayor business.'

The smile she flashed seemed sincere. I had to remind myself that Dad's glimpses of a redacted document were not enough evidence to paint her with the same brush as Chancellor Stevens. Having her present at my testing was an honour. My back straightened as I accepted the praise.

'I didn't realise you attended these things.' Dad finally spoke up. His synthesiser couldn't keep out the tension he tried to mask.

The mayor's energy didn't waver. 'I wanted to show my support for Akaego's efforts. And we have the added bonus of her and my Ki-Joon being friends.'

I felt the weight of Mum and Dad's gaze on me. This was news to them. We had been getting along, but I didn't think he was quite at parents' conversation level of name-dropping.

Mayor Bernard must not have noticed because she carried on. 'I took the liberty of making a celebratory lunch reservation at Crystal. I hope your family will join us.'

'That's kind of you.'

'You really didn't have to.'

Mum and Dad's words clashed, and they looked at each other, brows raised.

'It's the least I can do,' the mayor said. 'Or have you got other plans?'

I could sense how badly Dad wanted to turn her

down. But they'd both cleared their Saturday for the test. Mum would guess something else was behind the refusal.

'There will be no press coverage?'

His question suggested acceptance, but it was definitely a concern. Having lunch with the person you were secretly working against wouldn't look great if your allies heard about it out of context.

'Of course not. This is for them.' She pointed at me and Joon.

I glanced at Joon, and his smirk almost made me chuckle. If it really was for us, we should have been asked beforehand.

Dad begrudgingly thanked her. The other adults heaped more praise on me before we made our way out. The rep from the Ministry would run further analysis on the test plants and all the seedlings I'd practised on with Mr Ericsson before sending an official confirmation that the results were as expected, but it was only a formality. It was clear what I could do.

Three members of the mayor's security detail approached us in the corridor.

'We'll take my vehicles,' the mayor said, leading the way.

I desperately wanted to text Jaden. I'd never been in a car, and neither had he. They weren't cheap to maintain, even when run on solar-hydrogen power, which meant they were mostly used by specialist outdoor workers and, apparently, Level Four officials.

We took a lift to the academy's rarely used underground car park, not needing to set up our hydration suits. One good thing about outdoor vehicles was that they were well insulated, having to run above ground where the heat, cold and dust were felt the worst.

Teardrop-shaped metallic cars drew towards us in the otherwise empty space. They were low to the ground, and I heard Mum wince when she got in. Sliding in beside her, I placed my hand on her knee, and she squeezed it gratefully. The door to the airlock swished open seconds later and we were on our way.

The ride was a-m-a-z-i-n-g.

We whizzed by so fast, the view outside was a blur. Although the speed didn't quite match that of the trains we took to visit Grandma, the small size of the vehicle made it so my heart felt like it would leap out of my chest as we took each turn. I was truly gutted when we arrived at Crystal in no time.

With credit limits capped for everyone and based on status, restaurants had to serve meals within set price ranges or they wouldn't attract customers. The only way to stand out was through menu creativity and interior decors. I knew the second we walked through the airlock doors that Crystal was one of the few places that did classy well.

The main space was almost entirely constructed of reflective surfaces and glittering hanging lights. But as stunning as it was, it was a little overwhelming, and I was relieved when we were led to a room with opaque walls and low lighting.

'Before we continue,' Mayor Bernard said when we were seated, 'I would like to apologise for the lapse in security on the first day Akaego came to our home.'

I froze. It was the first time she'd mentioned the incident in all the time I'd spent with her. I glanced at Joon. Had she found out about my involvement? Or had Joon ratted me out? I prayed his straight face meant he hadn't.

'It was not to be helped. Rebels find a way of infiltrating any place they set their sights on.' Mum spoke with the authority of someone who listened to a lot of news.

'It shouldn't have happened,' the mayor said. 'Not with the best of our children gathered.'

Silence fell upon us as we contemplated that alternative ending. I wished I'd been able to chuck the disc before it was set off. Thoughts of what could have happened to her still haunted me.

'And what are you studying, Joon?' Mum asked politely, changing the subject.

'I'm a drummer.' Joon sat up, puffing out his chest. 'And not just drum kits. I couldn't believe it when I found a janggu sitting in storage at the academy. It's a traditional Korean drum. I've been teaching myself how to play it.'

'That's interesting.' Mum seemed impressed. 'You must have a passion for it.'

'Passion is not always what's important,' Mayor Bernard answered for him.

The look Joon gave his mother was one of seasoned frustration. 'She hates that I'm not more politically minded.'

'I don't hate it, sweetie.' The mayor sounded hesitant for the first time. 'I just wish you applied yourself to something more meaningful.'

Joon kept his gaze fixed on a spot on the table this time. 'Drumming is a dying art. People use synths and think they have the sound down, but you have to—'

'Nobody is going to vote a drummer into any position of authority,' his mother interrupted with a strained smile.

Joon stood so abruptly that the table rocked.

'Where do you think you're going?'

'Toilet,' Joon shot back.

Mum, Dad and I exchanged awkward glances. The mayor fiddled with her glass before refilling it. After a few seconds, she rose too.

'If you'll excuse me.'

'What's going on with them?' Mum asked, her gaze fixed on the door after the mayor left.

'We shouldn't have accepted this invitation,' Dad mumbled.

'Why not? It would have been impolite to refuse,' Mum reasoned.

Before Dad was able to respond, I got up. 'I need the loo,' I announced. I didn't want to hear Mum and

Dad argue. The atmosphere was already weird enough, and I wanted to enjoy this lunch.

The toilets were at the end of a busy corridor, but when I got in, I was alone. At least, I thought I was until I approached one of the furthest cubicles from the door and heard sharp whispering.

'You've had the specimen from my garden for weeks. We already knew what she was capable of. Just fix it so the levels look normal. I'll call you back tonight.'

There was no mistaking the mayor's voice. She could have been talking about anything, but it sounded a hell of a lot like she was trying to cover something up. And I couldn't ignore the sinking feeling that the person she could be talking about was me.

If the specimen she was referring to was the rose bush, then were the levels that needed to be fixed my test results? Or was I reaching? Surely the mayor had more important things to worry about than my test results.

I rushed out of the toilet at the sound of flushing, ducking into an adjoining corridor to give her time to return to our private room before I made my way back.

'You had to escape too, huh?'

Joon leaned against a wall in the empty, narrow space.

My mind was still trying to process what I'd just heard. It occurred to me that if the mayor wondered where I'd been, I could pretend I'd been talking to him and never made it into the toilet to overhear anything.

188

'Look at you, walking out on the mayor,' I joked, not knowing what else to say.

Joon grinned and scratched his chin. 'I think I'm the only person allowed to do that.'

'You're allowed? My mum would have chewed my ears off.'

We both smiled.

'I don't think your family want to be in there any more than I do.'

'We're more of a home-cooking type of family.'

'Even for celebrations?'

I shrugged and rested my back against the wall beside him.

'Why did you come, if you knew you'd hate it this much?' I asked.

'Would you be surprised if I said I wanted to see you?'

I turned to take in his profile. I couldn't tell if he was teasing, but I found myself hoping he wasn't. He'd shut his eyes for a moment, and all I could think was how incredibly hot he looked.

'How do you do it? How are you always so confident and relaxed in the face of . . . everything?'

'I'm not.' Joon opened his eyes. 'I just remind myself that everyone is the star in their own show. You're not the sidekick in your life story, so why act like one?'

'I am not the sidekick in my life story.' I repeated the words slowly. After I was told I could be a Mechsim, I knew I wanted to create health parks everyone could

189

enjoy, but deep down, making Mum and Dad proud was a bigger driving force. That was how I'd been raised: with the shadow of my grandfather's hopes for his lineage to accomplish more than he had looming in the background.

I had been a secondary character in my life for so long, I never pushed for what I wanted. When the mayor asked about my ambitions as part of the internship programme, I had felt seen in a way I had never imagined before. Maybe I needed to lean into that feeling.

Joon's hand brushed against mine. I looked up. I didn't pull away from the warmth of his touch.

We heard a door slam open, and our heads shot into the main corridor just as Dad stormed out of the room we'd been in.

'Dad?'

'We are leaving,' he snapped, walking past me with a determination that said I wasn't allowed to argue.

Mum emerged, chasing after him. 'Eloka, why are you being like this?'

Their voices faded. Whatever had happened in there was not something Dad would want to share with the rest of the restaurant.

I sent a reluctant wave Joon's way before I rushed after my parents.

CHAPTER NINETEEN

91 days to Augmentation Day

Joon: Hey, just checking you got home okay.

Akaego: Yeah, we just did.

Joon: Not sure what all that was about.

Akaego: I think it's fair to say my dad didn't vote
for your mum at the last election.

Joon: That bad, huh?

Akaego: Sorry it got awkward.

Joon: I'm sorry too.

Joon: Can I see you on Monday?

Joon: I promise it'll be quick.

Akaego: Sure.

I reread the messages from Saturday as I waited in the
recital room where I'd been tested. Joon had suggested
it. Standing there so soon after, knots formed in my
belly even though the plants had been cleared away.
The room was forever tainted with the memory of my
anxiety. I suspected I wouldn't be able to shake the same
feeling if I ever went back to Crystal.

The journey home that afternoon had been silent.

When I asked Mum what happened, she clucked and said Dad was overly sensitive to the mayor's comment on Level Fours' access to cars.

I cornered him in the kitchen later on and gave him a hug.

'I'm sorry,' I whispered, knowing he could tell my apology had nothing to do with the mayor.

'It's okay.' His voice was soothing as he moved loose braids away from my face. 'The only way you could have avoided it was pretending you hadn't found your frequency.'

I had considered that. Training for even ten years wouldn't guarantee I could replicate what I had done at the skills lab or with the rose bush. The disappointment would be heavy, but everyone would get on with finding other Mechsims. The problem was, lying wouldn't aid my vision of getting health parks built for everyone to use. I had to focus on figuring out a way to dampen the Deathsim effect if I got Augmented.

'But it's good we now know what we're dealing with.' Dad's face scrunched. 'With your frequency isolated, I can finish the disruptor before the mayor makes her move.'

If she makes her move, I thought. I didn't know if the mayor had lied about the roses being moved for rehabilitation, and her words in the toilet hadn't inspired confidence, but I wasn't sure if it was a good idea yet to tell Dad any of it. Until I was certain, I planned on keeping my concerns to myself.

'Did you have to make it so obvious you don't like her though?' I asked.

'I thought I would be able to hide it better, but I couldn't sit through that lunch wondering if everything she said was a lie.'

'Or maybe you're wrong and she has nothing to do with the EE-code.'

I desperately wanted this to be the case. Especially after whatever that was with Joon earlier. As much as I tried to dismiss it, my lips curled up unconsciously whenever I thought of him. I was becoming comfortable around him in a way I wasn't with anyone else. Not even Jaden. If his mother ended up being who Dad thought she was, where did that leave us?

Dad didn't acknowledge my rationale with a direct response.

'What is your relationship with her son?'

I had been waiting for that question.

'The mayor asked him to volunteer as my integration buddy.'

I'd thought hard about whether to reveal this and decided it didn't help if I kept facts like that from Dad.

'And you don't find it suspicious?'

'If it was meant to be a secret, he wouldn't have told me. Doesn't that say something?'

'Until we know for sure, let's not drop our guard. Stay away from him.'

I took a step back.

'Really, Dad? What reason would I have to suddenly cut him off?'

'Find one, Akaego,' he snapped. 'Lives are at stake. You have to take this more seriously.'

Mum walked in before I could defend myself. At some point, our voices had crept up.

'Nsogbu a di?'

'I was telling Akaego to be careful with that boy,' Dad covered quickly. 'We don't want her getting carried away by Level Four privilege.'

It was a weak excuse, but Mum seemed to buy it.

'Ah, Eloka.' She smiled. 'You need to give her some credit. Besides, I won't lie, I enjoyed that car ride, and I'm sure you did too. I saw the look on your face once we hit the road.'

After her mild chiding, we somehow got through the rest of the weekend without bringing it up again. Dad wasn't going to want to hear me argue about hanging out with Joon. I'd already agreed to meet him, and I couldn't think of a good excuse to back out. I didn't want to either. And Dad never had to know.

At school, I found Mr Ericsson in the staffroom just before lunch and thanked him for his help, hoping he would let slip any news about the plants. He'd assured me there was nothing to worry about. We would hear back from the Ministry if there was a problem. His words gave me hope there would be no issue if I went ahead with my enhancement.

'And there's no way it could be the wrong result?'

I couldn't help asking, the mayor's call at Crystal in mind.

'You're clearly a Mechsim, Akaego,' he replied, misreading the reason for my apprehension.

I made my way to the recital room. I'd managed to resist the urge to text Joon over the weekend to find out why he wanted to meet. He didn't keep me waiting long, showing up with his easy smile.

'I feel like I need to apologise again.' He shut the door and came to meet me at the back of the room. 'Mum forgets herself sometimes and tries to control everything.'

This wasn't the first time I'd been alone with him, so why were the organs in my chest flip-flopping? I had a terrible feeling he could tell because he smiled slightly and shifted from one foot to the other.

'I should apologise too.' I heard the lift in my voice. 'Dad shouldn't have walked out like that.'

'You'd wonder who the adults were, right?'

We grinned, their behaviour only amusing now we were removed from the emotions of it all.

'So what's up?' I asked.

Joon bit his lip, and I think I may have heard a gulp. I had never seen him look so uncertain.

'Nothing, really. I only realised after you left that I didn't congratulate you.' He pulled a small box out of his back pocket and passed it to me.

'What is it?'

I didn't stretch my hand out, confusion taking hold.

Joon opened the box, and my frown deepened. Inside, a band of polished green stones lay on a cushion. Was this for me?

'Joon, I—'

'You're not allowed to say no.' He placed a finger close to my lips. 'It'll be the equivalent of spitting in my face.'

'That's not a thing.' I laughed despite myself, moving his hand away.

'It could be.' He grinned, taking my hand and placing the box in it. 'You said you liked my necklace, and I wasn't doing anything with this. I thought you would put it to better use.'

Now I was really stumped. Was the bracelet part of a matching set? From his grandmother, if I remembered correctly. The gesture felt intimate, and I didn't know how to process it. I considered giving it back, but I knew he wouldn't have it. At least not that minute.

Slipping the bracelet on, I turned my hand to admire it, knowing I wouldn't be wearing it for long. There was no way I could explain something like this to Mum and Dad.

Joon's smile was catching. I found myself beaming back.

'It's beautiful,' I said. 'Thank you.'

I meant it. At home, we hadn't celebrated my success because Dad didn't see it as one. He was so worked up about me being a Deathsim, he'd put Mum off making a big deal about the test by saying we would celebrate properly on Augmentation Day. Jaden had sent a jokey hurrah message, but it didn't compare to this.

I rolled down my sleeve over the bracelet. I always felt ridiculous wearing long sleeves when it was so hot outside, but other than Mr Ericsson, most teachers kept the filtered air cooler than I preferred. At least today my outfit had another purpose.

'I'm guessing you haven't had lunch,' Joon said with renewed enthusiasm. 'Want to sit with us?'

When he frowned, I realised I must have made a face.

'What? Is it Luna?'

I wasn't aware he'd noticed I hadn't warmed to her.

'No, that's not it,' I lied.

'You don't have to worry about her,' Joon said, obviously not buying my fib. 'I don't know why she gets so weirdly territorial.'

I gave him a hard look. Did he honestly have no clue? Or maybe Luna just acted up with anyone new to their circle. I hadn't considered that possibility, and now I hoped it was true. It wasn't my place to out her feelings anyway.

Without waiting for further objections, Joon motioned for me to follow him. Abigail spotted us when we walked into the cafeteria, waving frantically.

'Did you hear the news about the raid at a Freestakers gathering last night?' Matt was saying when we drew closer.

My feet stopped before we reached the table.

197

'Yeah, I heard there were arrests and some people were hospitalised,' Abigail replied casually, like it meant nothing at all. Which I guess, to her, it didn't. Now I knew some actual Freestakers, news about them no longer felt like a distant reality to me.

Joon carried on past me, and he patted Matt's shoulder. 'About time they flushed those bastards out properly.'

Everyone nodded knowingly, aware of how his father had died.

'Some kids were rounded up.' This came from a harpist called Malik.

'I don't get it.' Matt shook his head. 'Who teaches kids to set off bombs?'

I finally forced my legs to move before I began to look odd. I couldn't say Freestakers weren't all the same without explaining how I knew this. It had been weeks since the meeting at the arcade, and I hadn't heard from Carl or Rosita. Jaden obviously thought it was for the best. Now I wondered if I should check on them.

'Akaego.' Luna patted the space by her, giving me no option but to sit there.

The second I did, although there was hardly any space between me and Estrella on the other side, Joon squeezed in between us and winked at me. Luna's mouth hung open for a second before she remembered to shut it.

'We heard you found your frequency.' She didn't sound thrilled. 'I guess congrats are in order.'

198

To my surprise, Joon beat me to a response.

'You guys should have seen her,' he told the table. 'It was amazing. One second the flowers were tiny buds, the next ...' He mimed them opening by splaying his fingers from a clenched fist.

Luna's glance from my face to Joon's was one of shock. 'You were there? I thought those evaluations were closed sets.'

'Usually, but I went with Mum. Figured I should support my friend.' He grinned at me.

As I placed my hand on the table, my sleeve rolled back a little, and Luna's gaze dropped to my wrist. I braced myself for a comment, but she just took a mouthful of pasta as the rest of the table chatted on about how amazing the pageant would be if Joon's description was accurate.

Only Abigail seemed to notice Luna's mood shift. She kept glancing her way, trying to pull her back into the conversation.

Once lunch was over, I slipped off the bracelet. There was no point creating any more unnecessary drama. Classes sped by after that. My after-school session was shorter than usual because Mr Ericsson said we could cut them down now it was only vocal strengthening to be done.

I got home early and figured I could use the time to look into the weird sounds the air fryer had started making last night. I was engrossed in fiddling with its controls when my slider vibrated on the counter. I

199

almost accepted the call before looking, but the device nearly fell from my hand when I saw the name on the screen.

Why was Joon calling? No, not calling. Video calling. Did he get home, take a look at his necklace and immediately regret giving its other half away? I had changed into Dad's old shirt and tucked my hair under a satin bonnet. Definitely not first-time video-call attire. Panicking, I let it ring out before calling him back on audio.

'Akaego?'

Why did he sound surprised?

'Hey, sorry my hands were tied. Not literally tied, I was just busy.' I kicked myself for adding that last bit.

'I didn't . . . Oh, wait. Looks like I butt-dialled you.'

Of course it was an accident. Why did I think he would video-call me?

But Joon wasn't done. 'It must be fate though, I was just thinking about you.'

Butterflies rushed from my belly and flooded my throat. What was up with today? First the bracelet, then the thing with Luna, and now he was admitting this. I recalled the feeling of his hand on mine on Saturday. Was he doing all this because I hadn't pulled away?

'I hope nothing bad.'

'Never.' I could hear a smile in his voice. 'I was wondering if you'd thought about singing your frequency. It could be really something if you did that at the pageant.'

I frowned, remembering how I'd wondered if Dad had chosen to let his frequency out on his testing day by singing it. I just never pictured myself putting a tune to anything that came out of my mouth. Certainly not with an audience.

'I don't know. I'm not musical.'

'So you say, but it's not too late to try.'

I was thinking of a way to get out of it when he spoke again.

'Is it okay if I call you back? I was in the middle of something.'

Suppressing a sigh of relief, I nodded, even though he couldn't see me. 'Call back anytime.'

I slammed my face into my palm as I cut the line. I'd sounded like I had nothing better to do than wait for his call.

I kept glancing at my slider as I pretended to fix the fryer. After a few minutes, I realised his call probably wasn't coming anytime soon and focused on my task. But when my slider buzzed ten minutes later, I jumped at it.

Jaden: Hey.
Akaego: Thanks again for the bracelet.
Akaego: It was really sweet of you.
Jaden: What bracelet?

I blinked at the name on the screen. This time, I wasn't able to hold on to my slider as it crashed to the counter.

No, no, no!

Why did both their names have to start with the same letter? And why was I friends with people who didn't use avatars?

Jaden: Did someone give you a bracelet?
Jaden: Wait, was it Level Four?
Jaden: Oi, I can see you've read this.

I'd told him Joon had stopped calling me Engineering, and he wasn't acting as bossy as before, but Jaden still wasn't sure about him. It was difficult to convince him otherwise when he'd only met Joon that one time.

Akaego: It was just a little gift for doing well at
the test.

I could hear his sigh all the way from his house.

Jaden: You can't trust him.
Akaego: What if he's just being friendly?
Jaden: I'm your friend and I didn't buy you a
bracelet.
Akaego: Maybe you should have.
Jaden: I'd rather you just came clean and said
you fancy him.

Storming to my room, I flung my slider on to my bed and collapsed into my desk chair. What nerve! Did he think I wasn't capable of forming friendships outside the one I had with him?

I also realised I was annoyed at the fact he'd sussed what I hadn't admitted to anyone yet. That I probably – nope, scratch that – definitely fancied Joon Bernard-Jeong. The one person I shouldn't have butterflies in my belly about right now. With suspicions about his mother still hanging in the air, it really wasn't the best time to catch feelings. But I had.

My slider vibrated again, and I groaned. Jaden and I never fought. We argued, but not over anything at the level we'd been facing recently. I loved the way things were between us because he never pushed me to be more than who he knew I was. Now it felt like we were losing that.

It was only when my slider buzzed again that I got up and grabbed it. The text came through as an unfamiliar blocky script. It took a second for me to remember it was Roulette's way of encoding notifications. I typed in my password, and the words morphed.

xcarlitox: We're back on!
xcarlitox: Details coming your way soon!

CHAPTER TWENTY

89 days to Augmentation Day

'What do we do now?' Carl's hands fell dramatically to his sides.

It was a bit of an overreaction, but I shared his frustration. Getting kicked out of the bowling alley we'd settled on for our meetup was not on the cards.

'Maybe next time you could pick somewhere with better inspection policies.' Rosita's comment was for me.

How was I to know the venue's air filtration system would get damaged? We'd been assigned the perfect lane as well, one at the end of the room. The continuous sounds of Jaden's and Rosita's bowling balls bashing into resin pins would easily mask our conversation.

'Cut her some slack,' Jaden said. 'This could have happened to anyone.'

He didn't return my smile of gratitude. To be fair, he hadn't made any more snarky remarks about the bracelet.

'Do you have a plan B?' Rosita asked, glancing at the other stragglers sharing the pavement with us. Her

204

only condition when she agreed to Carl's training was that she be present. Now I bet she wished she had tacked on more rules.

I had to think fast. Even though it was inching towards autumn and we were lucky enough to have a slight breeze, our suits wouldn't last long in the heat if we didn't start heading for the station. It was a three-minute walk, but we'd been standing outside for two.

I checked the time. Quarter past four. The bowling alley's incompetent management was making me waste my lie to Mr Ericsson. I couldn't play the cramps card more than once a month. I was thankful he hadn't asked me to slap on a hormone-balancing patch and carry on as usual.

'We could go to my place.'

My words hung in the air.

'What have you been smoking?' Rosita didn't mince her words.

It was a Wednesday, which meant Mum would be at her office for her weekly drop-in and wouldn't get home until after six. Dad had gone back to the biodome yesterday. As long as I got everyone out before six, we were good. I explained, then held my breath.

'We'd better get going before we melt.' Rosita fanned herself like she could already feel the heat.

I frowned, thinking my proposal had gone down a little too easily. Maybe she had decided this would be our only session and she was trying to move things along. Whatever, I wasn't going to protest.

Stepping closer, Jaden offered her a hand. 'If you're feeling faint, I could help.'

Rosita's laughter pierced through my helmet.

'Let me be clear, Jaden, you're not my type.'

'And what is your type?' he asked, not missing a beat.

Looking him up and down, she shook her head. 'Not you.'

I was glad my helmet hid my smile. Jaden spun on his heel and started marching briskly towards the station. Carl fell into stride beside him, striking up a conversation about something I couldn't hear. When Rosita slowed down, I did the same.

'What changed your mind?' I asked.

She didn't say anything at first, but when she did, she sounded deflated. 'Did you hear about the raid?'

I nodded. 'I was worried you guys were involved.'

'We were surprised,' she admitted. 'Everyone's nervous, but I didn't want to just sit around doing nothing.'

'Do you think they'll give you up?' I couldn't imagine the government wouldn't try to get something out of their captives.

This time Rosita's laugh was sympathetic to my ignorance.

'Even if they wanted to, they wouldn't know who to rat on. There was a time when everyone knew each other, which made it easier for the authorities to capture hundreds of people from a single raid. Now we work in smaller groups and communicate with others by code when necessary. It's safer that way. The only thing I know for certain is there are a few groups in London, and dozens nationwide.'

We'd been led to believe Freestakers were one big force pushing hard against the government and destroying the fabric of society by their underground movements. Was it possible they really didn't even know what was going on amongst themselves in one city?

'What'll happen to them now?'

Rosita shrugged. 'It depends. If it was only a meeting, they'll probably get tagged and added to a watch list. If they were caught with any equipment or there were signs of intent, that'll be manual labour in one of the food-growing biodomes. They'll only have access to the most basic food credits.'

'Even the kids?' I didn't hide my shock.

'That's the messed-up part. Most Freestakers are Level Ones by choice, so they force their children to get Augmented. Imagine having to become an active contributor to a system you're trying to break.'

I tried not to cringe. I wasn't planning on coercing Carl to get Augmented, but I *was* offering him my help because I hoped to sway him to swap sides. I shook my head. No, that wasn't the same. If he understood the good he could do, he would make the right choice.

What I really couldn't get my head around was knowing that these were the penalties and yet people kept joining. It had been over thirty years since the first Freestakers surfaced, and they had never fully been silenced. The public outcry after the explosion in Croydon came close, but even that wasn't enough to quash their cause.

We got to my house in under fifteen minutes. Having just over an hour wasn't great, but it was better than cancelling altogether.

'You have a cat!'

When we went past the airlock, Carl gawked at Clifford like he'd never seen anything like him before.

'He's jealous,' Rosita said, correcting my thoughts. 'He's always wanted a pet.'

I picked up Clifford and handed him to Carl. 'Did you know scientists tried finding plant-growth frequencies in animals?'

'Really?' Carl's eyes were wide as saucers as he stroked the cat.

'There weren't enough left to test, so they gave up. Besides, controlling sounds from humans is easier. Imagine trying to get a dog to bark at the right pitch each time.'

He turned to Rosita. 'See, this is the kind of stuff she can tell us.'

'Is it really?' Rosita raised a brow. 'And how exactly will knowing about singing cats and dogs help you find your frequency?'

Carl shook his head and gave me a look that said he was sorry for her childishness.

I chuckled. 'You guys are so lucky. I've always

wanted a brother or sister.' Jaden was a good stand-in, but it wasn't quite the same.

'Only because you haven't had to share a room with one,' Rosita grumbled, but she was smiling when she ruffled Carl's hair.

'One kid would be plenty.' Jaden's nose crinkled. 'I don't understand why anyone would apply to get moved to the three-child tier. It's not like they get more spending credits.'

I couldn't argue with that. Although it would have been nice to not always feel like I had to embody all Mum and Dad ever hoped for in an offspring.

'Chop-chop.' Rosita tapped her wrist.

'One sec, I need to reset my location.' I raised a finger at her before moving my falsified co-ordinates from school back to my actual GPS reading.

'You're good at this after all,' Rosita scoffed. 'I thought it was just talk.'

'She was top of our class before they stole her away.' Jaden came to my defence. I could tell he was still smarting from earlier.

'Of course you'd say that,' Rosita laughed.

'No, really,' he insisted.

I signalled for Carl to follow me, leaving them in the living room to bicker. Jaden knew his way around the house, and I trusted he would make sure Rosita didn't go snooping.

'Don't touch anything,' I said to Carl when we entered Mum's study.

Mum would flip if she knew I'd brought anyone here, but it had the best acoustic isolation in the house. I noticed Carl eyeing her monocle. I didn't blame him. Sometimes I wished I could take a peek. The monocles Jaden and I used for gaming were basic entertainment issue, which we could afford with our credits, but Mum's sleeker-looking version held classified information for her work as an analyst which could only be accessed by retinal detection.

'First point –' I began pacing like Mr Ericsson sometimes did – 'most plants respond best to sounds at frequencies between a hundred and three hundred hertz. Like I was saying at the arcade, every Mechsim affects plant growth differently, and that's because there are thirty-four identified active frequencies within that range.'

'Thirty-four?'

I could see Carl calculating how long it would take to practise each frequency before ruling it out.

'Second thing, and this is important for when you start working on seedlings – silence is golden.' I paused, realising I sounded a little too formal. I perched on Mum's desk and softened my tone. 'Even room surfaces need to be considered. But it won't make much difference when you've isolated and strengthened your frequency.'

'I have questions,' Carl interrupted.

For some reason, I hadn't been expecting that. I simply made notes whenever Mr Ericsson droned on.

'What happens if two Mechsims try to grow one plant at the same time? Does it grow faster?'

'Why? Are you hoping to build a sonic team?' I joked, trying not to dwell on the possibility of him accidentally creating a hybrid Deathsim group with that thinking.

Carl's nod confirmed he had been thinking in that line. Not the Deathsim bit though. At least I hoped not.

'It's not a great idea. If the two of them happen to have similar enough frequencies, the sounds could distort each other. The same frequency projected at an equivalent amplitude could create destructive interference.'

'They cancel each other out?'

'You know about this?'

'Not really, but the physics works.'

He was clearly a lot brighter than I'd been at that age.

'So no supergroups for you.' I smiled. 'Sorry.'

'Akaego Eke, what is going on here?'

We turned to the door. My heart pounded. Mum's eyes were on Carl, who had jumped up from the swivel chair and was looking nervous. I couldn't understand how she was home. It wasn't even half five.

Before I could speak, Rosita appeared in the doorway, clutching Jaden's arm. She squeezed past Mum, pulled Jaden close and let out a sound I had never heard from her before. A giggle.

'I'm so sorry, Aunty, this is my fault.' Rosita

masterfully bridged the gap between herself and my mother by referring to her with that term of endearment.

When she blushed and gently stroked Jaden's cheek, he wasn't the only one staring at her in shock. It suddenly occurred to me what she was doing.

'Mum, this is Roz.' I recalled the pet name Carl used for her. 'Jaden's girlfriend.'

I wasn't planning on introducing her as my friendly new Freestakers mate, but this was a good explanation for me bringing home strangers without having to say more. I hadn't thought *that* far ahead.

Luckily, Jaden's brain unstuck and he pulled Rosita closer, slipping an arm around her waist. If Rosita hated it, she didn't let it show, burrowing into his side even more. They actually made a really cute couple. Cute enough for Mum to buy the act.

Her frown twisted into a smile. 'Ah, look at little Jaden having a girlfriend. The young shall grow.'

I don't know how we all managed not to cringe on his behalf.

Mum's glare returned, and her attention shifted back to me. 'What were you doing in here though? Who is this young man?'

'They were giving us some privacy, Aunty.' Rosita continued to lie her way through the crisis. 'I was meant to watch my little brother today, and Akaego offered to help.'

Mum's brow slowly unknitted. 'Well, you should be watching him somewhere that isn't my workspace.' She directed this at me, and I dipped my head in genuine remorse. 'You know I keep sensitive material in here.'

'I'm sorry, Mum, we were wandering around and Carl was curious about your monocle, so we stopped.' It wasn't an outright lie. 'I didn't think you'd be back so soon.'

'Is that your excuse?' Mum scolded, but I could tell she wasn't really angry. Her monocle was perched on her desk exactly as she'd left it.

'We should head out.' Rosita didn't wait for more questions to be asked, not least what she and Jaden could have been doing that required privacy. 'Really sorry again, Aunty. It was lovely to meet you. Come on, off we go.' She signalled to Carl.

Mum watched silently as the three of them rushed out of the room, leaving me behind.

'I'll see them out,' I added, to delay the telling-off I was bound to receive.

I found them in the hallway, scrambling into their suits and trying to avoid stepping on Clifford.

'That was close,' Jaden whispered cheerily. I thought he'd be upset, but the adrenalin was clearly having a different effect. 'And hey, a little warning would be appreciated next time you decide to feel me up.'

'Don't flatter yourself.' Rosita didn't look at him as she set her suit to chill. 'That's the last time you'll be that close to me, so I hope you enjoyed it.'

'I do love a challenge,' Jaden countered, receiving an eye-roll from her.

'I'm sorry, guys.' I shook my head. 'She's never back so early. I would never have brought you here if I even—'

'Let's hope this was not a sign from above.' Rosita was very calm about it all, but I supposed she'd been in tighter spots before. 'Next time, I'll pick where we go.'

I couldn't contain my smile when Carl threw himself at her for a hug before flashing a double thumbs up my way. All that mattered was that there was going to be a next time.

I returned to the study feeling a little lighter, yet fully prepared for Mum to rip into me. She had moved to her desk and was tapping away on her slider.

'I'm sorry,' I repeated sheepishly.

To my surprise, Mum just looked distracted. Something must have come up at work. 'That girl seemed interesting. What was her name again?'

'Roz.'

'And?'

'Carl.' I didn't see the point in lying. With any luck, she'd never meet them again.

Mum put down her slider. 'It's good you and Jaden are making friends. You should spend more time with them.'

I suspected she was relieved Jaden had a girlfriend. That way she wouldn't keep wondering what we got up to all the time. From the moment I hit a C cup, she couldn't fathom the thought that he only saw me as a friend. It didn't help that she'd caught him jokingly holding me in a headlock when we were fourteen, even though we had an open-door rule and absolutely nothing was happening.

'Am I still grounded?'

'You know that decision was your father's.' Mum sighed. 'How many weeks has it been? You need some freedom to develop friendships at your age.'

She'd hinted before that she thought Dad was overreacting since there'd been no other drama after the incidents at Rush and the mayor's reception. At least, nothing she was aware of. But I hadn't realised she would be willing to encourage me to disobey him. This was my chance to meet the others without hiding.

'I'm glad you brought them home instead of sneaking around,' Mum went on, 'but you should be able to go out with them. Don't worry about your father. I'll deal with him.'

There had to be a limit to how guilt-ridden I could feel in one day.

'Just make sure you don't give those two any more privacy in my house. Do they think this is a motel?'

I laughed and went over for a hug. I hated lying to Mum, but I couldn't let her suss out what was really going on.

I had to protect her from the insanity that had taken over my life. Despite Mr Ericsson saying my test results seemed fine, the mayor's call still worried me. The timing of it. The words she used. Next time I was in Regent's Park, I would do my best to find out if she was who everyone feared she was. Whatever it took.

215

CHAPTER TWENTY-ONE

86 days to Augmentation Day

It was one thing having a mission, and another figuring out how to implement it. I'd spent the past few days working out how to ask the mayor about what I'd heard at Crystal without implicating Dad or anyone else. After all, why would I believe the test result or the garden specimen she mentioned had anything to do with me if I didn't have other suspicions?

I finally settled on a potential in.

Sitting across from Mayor Bernard, I cleared my throat. She was talking to Darren, and they looked my way.

'Sorry to interrupt –' I tried not to sound nervous – 'but did you get a chance to speak to the people who have the rose bush? I was hoping to see it today since this is my final session.'

The mayor's smile was as easy as always. 'Ah, how's that coming along, Darren? You spoke with the team at the nursery?'

From the glare he shot me, I sensed Darren thought I was wasting the mayor's time. 'They've been

216

incredibly busy. I'll chase them, but you'll have to come back another day.'

I nodded. It wasn't a refusal, but it felt like a fob off.

'Sure, thanks. It's just, what if the roses are all gone by then?'

The mayor frowned. 'Ki-Joon showed you photos, no?'

'Yes, but—'

'When Darren hears from the team, he'll be in touch with a date.'

It was the first time she'd snapped at me. I knew not to push it. Besides, if this was a cover-up, it didn't make sense for them to postpone the viewing. If the roses were dead, they could have shown me another bush and I'd have no idea if what I saw was different.

Unless they never planned on following through. Maybe they were hoping I'd lose interest after the success of my testing.

I shook the thought from my head. I needed something concrete before I spiralled down that road. I had to move on to the second part of my mission. For this, timing was everything.

Like clockwork, the mayor had a cup of tea brought in at eleven. Ginger and turmeric. She'd offered me a cup on my first day, which I'd politely declined because, really, who drank anything so strong smelling if it wasn't on prescription? I eyed the yellow liquid today. It had been on her desk for a couple of minutes, which felt long enough for it to have cooled.

Pulling out my slider, I made a show of checking it before placing it on the desk. In the process, I moved my chair forward, kicking the desk with as much force as I could manage.

'Be careful,' Darren yelled, although it was a redundant plea.

The tea-filled cup wobbled, and I dived for it, praying they wouldn't notice I was helping it tip over, not saving it from that fate. The mayor sprang up, her floral-print dress drenched.

'I'm so sorry,' I cried. My heart raced so fast I was sure they could hear it as my hand flew to my mouth to convey the shock I didn't feel.

Darren was looking around for something to soak up the mess, but the mayor raised her hand, pulled off her monocle and tossed it on a dry section of her desk. I glanced at the device, noting a small flashing red light on its thin frame.

This could actually work. Dear Lord, let it work!

I walked towards her, pushing my slider closer to the monocle. The app I'd downloaded off a dodgy-looking open-source account on Roulette was specific about how close the device I needed to latch on to should be. Thirty centimetres. I hoped my slider synced with the monocle's signal before its retina-detection lock set in. Now I needed the mayor to leave it untouched to give me the five minutes required to shadow the server.

'It's okay, Akaego, accidents happen.' Mayor

Bernard waved away my apology. 'I'm only a flight of stairs away from my wardrobe.'

I joined in when she laughed, hearing it sound forced.

'I guess I'll just wait here?' I asked, mentally crossing my fingers and toes. If they told me to step out, this would have been for nothing.

My sigh was almost audible when she nodded. 'I'll be back in a tick.'

I held my breath until she left, followed closely by a scowling Darren, who said something about going to fetch a cleaning cloth. I didn't dare touch my slider. I hadn't noticed any cameras in the study in the past, but I'd never looked. It felt too obvious if I suddenly started glancing around for signs of recording activity.

'Please let it be five minutes, please let it be five minutes,' I mumbled, rubbing wet palms together and keeping my eyes on the door.

The next part of this scheme wasn't going to be easy either. Shadowing the secure server the monocle was connected to meant staying on the same network, to avoid looking like I was hacking the system. If I gained access, I'd have to trawl through the mayor's files for something to tie her to Dad's claims. I needed an excuse to remain on the property.

When Darren came back, it didn't feel like I'd had enough time, but I could only watch silently as he mopped up the liquid. I shoved my slider back into my pocket after he shifted the monocle closer to the mayor's chair. I'd know soon enough if it had worked.

The mayor returned shortly after in a pinstriped tailored trouser suit.

'I'm really sorry,' I apologised again. 'I'm not usually so clumsy.'

'No, it's fine,' she said. 'I had to change for an outing later anyway. Which reminds me, I thought you could join me on an external engagement today.'

'What?' I was stunned. Of all the days she could have chosen to include me, this was the absolute worst.

The mayor didn't seem to notice. 'The other interns had more productive experiences because we met on weekdays. Fortunately, I have a last-minute face-to-face meeting with the Minister for Crime Prevention at one o'clock. I thought it would be a perfect opportunity for you to come along to Greenwich Park Biodome. Not many non-workers get to go in.'

'But that's . . .' The words died on my lips. I wouldn't get a chance to search her files if we left the house. But was I really about to throw away the opportunity to meet a high-ranking official because I wanted to access information that potentially had no value?

Her look of confusion at my hesitance was understandable. 'I hope you haven't made plans because we've cut our other sessions short.'

'No, that's not it.' I thought fast. 'But . . . would it be okay if I have lunch before we go? I wasn't feeling too well this morning and skipped breakfast.'

'Of course.' Her frown turned to one of concern. 'Go to the kitchen. We don't want you passing out, do we?'

My slider came out the second I left the room. Clicking through, I opened the app and sighed with relief. A new icon sat in it. I tapped it, knowing there wasn't much time.

Please enter network access code.

Crap! I'd hoped shadowing the server meant I didn't need to connect to the network separately.

'Think, think.' I looked around aimlessly, like the code would materialise out of thin air.

There was one way of getting it, but it meant another lie. I was already neck-deep; one more almost felt normal.

Akaego: You home?
Akaego: Meet me in the kitchen if you are.

I made my way over there, not waiting to see if Joon replied. I had to pretend to eat something even if I didn't want to.

'If this is about the sandwich I didn't make you last week, I'm sorry to say I'm still banned,' Joon said when he met me outside the kitchen door.

There was no thrill in seeing his smile today.

'What's your network code?'

His brow scrunched at my abruptness. 'You haven't got signal on your slider?'

'There's a limited-edition Broxxie token coming out right now. Jaden's obsessed with him, and I was hoping to download it for his birthday. My slider's acting up though, so I can't join the queue.'

He came closer, craning his neck at my screen. 'Broxxie? Really? I love his tunes.'

I hadn't been expecting that response. He didn't strike me as a Broxxie fan, based on the pop rock and slow ballads I'd heard him play. I pulled back quickly. 'I just need the code before I'm locked out of the queue. Can I have it?'

'Sure.' He brought out his slider and sent the access code to me.

Once my screen flashed with a welcome message to the network, I checked the shadow server and smiled when it opened. I looked at Joon and he was frowning again.

'Aren't you going to send me the link to the token?'

'Eh, no, sorry,' I laughed, hoping he'd buy my light tone. 'It's invitation only and I can't have too many people clogging the queue. Thanks for this.' I waved my slider before ducking into the kitchen. I didn't like using him, but I had no choice.

As I waited for the cook to make me a grilled tomato sandwich, the only thing I reckoned I could stomach, I sat with my back against the wall to avoid anyone looking over my shoulder. The mayor's monocle had given me access to two folders, one named *Home* and the other *Work*. I went into the obvious one.

With little time to be thorough, I typed in the EE-code. It took ten seconds for a file to pop up.

EE-code evaluation – Classified

I stared at it, my hand trembling, my chest heaving.

Until that moment, I hadn't truly been expecting to find anything tangible. I didn't know if the file held proof of anything Dad said, but seeing the name on the mayor's secure system made it all feel more real. More possible.

When I tried to open the file, an encryption notice popped up. I copied it to my slider before typing in Deathsims for another search. Nothing. I would take my time to crack the encryption when I got home.

I saw the cook move the grilled tomatoes on to a plate and set the bread to toast. I estimated I had time for one more search. I moved to the Home folder, spotting a security footage subfolder. Scrolling through, I found a tab titled *Courtyard* and went back a couple of weeks. Muting my slider, I played a video from two days after the reception.

The camera position in the courtyard was angled so it showed the rose bush clearly. Same as in Joon's photos, the roses stood out in vibrant blots of red. Ignoring the pride that swelled in my chest, I moved to the next day. They were still there. A day after, wilting took hold. By the Friday, the rose bush had completely dried up. Leaves on a few plants around it also showed signs of yellowing.

Joon was right.

'Miss?'

My mouth hung open when I looked up at the cook, before I recovered and took the plate. I barely registered the taste of the sandwich. There was only one thought racing through my mind.

The mayor had lied. Not bent the truth a little, but straight-out lied about the roses.

It was inevitable I'd eventually find out my abilities were accelerated, so why lie? The only advantage I could think of for keeping that information quiet was that it had bought her time. But time to do what?

My walk back to the study felt like a death march. Was Dad really right about the mayor's intentions? I had to know what was on that encrypted file. It suddenly felt like the most important thing in the world.

'You're here.' The mayor frowned when I entered, standing and approaching me. 'I should have noticed you looked a bit peaky earlier on. You look even worse.'

I did? She must have mistaken my anxiety for symptoms of my feigned illness.

'You should go home. Dragging you to Greenwich won't do you any good,' she reasoned. 'It would have been fitting to mark the end of your internship, but we can organise a visit with me to another biodome, your choice. It won't be for a while as I'm quite busy over the next few weekends.'

I nodded silently. I understood now why Dad couldn't sit through lunch with her. It was difficult to look at her, wondering what else she might be lying about. All I wanted to do was get home and work on the file.

I fired off a message to Dad the second I got on the Tube.

Akaego: When are you coming home?

A response came through a few minutes later.

Dad: This evening.
Dad: Everything okay?
Akaego: I don't know.
Dad: Are you hurt?
Dad: Are you at home?
Akaego: I'm fine.

I wasn't, but I couldn't mention the mayor in case our messages were being read. If Carl could tap into my tracker, who knew who else had access to unencrypted data on my slider?

Akaego: You may have been right about Level
     Four luxuries.

There was a pause. He was probably trying to work out what I meant.

Dad: I'll see you soon.

I was still trying to decrypt the file when Dad burst into my room an hour later. The suspense must have been too much for him to bear until evening.

'What is it? What happened?' he panted, crouching by my desk, grabbing my shoulders and scanning my body.

'I'm okay, Daddy.' My words didn't match my

225

lunge at him as I buried my face against his shoulder. 'I'm okay.'

'Ego, what happened?'

Pulling my head up, I turned my slider to him. His eyes narrowed, then widened at the file name on the screen.

'How?' He looked up at me, his eyes even wider. 'Where did you get this?'

'I hacked into the mayor's files. You said you didn't have time to read through the redacted document you saw. Maybe this is it. Can you find a way to decrypt it?'

'Akaego, you shouldn't put yourself in danger.' He shook his head. 'Do you know what the penalty for hacking a government official's system is? What if this gets tracked?'

I was too far gone to worry about that now. 'I used a shadowing app, so it shouldn't get noticed. The mayor lied about the roses I grew, and I overheard her asking someone to fix test results. I need to know for certain if this has anything to do with me. This way we know for sure, right?'

Dad glanced at the screen again. His sigh was drawn out.

'I know someone who may be able to open it. But in the meantime, please, no more hacking or digging.'

I nodded. There probably weren't going to be any more opportunities to access the mayor's files now our sessions were officially over anyway. I wished I had thought to do this once Dad told me of his suspicions. I might have had time to dig more.

'Is it silly that I still want you to be wrong?' I asked, staring at the file on my screen.

'Not at all.' Dad placed a hand on my cheek and sighed. 'You don't know how badly I want to be wrong too.'

CHAPTER TWENTY-TWO

81 days to Augmentation Day

'Are you sure you want to do this? I'm pretty certain I'm tone deaf.'

'No, you're not.' Joon walked to the back of the room. 'Most people just say they are because they sing at the wrong pitch.'

Or they've never sung at all, I wanted to say. Instead, I watched him select an acoustic guitar from a rack against the wall.

'Don't tell me you play that as well.'

'Okay, I won't tell you.' Joon smiled, expertly strumming a note before coming to sit beside me.

Watching him tune the guitar by ear, his lower lip caught in his teeth as he worked his way up the metal strings, I had to agree with Rosita on one thing. Labels were wasted on people like him. It was a shame someone with passion and skill for so many different things was forced to choose only one.

'Right.' He looked up at me, a sparkle in his eyes. 'We need to come up with a signature tune. Something you can stretch or shorten to suit you. Do you mind singing your frequency to me?'

I knew what was coming, yet nerves struck. Joon wasn't one to half-arse things. After he'd suggested I sing at the pageant, he'd gone ahead and sent me practice details, having worked out we shared a free period on Thursdays.

Dad's contact hadn't come back with any news about the files I'd stolen off the mayor, apparently so far stumped by the complex encryption. One thing was clear though. The garden footage screamed Deathsim. I was still trying to process this information. I had no intention of singing on Augmentation Day, but I needed a distraction. Which was why I'd shown up as Joon requested. Not because the thought of spending more time alone with him warmed my insides.

Nope, not that at all.

'Is that a no?' Joon asked when I remained silent, a note of doubt creeping into his voice.

Taking a deep breath, I checked to make sure there were no potted plants waiting to betray me later on before I let out the sound I had come to both fear and revere.

Joon's head tilted. 'I don't remember it sounding so low.'

It wasn't. My anxiety was getting the better of me.

'How could you remember something like that?' I frowned. I'd kept my output brief at my evaluation.

'I always pay attention to things important to me,' Joon replied quietly.

I couldn't tell if time stopped or if it was my heart that skipped a beat.

It didn't matter which because I leaned forward. My eyes drank in every perfectly placed feature of his face before dropping to his slightly parted lips, which would have been utterly embarrassing if he hadn't been staring back at me so intently.

When Joon's gaze fell to my lips, I may have let out a sound. I couldn't really tell with all the blood rushing to my head.

Things.

The word pushed its way through my head rush and flashed in bright lights. He hadn't said people important to him. He'd said *things*.

He must have been referring to my frequency, not me. I hadn't questioned his presence at my testing, but what if his mother brought him along to pay attention to it? She could easily have requested the recording later, so my rationale was probably not accurate, but once the thought entered my mind, it was impossible to unthink it.

I sat back at the exact moment Joon inched forward.

'Don't tell me I have another lash on my face,' I chortled nervously, searching for something to break the tension.

Joon blinked with confusion. Whatever that was, even if it had started off with my misunderstanding, I hadn't imagined what nearly happened. Not with the heat in his eyes and the floating see-saw in my belly. If I'd stayed still for just a second longer . . .

'Akaego, I—'

'Attention, students.' The speaker at the front of the rehearsal room came to life, interrupting him. 'Due to the ongoing problems with the gym's plumbing, our Level One guests will be using other changing facilities in the building today. If you notice any unfamiliar faces over the next hour, please say hello and help our guests along.'

My slider buzzed just as Mrs Miguel's voice cut out.

'You're on Roulette?' Joon squinted at my screen.

I hadn't thought twice about pulling the device out in front of him. I was clearly terrible at this whole secrecy business. Thankfully, the text was in its usual unreadable script.

I paused, aware I could make this worse with my response. 'Yeah, just for this and that, you know?'

Joon's frown very clearly indicated he did not know. 'I thought people only used it for hook-ups and illegal deals.'

If only he realised how close he was to the truth.

'Not every hyper-encrypted platform is dodgy.' I hoped my laughter sounded more genuine to his ears than mine. 'We used it in my last school to improve code-cracking skills. Jaden sends me stuff to help him out.'

It was nonsense, but I hoped using something from a world alien to his would do the trick. And it did. Joon nodded like he understood before he put down the guitar.

'About earlier—'

'I think we should come up with more than one tune,' I cut in, not wanting him to take us back to that awkward moment. 'It'll be better to have options for the pageant.'

'Ten minutes ago, you weren't convinced you could even sing one.'

'Are you saying you don't want to go on?' I challenged.

His frown returned, and I thought he would push on, but he sighed. 'Okay, but this time, I need the real thing. We can't make it work if you're holding back.'

Nodding, I gave him my frequency.

'How about this?' He hummed a folky-sounding tune.

When I sang it back to him, he grinned. 'And you thought you were tone deaf.'

'That sounded okay?' I returned his smile, genuinely surprised.

'You won't be selling out Hyde Park any time soon, but you can carry a tune. Let's try something else.'

We carried on, and I found myself sharing opinions about his suggestions as he wrote down notes, crossing them out and tweaking them as we went along. Although this was related to using my frequency, it felt different. Applying a melody made it feel like I was singing for pleasure. Something I never did. Something I was really enjoying. I liked the idea that Dad had passed on more than his Deathsim ability to me.

When the bell rang, it didn't feel like we'd been there

for the better part of an hour, and the weirdness between us was almost completely gone. It was impossible to hold on to it when Joon's default mode was so easy-breezy. I made sure his hand didn't touch mine when we both reached for the door to leave the room. Safer to keep the butterflies at bay.

'How much longer are you stuck with Ericsson?' Joon asked as we walked down the corridor, trying not to bump into the crowd streaming towards the exit. 'I thought you'd stop your sessions after the test.'

'Why? You haven't had your fill of playing composer for the day?' I joked.

'There's a good karaoke place we should go to. Once you see how out of tune everyone is on that stage, you'll understand how brilliant you really are.'

I turned to see he was serious.

'Careful there, it almost sounded like you were asking me out on a date.' I let out a small laugh, playfully nudging his shoulder.

'Who said I wasn't?' He grinned, stopping and forcing me to do the same as he stood in my way. The last thing I expected was for him to reach for my hand.

It was official. The butterflies had free rein.

But as much as I wanted them to soar, this was my chance to turn him down. Accepting his bracelet was my first mistake, and had to be my last. I didn't think my heart could take it if I found out all this attention was an act.

As my mind raced, a group came up behind Joon.

Even if they weren't dressed in identical blue T-shirts and black shorts, the Level One students stood out by the way they huddled, their eyes scanning the faces of the academy students they walked past.

All but one pair of eyes, which were fixed on me.

Rosita's.

I should have guessed there was a possibility she'd be amongst the group, seeing as I had stalked her from the gym on a Thursday, but Joon had thrown me with his question.

Joon turned to see who had caught my attention before spinning back to me, his smile gone.

'That's the girl from the reception.' His voice was low, and still it sounded like it bounced off the walls.

'Who?'

'The waitress.'

The group moved past us and I snuck another glance at them. Rosita had ducked away. I couldn't understand how Joon recognised her without the nose prosthetic and blonde hair she'd had on that day.

'I don't remember what she—'

'Don't do that.' I heard a plea in his voice. 'I saw the look on your face. It was the same that day. Like you're afraid of her, or something else.'

'I really don't remember. I have to—'

Joon hadn't let go of my hand, and now he tugged me along, heading back the way we'd just come. He only released me after he shut the door behind us in the rehearsal room.

'What's going on?' He kept his voice low even though we were alone.

'Nothing is going on.' I rubbed my wrist, avoiding eye contact.

'Really?'

'Yes,' I insisted.

My mouth was dry as I tried to recall exactly what I'd said over a month ago. If he remembered Rosita, was that because he thought she had something to do with the attack? And if he thought I knew her, did that mean he believed I'd lied all this time?

'You know you have a tell, right?'

'A what?' I looked at him now, eyes narrowed.

'When you're trying to twist the truth, you can't help doing it.'

He didn't say what it was, but he seemed pretty convinced.

'I'm not lying.'

'You're doing it now.'

Okay, what the hell was it?

'Look, Joon.' I let out an exasperated sigh. 'I don't know what you think you know, but you're wrong about this.'

'So if I ask Mum's team to check up on the girl you claim not to remember, you won't care.'

What? Could he do that?

'What are you saying?' I crossed my arms to hide them trembling.

'I thought I saw her give you something, but when

you told me what I found wasn't related to the attack, I let go of my gut feeling. I'm now not so sure I should have.'

I wanted to scream. It was my own fault for not dumping the detonator quickly enough. Nothing from that night was planned. Yet there was no way to prove it without giving him more info.

'Is that why you've been acting nice to me all this time? Were you waiting for me to slip up?' That possibility hit me harder than anything else.

'Come on, Akaego.' Joon threw his hands in the air. 'I didn't tell anyone because I actually care about what happens to you. I'm trying to figure out what's going on.'

'Joon—' I couldn't keep the quiver from my voice.

He took a step back and shook his head. 'Freestakers killed my dad, and they attacked us in our home. How do you think I felt watching Mum that day, not knowing if something worse was coming? How do you think it feels wondering if you lied about what happened?'

He stormed towards the door, and panic rose in my chest. He managed to open the door a crack before I slammed it shut from behind him. My arms wrapped around his torso as I pressed my head against his back.

Joon froze, but I wasn't sure which one of us was more shocked. We stood like that for what felt like minutes but must have only been seconds. I followed the rise and fall of his chest, taking my own deep breaths as a hundred thoughts flooded my mind.

'It's not what you think.' The words weren't the denial I thought I'd continue with.

I let go when Joon twisted around in my arms. We stood so close together, I could feel his heart beating against my chest.

'Try me,' he said gently, his expression softening.

Was I really doing this?

I glanced at the camera positioned at the back of the room. The law on filming minors at schools prohibited audio recordings, but who knew what would actually happen if someone argued that national security was at stake?

'I knew how unbelievable it would sound if I admitted it when you asked initially. I'd only just met her. She said it was for show. No one was supposed to get hurt.'

The disappointment in Joon's eyes was hard to look at.

'And you believe her?'

'Yes, I do.'

I needed him to think the intention behind the attack was a prank. I had to convince him not to go to his mother with this, and I couldn't give him too many details in case he still did.

'I'd like to meet this person. Hear what they have to say.'

I almost laughed. 'That's not possible.'

Rosita would bail immediately.

'And what is?' Joon stood his ground.

To be fair to him, he was giving me much more leeway than I deserved.

'Can I get back to you on that? It's not like I can say the mayor's son would like to have a chat.'

Joon's nod was heavy before he reached for the handle again. 'Be careful, Akaego. Anyone okay with the killing of innocent people isn't the kind of person you should be putting your trust in.'

When he pulled the door open, Luna was there, flanked closely by Abigail. I reminded myself not to overreact because the rehearsal rooms were acoustically isolated. Unless the door was slightly open, they shouldn't have heard anything.

I hoped.

'Are you all right?' Luna asked, concern etching her brow, making me wonder how long they'd stood there for.

Joon walked off without answering. Luna didn't spare me a glance before she hurried after him. I watched them go, praying he wouldn't let something slip.

'Can we talk?'

I'd almost forgotten Abigail was still there. I couldn't think of what she could possibly want to discuss, but whatever it was, this was not the day for it.

'I have to meet Mr Ericsson,' I said, glad for the excuse.

'It won't take long.' She stepped forward so I was forced back into the room. 'It's about Luna.'

If anyone watched back the room's footage, they would definitely wonder what the hell was going on.

'I'm going to ask so I know how to deal with what I think is coming,' Abigail carried on seriously. 'Are you and Joon hooking up?'

'I'm sorry, what?'

'Look, I like you. I really do. The problem is Luna's fancied him for a very long time. I'm not saying you guys shouldn't do whatever you want, but maybe don't rub it in her face.'

'You think I'm rubbing it in her face?'

'Sneaking off together, wearing his bracelet, smiling at each other. You're not exactly hiding it.'

I opened my mouth and then shut it, no longer sure what part of the conversation to be annoyed by. If she had come to me on any other day, maybe I would have cowered and made an excuse. Not today.

'If we are hooking up, it's none of your business. And if Luna has an issue with it, she can talk to me herself. Better yet, she can ask Joon. They're supposed to be mates, right?'

Abigail must have expected a denial because her mouth hung open as I brushed past her and exited the room. I was tired of acting like I'd done something wrong. If Joon liked me, why was I the one having to answer for it?

There was no way I was going to survive a session with Mr Ericsson feeling the way I did. Fortunately, he took one look at me and said I could be excused.

Waiting for the airlock to decompress, I kicked myself for compromising Rosita and Carl by admitting my part in the attack to Joon. How was I going to tell Rosita that Joon was on to us? She'd probably start by ending my sessions with Carl. But that might be the least of my worries. If she told someone higher up, word of my involvement could reach Dad. He was shaken enough by my hacking into the mayor's system.

The entrance to the Tube station came into sight and I quickened my pace. But I didn't get far. Something – no, someone – hooked my arm, yanking me into an alley before I could let out a scream.

CHAPTER
TWENTY-THREE

81 days to Augmentation Day

'Don't be such a wuss, it's only me,' my assailant hissed.

The scream froze in my throat. 'Rosita?'

Her glare was seething.

'You realise we don't always have to hide to have a conversation.' I frantically scanned the narrow space we were wedged in.

According to my suit's wrist gauge, it was less than two minutes since I'd left the academy. We had about six minutes and counting to get to the station or head back to school.

'You'd rather talk about you-know-what at the station for everyone to hear? Didn't you get my message?'

Carl gave her access to his Roulette account after she took charge of organising his training. It must have been the message I'd received earlier.

'I haven't had time to check.'

'Obviously. You seemed quite occupied.' There was a touch of humour in her voice even though she still mostly sounded annoyed. 'I was teasing when I called him your boyfriend. I wasn't actually suggesting you go for it.'

'He's not my boyfriend.'

'Does he know that?'

I sighed, not wanting to drag on that line of interrogation. 'We're risking heat exhaustion for this?'

'If you'd read my message you would have seen my plan to make sure we didn't bump into each other,' she chided. 'What did he say? He clearly remembers me.'

I hesitated. 'He saw you give me the detonator. He mentioned you a few weeks ago.'

Rosita was actually lost for words.

'Why for the love of all things green are you telling me this now?' She finally found her tongue.

'Are you really okay working with a group willing to kill people?' Joon's accusation was fresh in my mind.

Once again, Rosita gasped, finding no words to respond.

'Crintex,' I refreshed her memory.

Rosita continued to look lost for a moment before recognition settled on her features. 'You've got it all wrong. It wasn't an attack that killed those people.'

'You're saying it wasn't you guys?'

'Why would we kill seventeen of our people and sixty-two innocent Level One and Twos? Make it make sense.'

'That's not true. There were sixty-two workers and five Freestakers.'

'Are you sure about that?' Rosita's head tilted.

'Non-stat victims weren't accounted for. And it really wasn't an attack. It was an accident which happened to take place on what was meant to be a non-violent protest, back when those were still allowed.'

'What are you saying?'

'Whoever has the loudest voice controls the narrative. Killing is not what we do. How come there's been only one massive fatality in decades? If we were out to murder blindly, don't you think it'd happen more often?'

A cover-up sounded far-fetched, although not impossible. The attack single-handedly gained the most public support against Freestakers and helped tighten the law on protests. But still, the idea that the government would go that far to sway opinions was hard to swallow.

'Can you prove it?' I needed something more than words.

'Even if we had footage, what was the first thing you thought when I showed you the video of the destroyed greenhouse?'

'That it was fake.'

'Exactly. If we hacked all the news channels and showed videos to the public, the government would counter them as fabricated. It'll be our word against theirs because the data forensic experts would be theirs. The only way to get people believing anything is if they see it right in front of them.'

She had a point. I still found it difficult to believe the mayor could be planning something insidious, even after overhearing her conversation and seeing videos of the dead roses.

'Think about it,' Rosita went on, placing a hand on my shoulder. 'All the footage from that day was conveniently deleted. The claim was that Freestakers were trying to cover themselves. The government was bound to point the finger at them, so what possible reason would they have to delete it?'

'Is all that true?'

This question didn't come from me. We spun around to find a dark-suited figure blocking the mouth of the alley.

Joon.

Rosita stepped back, realising her error as she glanced behind us. She'd chosen a dead-end alley, so the only way she could get past Joon was by tackling him. He wasn't as well-built as Jaden, but he would be able to stop someone as slight as her.

'You followed me?' I asked, although I should have seen this coming. I'd done the same with Rosita when I needed answers no one else would give me.

To my surprise, Rosita approached him. 'What exactly do you think you heard?'

Her confidence had to be feigned, but it was pretty convincing.

'We should talk about this properly somewhere else,' Joon replied, his eyes on me, anger and disappointment clear in them.

'We're not going anywhere with you.' Rosita squared her shoulders defiantly.

'You kind of have to. Unless you've figured out how to extend your suit's charge.'

He wasn't wrong. I could already feel the effect of the heat on my suit's sensors. If we stayed much longer, our systems would start to power down, and we'd be in real trouble.

'If I was going to give you up,' Joon insisted when we didn't budge, 'I would have called someone already.' He looked at me again, his features softening a bit now. 'I need to know why you're working with them.'

I stared at him, confused. Was that more important than getting clarity about what had happened thirteen years ago?

'I don't know how much you heard,' Rosita said, drawing his attention back to her, 'but every word I said was true. I'm sorry about your father, but we aren't the ones you should look at for answers.'

'It's okay, Rosita,' I heard myself say, knowing it wasn't. 'I'll talk to him.' I wasn't sure how I'd get him to keep quiet, but I couldn't let her mention anything that could implicate Dad.

Rosita's scowl said she was against me doing this. She had every right to be angry, but if she hadn't thrust the detonator at me, we wouldn't be in this position. We were at Joon's mercy now, and it was her fault.

Joon didn't stop her when she walked past him, disappearing in the direction of the station.

My slider buzzed, and I checked it quickly this time. The message was brief.

xcarlitox: Fix this.

'Coming?' Joon asked, his hand stretched out to me.

'Where are we going?'

'Next door.'

He must have been referring to the restaurant to the right.

'We can't,' I said, confused.

Venues needed bookings confirmed at least fifteen minutes before arrival so their air filtration systems could adjust for optimum efficiency. We did not even have two minutes. Our best bet was the station or school.

'Yes, we can.'

He took my hand and, too hot to argue, I let him lead me to the entrance. The airlock door opened when he scanned his slider and an orange circle flashed. It had to be another Level Four perk. No reservations required.

Before the hostess could ask questions, Joon whispered something to her and she took us to an empty room at the back.

'You have ten minutes.'

Once she left, I sagged against a wall, surprised at how knackered I felt. It wasn't just emotional fatigue. Enough heat had seeped into our suits before we'd escaped the outside air. Glancing up at the camera in the corner, I understood why he'd brought us there. Audio recordings were illegal in private eating spaces.

'I know Mum is hard on Freestakers because of what happened –' Joon chose his words carefully, through gritted teeth – 'but your friend can't have her facts right. She's saying my mother could be tied up in a cover-up that has left millions of people believing a lie. Including me.'

Although the explosion took place before her regime, it was difficult to believe the mayor hadn't delved into the details of something so close to her when she had the power to do so. If she was seeking payback, she couldn't possibly think it had been an accident. Which meant if there was proof it was one, maybe it would be enough to convince her to stop the Deathsim project.

That is, if the project existed at all. The thing was, I would have been inclined to dismiss Rosita's claims if the mayor hadn't lied to me about the roses being dead. Something that shouldn't have raised alarms if she thought it had no significance.

'I'm sorry for putting you in this position,' I said quietly. 'I can't tell you anything else, but I promise you I didn't go into this lightly.'

I couldn't explain that I was working with Rosita because I was hoping to bring Carl on side. And I obviously couldn't mention Deathsims. The less he knew, the better.

Joon looked sadder than I'd ever seen him as he came to lean beside me. My mind returned to that moment in the corridor at Crystal. Judging from the wistful look that crept on to his face, he was thinking the same thing.

'Do you know the worst thing about this?' he asked rhetorically. 'The fact that a part of me keeps wondering if you were using me to get to my mother.'

'Joon . . .'

I hadn't thought about it that way.

'I don't think we should spend any more time together.'

There was no point arguing. He was giving me the space I should have asked for all along. So why did his words cut so much?

'Does that mean you won't tell anyone?' I sounded more hopeful than I felt.

'What am I going to say? That I think I saw someone hand you something at the reception? You'll only deny it.' Pushing himself off the wall, he laughed drily. 'It's you who needs to do the right thing and report what you know to the authorities.'

He could easily have gone to his mum, but he was giving me a chance to do the right thing. Reporting Rosita for the attack was something I wasn't willing to do.

I didn't expect a sob to catch in my throat, my frustrations bubbling over, seeking an escape. Joon must have been startled too because his face twisted from concern to anger, then back to concern before he stepped closer. When he reached out and drew me against his chest, I welcomed the contact.

'Be careful,' he whispered into my hair. 'I don't want to lose you too.'

I pulled my head back. I hadn't realised I'd become

someone he was afraid of losing.

Caught in the moment, I reached up to place a peck on his cheek at the exact instant Joon dipped his head. My lips hit the corner of his, and our bodies went rigid. I was about to pull away again when he placed a finger firmly under my chin, his left eyebrow rising with an unspoken question as his eyes dropped to my lips. My nod followed quickly.

Tilting my head slightly, he planted his lips firmly on mine, shutting his eyes.

With a sigh, I shut my eyes and gave in to the butterflies.

CHAPTER TWENTY-FOUR

79 days to Augmentation Day

Time felt like it was crawling as my worries mounted.

I'd messaged Rosita to let her know Joon had promised not to rat on us, but she hadn't responded. My attempts to crack the file encryption as we waited for Dad's contact had led nowhere, despite me downloading six different apps on Roulette. But my main concern was if Joon would keep his word.

I didn't have to avoid him yesterday because he'd ignored me instead. Not completely. His friends would probably have asked a ton of questions if we suddenly stopped talking, so we smiled and said hello in the corridors. When I got home on Thursday, I slipped on his bracelet and curled up in bed. He hadn't asked me to give it back, but keeping it didn't feel right.

Seeing him after our kiss was harder than I'd imagined. My palms always went clammy until I finished the backwards counting technique I'd adopted to stop my heart racing. Joon ignoring me sent a clear signal that it had been goodbye, not an opening for something more. I knew it was better this way, but my foolish heart yearned for more.

Kissing Joon wasn't how I thought it'd feel. It was certainly nothing like how I'd felt when I tried it with Jaden when we were fourteen. He got it into his head that we should experiment so we wouldn't be terrible when we found someone we fancied, but we got about an inch away from each other's lips before we burst out laughing.

The other weird thing yesterday was hearing back from the Ministry. Although the results noted my frequency had an exceptionally strong effect on the plants, it was not classed as remarkably unusual. Mr Ericsson had frowned, admitting he would have thought there'd be more details in the report, but he said I shouldn't worry. Even with his assurance, the mayor's words haunted me. Did this clean bill mean the results had been fixed? I still didn't know if she had been talking about me at Crystal. And if so, what did she gain by having the data changed?

'Are you ready?' Dad broke through my chain of thoughts.

Dad had returned last night. The pattern of his comings and goings was almost back to normal, and I wondered if that meant he was spending less time on the disruptor. He'd told me he could only work on it when his colleagues wouldn't catch on. I didn't like discussing the device that could take away my ability to create the type of world I wanted to live in, so I didn't bring it up.

I hadn't figured out how to ask him to make it a dampener and not a destroyer, but what Jaden had said to Rosita when they came to the house had stuck with me. I wasn't a tech genius, but I was pretty decent at coding. If what Dad created could be hacked, maybe I would be able to come up with a workaround.

Now, standing outside a barber shop, I was trying to understand why he'd insisted we make the trip to Shepherd's Bush when his regular guy was in Tottenham. It was Mum who suggested I go along, although I suspected the seed was planted when Dad noted he hadn't spent much time with me recently.

'It would help if I knew what we are doing here,' I repeated for the fourth time that morning.

Dad placed a hand on my shoulder. 'Saving you, Ego.'

I followed him in, confused about how his haircut could possibly save me. Ever since the mass shift from in-store shopping to home deliveries, most malls had moved to housing services like the barber shop under one roof instead of having them inefficiently dotted around on streets. Small businesses couldn't afford the upkeep of sealed spaces on their own anyway.

The room buzzed with conversation as customers and staff ranted and laughed about one thing or another. No one looked at us when Dad told a man that he was there for his regular. We were pointed towards a side door, and Dad led me into a storeroom.

We were clearly not there for a haircut.

Before I could ask any more, Dad took a small silver cube from his pocket and placed it on the edge of a heavily laden shelf. I blinked in shock when a beam of blue light shot out of the cube, scanning our faces. The back wall slid open by about a metre. Dad picked up the cube and walked through the hole in the wall. I followed, glancing back the way we came, my heart pounding. This was next-level stuff.

The dimly lit corridor we stepped into went on further than I could see. If I had to guess, it was some sort of abandoned service route which ran behind the shops. We walked in silence for about three minutes before Dad stopped, and this time I wasn't surprised when the wall to our left parted.

The room we entered was a little larger than the storeroom. Shiny, metal-sheet-lined walls, and a half dozen humming machines filled the space. A long-haired man was hunched over a workbench.

'You're late,' his deep voice chided. He didn't look back at us.

'Only by two minutes,' Dad replied with a hint of annoyance.

'Two minutes can make all the difference, Eloka.' The man turned around with a grin, which made me wonder if this was just their usual banter. 'You must be Akaego.'

I didn't know what to think. This was getting weirder and weirder.

The man was broad-shouldered and shorter than

he'd initially appeared, probably only an inch or two taller than me. He looked vaguely familiar, but I couldn't place him. It wasn't just his hair that was long; his face was covered in a thick sandy growth that could have done with a trim.

It was his eyes that held me though. He looked right at me, yet I felt like he was looking through me.

'I can't see you, if that's what you're wondering,' he said, making me embarrassed for being so obvious, 'but I don't need that sense for this.'

He extended his hand and I turned to Dad. I shook the man's warm hand only after Dad nodded. If Dad had snuck us into this back room to meet him, we probably needed him for something important, so I played along.

'This is Manuel. He'll be helping with the disruptor's implantation.'

My heart sank. 'You've finished it?' Augmentation Day was over two months away, so I thought I'd have more time to prepare a solid counterargument.

'Not quite, but after what happened with me, I'm not taking any chances. We need to test it first.'

I stifled a sigh of relief.

'I was glad when your father reached out,' Manuel said. 'Attempting the implant on his own could have consequences none of us want replicated.'

Manuel motioned for me to sit in the chair he had vacated.

'You're going to perform the procedure?'

I side-eyed the chair. The relief I'd just felt evaporated. What part of not taking any chances did Dad see as logical when his friend was blind?

Manuel's laugh was light as he picked up what he had been working on when we entered. A dark metal collar similar to the one used at my testing. This one had a second button crudely grooved into its side, with a few loose wires sticking out.

'I'll be mostly a guide. Would you be more reassured if I said I had eleven years of general surgery experience, and a few years of research after that?'

He must have sensed my deepened frown because he laughed again.

'Sight loss was part of the deal I got with my brain tumour. We caught it early, but when the options I had were ninety-two per cent loss of sight or six months of life, it wasn't much of a choice.'

'We don't have much time, Akaego,' Dad cut in. 'If we stay out too long, your mother will worry. I'll have to pop out at some point and actually get a haircut for our cover, but you'll be in safe hands with Manuel.'

'Dad,' I started, then stopped. I had to let him know this couldn't be the way forward.

'I don't think the girl wants to do this, Eloka.' Manuel turned to Dad, catching on quickly.

'That's nonsense.' Dad didn't entertain the notion for a second. 'She understands it is necessary.' He sounded dismissive until he saw my grimace. 'Akaego?'

I wanted to shrink away to avoid the puzzlement

on his face, but I forced myself to stand firm. 'I'm sorry, Daddy, I should have said something sooner. I'm not ready to risk losing this when we're not even sure anyone's looking to weaponise me.' My hand went to my throat.

'You haven't shown her the file?' Manuel asked when Dad gaped at me.

My heart skipped a beat. 'It's been decrypted? Why didn't you say? What was on it?' All this came out in what sounded like one breath.

Dad's head dropped, and my gut clenched.

'Was it that bad?' My voice was a whisper.

'I was going to show you later,' he said, his voice not much louder than mine. 'There are records of things on there that I did. Things I'm ashamed of, even though I didn't understand their impact at the time.'

I swallowed hard. 'Please, show me.'

Dad hesitated before bringing out his slider. The page count for the document he turned to me was three hundred and forty-one. He didn't say a word as he clicked in.

Findings from the experimental procedures carried out on advanced ability Mechsim test subject, Eloka Eke, referred to as EE hereon.

'I know you don't want it to be true,' Dad said as I flicked through pages with words and figures that didn't make sense to me, 'but she knows everything that happened back then. The document doesn't say what she intends to do with the information, but there's this.'

He skipped to a section close to the end.

Effect of frequency on mice pain reception – see supplementary document for a summary of findings. With the loss of the asset, more tests required from potential subjects to ascertain full impact on larger species. PB to approve.

PB? Patrice Bernard?

'The document wasn't attached,' Dad explained when I looked up at him, 'but this was.'

There were locations around the country with numbers assigned to them. Hove, Ely, Salford, Crewe, Rye, Ascot, Haslemere, Shrewsbury, Mansfield. The list went on.

'We've identified these as safe spots for non-stats in surrounding areas. The numbers match the co-ordinates for greenhouses. I doubt they have it appended to this document for no reason. The problem is, we can't notify people without alerting the authorities to the hack.'

Dad placed a hand on my shoulder. 'We can't just wait and see what could happen, Ego. We have to protect you if there's even the slightest chance someone hopes to resurrect any of the actions of Chancellor Stevens's team.'

I stared at the screen. I had glimpsed phrases like 'isolation of the genetic code', 'potential for catastrophic destruction' and 'effective wipe-out of multiple specimen', and now I scrolled back to the pages with photos. Dozens of images of plots laid to waste.

Dad wasn't present in any, but he was responsible for the damage. I could see why he didn't want this future for me. And he most certainly didn't want me becoming a test subject for whatever they'd started on animals.

Walking to Manuel's chair, I sat with a heavy thud. Dad needed to have the option of the disruptor for his peace of mind. I still intended to find a way to muffle the effect of my voice, but I could give this to him until I did.

'Is that an Augmentation simulator?'

Dad nodded, letting out a relieved sigh at my compliance. 'I had the idea to adapt one during your test. It took a few days to get my hands on an old model no one will miss. I don't think I'll be lucky enough to find another.'

'The plan is to amplify your frequency to make sure we can cut it off effectively,' Manuel said. 'The device your father is working on will need to be inserted after your Augmentation surgery.'

Manuel strapped the collar around my neck with no assistance. Next, he felt around below my jaw for a few seconds. I shifted, not enjoying any of this.

'That's mostly where I come in. You'll swallow it as a capsule which we'll track and guide. Once it reaches your larynx, we'll stop it just above your vocal cords and expand it in place. We need the disruptor to go unnoticed if you are examined later. The size and tension of cords affect frequencies. It will emit a signal that temporarily changes the shape of your cords when it detects your frequency in its enhanced state.'

I followed all this with a pounding heart. Dad said I wouldn't need surgery, but this sounded a bit trickier than he'd implied. I could see why he didn't want to do this on his own.

'And it'll be permanent?' Maybe we could reverse it once we were sure there was no danger.

'Unfortunately, yes. Vocal cords are sensitive tissues. The moment we disturb them, they'll never be quite the same. Now tilt your head back and let out your frequency so we can calibrate the simulator.'

I did as instructed, waiting as Dad adjusted something on a screen beside me. There weren't any plants in sight, so I assumed he could read my frequency instead.

'Your amplified reading is off the charts.' Dad sighed, struggling to hide his disappointment.

I shut my eyes, now convinced the mayor's conversation in the loo was about my test.

'Mayor Bernard may be waiting for the post-surgery assessment before she reveals her hand,' Manuel said. 'There would be no point in drawing Akaego in if something goes wrong before then.'

'Or someone else could be behind this,' I offered, still hoping my friend's mother was not the villain they made her out to be. 'She has the file, but she may not be the only person who could have been inspired by his vision.'

Dad ignored me. 'Let's try this with the disruptor simulation switched on.' He pressed the added button on the collar, and I felt the metal warm up slightly.

This time, I paid closer attention to Dad's screen. I wasn't sure what the numbers and constantly spiking lines represented, but if I had any hope of fiddling with the disruptor in future, I wanted to memorise as much as I could. I'd need access to the software, but I'd cross that bridge when I came to it.

'Hold the note,' Dad demanded when my straying eyes caused the numbers to waver.

I was trying my best, but twenty seconds was pushing it. The increasing heat from the metal wasn't helping. My neck felt like it was being shoved in a furnace. Movement registered on the inactive left half of the screen just before I gave up. Dad waved his hand for me to repeat the sound. We were on our sixth attempt by the time Dad looked up, hope unfurling on his brow.

'That's it!' His smile was so wide, his face could barely contain it.

I leaned in to see what had convinced him of this fact, and just as I began cramming the lengthy numbers I hoped he was referring to, the collar gave an ear-splitting hiss before startling me with a spark. A hint of smoke hit me as Dad unclipped the device, slamming the makeshift button. I probably should have said something when it had continued warming up with each try.

'Damn it!' Dad turned the collar around, assessing the extent of the damage.

'Is it broken?' I rubbed my neck, certain there would be a welt if I looked in a mirror.

'I hope not. We won't be able to replace it.'

I frowned. I knew how badly he wanted this to work, but I couldn't help feeling like this device was more important to Dad than my immediate welfare.

'Are you okay?' Manuel asked.

Dad looked at me in horror, realising what he was doing. Dropping the collar, he tilted my head to check if I was hurt.

'I'm sorry, Ego. I wasn't thinking.'

'I'm okay, Dad,' I assured him. 'At least you know the disruptor isn't completely hopeless,' I said, attempting a joke.

'Maybe this would be a good time to get that haircut,' Manuel suggested gently. 'Give the girl a breather. I'll fetch some salve to prevent any marking.'

It was only after Manuel began to apply the lotion that Dad reluctantly left to provide us with our cover.

'Are there many places like this?' I asked, looking around the room and noticing a folding bed in the corner. I also needed something to distract me from dwelling on the possibilities of what I'd read earlier.

'A handful. We pooled as many credits as we could and set them up for emergencies after raids became more frequent. They've been worth the financial sacrifices our members had to make over the years. Too many questions get asked in hospitals. This is more of a research space though. It would be equally difficult to explain bloody victims entering the mall.'

I didn't recognise any of the equipment, but I could see how they could be medical.

'You're a lot more relaxed about all this than I expected,' Manuel said, putting away the first-aid kit. 'My daughter made it sound like you aren't prepared for what could come.'

I didn't ask who he meant. I had begun to suspect who he was. Did he know I'd met Rosita more than once? Or that Carl was in that bracket?

'I'm not really,' I admitted, 'but her courage makes me want to do better.'

He smiled proudly, even though I hadn't intended it as a compliment. 'My apologies for how this began.' He glanced at the wall Dad had disappeared behind, as if he was worried about being heard. 'Your father was particularly difficult about telling you the truth. We felt we had to send that letter to kick things into gear.'

I nodded, grateful they hadn't been Freestakers of the kidnapping kind. 'Can I ask a personal question?'

'Go ahead.'

'Rosita mentioned you're Level One, but you trained as a surgeon. I thought you couldn't drop a level even with your disability.'

Since double enhancements were not permitted, any life-changing event that resulted in a Level Two's inability to continue performing their role usually meant one of two things: a shift to a teaching position or to a political one.

Manuel's smile faded. 'You can if you make it impossible for them to define your path. I chose to be a surgeon so I could help non-stats who can't receive medical care under the system. My tumour took that away, but if I am to train anyone, it should be the people who need it the most, not those who already have all the support they need.'

'Your Level One status is a front,' I said with a nod of understanding. That was probably why Rosita felt she could do more behind the scenes as a Level One than any place higher.

'The authorities claim the system is efficient,' Manuel continued, 'yet it wastes human resources just to maintain control over citizens. I understand why the policies we oppose now were implemented years ago. Nobody can deny something drastic had to be done to shore up our dwindling economic state. But if there are other sustainable ways for people to live outside of the system, why can't both exist in parallel?'

The wall slid open before I could ask anything else. Dad, with his freshly faded hairline, eyed the both of us. He didn't question our discussion, just went to the workbench and picked up the collar.

'There's not much more we can do today,' he said. 'I'll use the last set of readings to stress test the tech better, but you've got what you wanted, Manuel. You can see she will be able to handle this.'

I glanced from one man to the other. I hadn't realised I'd been under assessment. Dad might have gone to Manuel out of necessity, but if I was now officially meeting a rebel, and not just Rosita and Carl behind the scenes, they would want to vet me.

263

'You'll do fine, Akaego,' Manuel said to me, patting my arm lightly. 'Your father worked hard to protect you all these years, and he almost pulled it off. Just keep focused for this last stretch.'

Calmness washed over me. He gave off an assured energy which made me want to believe everything would work out okay.

The journey home was quiet. I was emotionally and physically drained. When Mum asked for my help making dinner, I forced myself to perk up. Explaining my exhaustion would have been difficult if all I'd done was sit and watch Dad get a haircut.

I'd left my slider in my room for dinner, so when I returned to find a Roulette message, I clicked in hurriedly.

xcarlitox: Darma's, Monday at four.
a-k-go: Why?
xcarlitox: My father caught Carl doing one of
    your warm-up things yesterday.
xcarlitox: The little runt spilled everything.

If Manuel knew about our arrangement, was that partly what today had been about? Some sort of test of my personality? He couldn't possibly have told Dad about my extracurricular activities with his kids or I would have had an earful.

xcarlitox: Shock of all shocks, Dad agrees
    with Carl.

Was it possible Manuel wasn't as upset about it as they'd thought he would be, now he'd seen Dad's disruptor could potentially work? If we confirmed Carl was a Mechsim, and he also turned out to be a Deathsim, he wasn't doomed to remain one. There was a viable solution. Untested, but still likely to work.

> xcarlitox: Don't get me wrong, your boyfriend is
>   still a problem.
> xcarlitox: Dad doesn't know he knows about me.

I could see why she wouldn't want her father knowing her actions at the reception hadn't gone as smoothly as she hoped.

> xcarlitox: Nobody's come knocking on our
>   door yet.
> xcarlitox: You must have charmed your man
>   very well.

I sighed and shook my head. She was never letting this go.

> xcarlitox: Either way, we can't wait around for
>   something that may never happen.
> xcarlitox: You still want to help Carl?

I paused. The mayor was aware of the Deathsim experimentations. I wasn't so sure about telling her I had discovered a new Mechsim if Carl ended up being one. In fact, I was pretty certain I wouldn't. But I still wanted to help him do what he dreamed of for undocumented immigrant non-stats, just like I'd promised.

It wasn't just that though.

Carl's enthusiasm was infectious, and despite Rosita's sulking, I knew her actions came from a place of good intentions. And I found I didn't want to end my time with these people I was finally becoming comfortable with, even though the way we'd come together was so unconventional.

Smiling, I tapped my screen.

a-k-go: I was never going anywhere.

CHAPTER TWENTY-FIVE

62 days to Augmentation Day

Three months ago, if anyone had told me I would soon be leading a double life as a sort of rebel, I would have laughed in their face.

Hard.

And yet here I was, juggling multiple deceptions. Keeping Dad's secret from Mum was difficult enough, but lying to Dad about helping Carl with his lessons was also weighing on me. Dad would not want me hanging out with rebels. He'd made it clear he only associated with them out of necessity. It helped a little that he was away some days. But for the stretches of time he was home, I had to be extra careful meeting with Carl and Rosita.

At least I could talk to Jaden.

'I knew getting close to him was a bad idea,' was what he said after I told him Joon recognised Rosita and had withdrawn from me. 'But it kind of worked out. You don't have to worry about slipping up now. Just stay away.'

I didn't tell him about the kiss, or that I would

have swapped all the stress of worrying if it meant Joon could look at me the way he had done those last few days before we agreed to keep our distance. My belly still clenched when I saw him, but my heart had learnt to slow its beat.

Jaden was also not super excited to hear we were continuing Carl's training, but he didn't make too much of a fuss. I suspected Carl had grown on him a little. Or, more likely, Rosita.

We'd had three sessions so far in venues which got more random. A roller disco, a ball-pit club, a skatepark. Places busy and loud enough for us to mostly go unnoticed because anyone looking on would simply see four kids hanging out.

Rosita and Jaden even started to play their fake couple routine in public, although Rosita always disentangled herself once any onlookers lost interest.

'Are you free next Tuesday?' Carl had asked last Friday evening as we left the indoor skatepark and walked to Paddington station.

My ears were ringing from all the clattering. I was definitely going to suggest we never go back there.

'Should be.' I nodded. My after-school sessions were down to once or twice a week now the Ministry had officially confirmed my results, and Mr Ericsson was less precious about me asking for last-minute reschedules. 'Want to plan another session?'

'No.' Carl suddenly looked a little unsure. 'I know we aren't supposed to be friends or anything, but it's my birthday and I'd love it if you came along. Dad's friend runs a pub in Camden and he's letting us have a space for free since the weekend is all booked.'

It was on the tip of my tongue to tell him I truly thought we were friends.

'Of course, Carl.' I smiled at him. Another thing to hide from Dad, but he was away again, so it'd just be another day out for me. Ever since Mum met Carl and Rosita, she'd let Dad's restrictions on my time outside the house slide if I said I was seeing them. 'Thirteen, right?'

'Maybe now someone will finally start taking me seriously,' he said, grinning.

This earned him a smack on the back, but Rosita's smile took away the severity of it. 'He's inviting you because I'm officially his only friend.'

'Hey.' Carl stopped and raised his hand dramatically, starting to count off his gloved fingers. 'Mo, Agnes, Phoebe, Bjorn. That's plenty. You're the one with no mates.'

'Fine, you're a celeb. We get it.' Rosita pulled him along with a sigh. 'And correction, I choose not to have friends. It just complicates all the other important things I have to do.'

I hadn't given much thought to their lives outside when they were with us, but discovering Rosita wasn't social surprised me. She'd seemed to get along well with the kids I'd seen her with in the gym that day. I couldn't help wondering what else I had misjudged about her.

Was she beginning to see us as friends, or was she only here to protect Carl?

'Sorry, Jaden,' Carl went on, 'my parents don't know about you. It's just Akaego they'll be expecting.'

I found it difficult to believe Manuel hadn't done some digging after he found out about our sessions, though I didn't think Jaden would mind not being invited because I knew he had an online tournament on Tuesday. But he was scowling when I turned to him. He tugged at my arm, letting Carl and Rosita walk out of earshot.

'Are you sure this is a good idea? The four of us hanging out is one thing, but meeting up with their dad in public seems a bit . . . ballsy.'

'It's just a party, Jaden.' I jabbed him in the side. 'It's not like it's a Freestakers annual convention.' I was almost never invited to parties, and I really didn't want to miss out on this opportunity.

'It's not necessary for you to be there,' he sighed, not convinced by my humour. 'Your dad will be livid if he finds out.'

He said this so seriously, I frowned too, wondering if I really was being reckless with my decision. But if a few kids couldn't meet up to eat birthday cake on a weekday evening, something was terribly wrong with the world. Besides, I doubted Manuel would put his family at risk by letting me attend if he thought there was any danger.

Mum didn't bat an eyelid when I told her I was

meeting them. She was the one who reminded me I should take a gift. I knew right away what I'd give Carl because he hadn't stopped going on about Clifford. I spent an entire evening creating a video montage of him generally being a cat, attacking pretty much any balled-up fabric I threw near him and getting super excited when I shone a beam of light on my bedroom wall.

'I'll be back before eight,' I called to Mum, dashing out before she could give my outfit a once-over.

My jeans and print blouse weren't what I was worried about. I'd slipped on Joon's bracelet at the last minute because it perfectly matched the petals on my top. Jaden wouldn't be there to judge me for not returning it.

It wasn't that I hadn't tried. I'd taken it to school a week ago, fully intending to force it on Joon.

'Are you here to spit in my face, Engineering?' He'd started using the term again, and it made the distance between us feel all the wider. It felt like I was the one whose face had been spat on.

He'd walked away without waiting for a response. I didn't have the heart to try again after that. If I was being honest with myself, I wasn't quite ready to part with the only physical reminder of our non-starter romance.

I arrived at Camden Town station earlier than planned and followed my slider's directions to the pub in a quiet street seven minutes walk away. The air was now cool enough for me to adjust my timer to ten minutes.

'You made it!' Carl squealed when I popped my head into the back room I was shown to. He ran to the door and pulled me in. 'Thanks for the video. Hands down the most original gift I've ever received.'

'I figured you'd like something no one else has.' I grinned.

'You got that right. New cat videos are gold dust. I could make a fortune if I share it online.'

I was still laughing at his excitement when a woman walked over. I knew right away she was Carl and Rosita's mum.

'You must be Akaego,' she said in a deep voice almost identical to Rosita's. 'I'm Ana. I've heard a lot about you. And don't worry, all good things.'

Her smile was so easy, I wondered if Manuel had shared anything with her about me. Everyone seemed to be keeping secrets.

'Thanks for letting me join you,' I said, shaking the hand she held out as Carl rushed off to speak to someone else.

'We're only here for a couple of hours, but we wanted to mark the day with something more than a home-cooked meal. Carl never asks for much, and he deserves to be celebrated.'

I understood where she was coming from. Getting the room for free cut costs, but it wouldn't be cheap for Level Ones to host the twenty people present. They'd really made an effort. Someone was singing on a karaoke machine, and the food looked like it wouldn't run out for a while.

I hung my suit up and poured myself a soft drink from the only active pump at the counter before moving to the side. Rosita waved from the opposite corner, where she was chatting with a woman, and Manuel was engaged in conversation with a group of adults. I took that as a sign we were playing it cool today.

If there were other Freestakers present, it would be impossible to know without walking around asking directly. I had to remind myself that just because I knew the family's secret didn't mean they didn't lead a normal life.

About ten minutes in, I finally felt settled enough to join in on an activity, a game of Never Have I Ever. It wasn't one I had played before, although I'd heard it was popular at the parties I'd not been invited to at my old school.

'Carl gets to ask the questions.' Rosita sounded exceptionally chirpy. 'And since we can't have a drinking penalty, whoever gets the worst tally has to perform a duet with him.'

Scanning the room for plants, I was happy to find none. I couldn't see any harm in joining in, even if I lost. Which looked likely to be the case five questions in.

Carl had just asked if everyone could roll their tongues, and I was trying not to show myself up by being the only one who couldn't when a round silver object

273

flew through the room, landing right in the middle of our circle.

A shout came from behind me. 'It's a raid!'

As if on cue, the silver ball twisted, letting out a plume of yellow smoke. Smoke so thick and acrid, my eyes watered and my throat began closing up within seconds of inhaling it. Our coughs were quickly drowned out by the disorientating blare of a smoke detector.

I choked against the back of my hand. Why would anyone raid a child's birthday party? This had to be a mistake. Though no one was standing around to ask questions. Through stinging eyes, I just about made out silhouettes frantically weaving towards an exit sign at the back of the room.

I was caught in an actual government raid.

This acknowledgement kicked my other senses into action. The quickest way out would be the delivery airlock at the back, where there would be an emergency override switch to release us in a fraction of the usual decompression time, temporarily flooding the rest of the building with hot air. But it was pointless without time to grab or put on our suits.

A white light beam came next, cutting through the smoke, pointing at faces, searching for something.

'Dad!' Carl's scream carried above the alarm.

Unlike the rest of us, he was heading to the centre of the room. I followed his hazy path and spotted something crumpled on the ground. Not something, someone.

Manuel.

I couldn't see if Manuel had ducked to avoid the rising smoke or if he was in distress, but Carl was not waiting to find out.

'Carl!' Rosita's voice was muffled as she tried to push aside a woman who'd tripped over her. 'Watch out!'

A man in a black hydration suit had emerged from the smoke. In one hand was the source of the light beam, and in the other was a slim black rod.

Carl turned a second too late. Two sprigs shot from the weapon, connecting with his back, sending waves of electric current through him. We watched in horror as his convulsions knocked him to the ground. Except he didn't quite hit it. A unified gasp sounded from our side of the room when his forehead slammed against the edge of a chair.

'Carl!'

Next thing we knew, Rosita had ripped the karaoke machine from its cord and was racing towards Carl's assailant. He must have been as stunned as we were as she swung the box with all her might. It made contact with his helmet with enough impact to stagger him. Rosita didn't stop there, moving the device again, this time aiming for the man's knees. When he was down, she struck his head once more.

I had never seen anything like it. The sheer power from such a small frame.

Suits.

I had to get the suits. That was what popped into

my head when Rosita reached for Carl. Ana had already rushed past me to help Manuel, who appeared more startled than hurt. If I didn't do something, others could be close behind the man.

I ran to the rack, pulling off as many suits as I could, not knowing if any were mine.

'Hurry,' Ana yelled.

I couldn't tell if she was talking to me or Rosita, but I ran to them, the suit helmets slamming against each other. Even overladen with all that gear, I could see they needed a hand. The smoke had almost completely cleared now, yet no other armed attacker had entered. They must be waiting at the back, I realised.

'There's another exit,' Manuel whispered, reading my mind.

Someone must have engaged the airlock override because heat struck us the second we entered the corridor. Nothing severe, but definitely not what the controlled air should have been. I couldn't work out how anyone could have left without a suit. Had they been dragged into a vehicle outside?

Manuel turned right, away from the airlock. He must have been there enough times to know the way from memory, or else he'd done his research before coming today.

We entered a storeroom and I locked the door behind us, hoping it would buy us time. While Ana checked on Carl, Rosita crashed on to the floor, quiet sobs coming from her.

'Did I kill that man?' The adrenalin was probably still coursing through her body, but she must have just realised what she had done in there.

'You did what was needed,' Ana assured her, not looking up from Carl.

I leaned against the door; my own adrenalin was settling enough to permit questions. What the hell had just happened? Why would anyone raid Carl's party? He was just a kid. This had to be an error. Mistaken identity or something similar.

There was a deep, bloody gash above his left eyebrow, and his face was deathly pale. But he was breathing. Shallow breaths, but he was with us.

'Manuel Ortiz and Akaego Eke, you are under arrest for unlawfully obtaining and sharing classified information. Show yourselves to an officer immediately.' The voice boomed through the corridor we had just exited, startling us all.

Classified information?

I turned to Manuel. That could only mean one thing. The file I'd downloaded off the mayor's server had been tracked, and somehow they knew Manuel had accessed it too. But that also meant Dad would be in trouble. He was the one I'd transferred the document to. The one who had shared the file with Manuel and whoever decrypted it.

This was happening because of me!

'Manuel, what is going on?' Ana looked up from Carl, confusion briefly taking over from concern.

277

'We need to get out of here,' Manuel said calmly, walking to an almost empty high metal shelf like he'd definitely been in there before. 'Help me with this.' He indicated we needed to move the shelf.

'I'm sorry, this is all my fault.'

'Save that for later. We don't have much time,' Manuel snapped.

I obeyed without hesitation, and we leaned our backs against the shelf and pushed, revealing a metal door. It had likely been blocked off when the building was upgraded, so only a few people would know of its existence.

'We should suit up before we unseal it. The door isn't locked.'

He ran his fingers along the door's edges to check it was something we could open, and I rifled through what I'd grabbed. Seven suits, but only five with helmets still dangling from their sleeves. That wasn't what worried me.

'Carl won't fit in any of them.' Rosita had recovered enough to come help me. 'He won't make it to the station.'

'There's a safe house two streets from here,' Manuel said, making me wonder if the pub was used for Freestaker gatherings. It would explain why he had an escape strategy. 'Wrap some towels around his neck and it should hold the helmet until we get there and figure things out.'

Miraculously, I had brought Manuel's and Ana's

suits, so we helped Carl into the smallest suit and used dishcloths we found on a rack to pad his neck. Rosita would also struggle with her size, but she was conscious and would be able to evaluate her situation.

Manuel had moved on to ripping the clear gel sealant from the door when we heard a bang on the door to the corridor. Realising we weren't coming out, they must have started searching rooms. Someone tried the handle, and I rushed to help Manuel, leaving Rosita and Ana to bring Carl closer.

'You haven't set your suit.' Rosita pointed at my wrist gauge's blank screen.

I yanked the door open, letting in a gust of hot air. Now wasn't the time to explain that my slider had fallen out in the chaos. The only way to override someone else's suit was by entering a code from your device, which Rosita had done for herself and Carl. Theirs would be cooling already, even if not fully. I just had to make it to the safe house, somehow.

'All clear,' I confirmed, poking my head into the narrow alley, shoving a heavy metal bin aside.

'Akaego, you can't be out here like this,' Rosita whispered fiercely.

I ignored her, feeling my skin prickling in the already warm suit. We couldn't stop now, not because of me. I could last a few minutes longer. I carried on beside Manuel, imagining shots of cool air inside my suit.

Mind over matter.

I could do this.

'Akaego!'

I felt myself swoon before someone caught me. I turned sharply, sure it was one of our pursuers.

'Jaden?'

I blinked. How was he there? He was supposed to be at home fighting opponents in a game, not in a back alley, holding me upright.

'Her suit's not set,' Rosita said, coming forward to help her dad.

'What?' Jaden cried. 'You have to get inside.'

I yanked myself free of his grip when he began leading me back to the door.

'I lost my slider,' I explained breathlessly. 'How long have you been outside?'

The others had carried on, with Manuel giving Rosita directions. He had said the safe house was two streets away. I needed to check if this could work.

Jaden opened his mouth, then shut it as he clocked what I was hoping to do. 'Not long,' he said, his slider appearing in a flash.

He handed it to me. If his suit was chilled enough to last until we got to safety, I could disengage his slider and connect it to mine. Sweat poured down my face into my eyes, but I was unable to wipe it away as I checked his capacity. Sixty per cent. I looked up at Jaden.

'Just do it,' he hissed as the others turned the corner, disappearing from sight.

I made the connection, grateful for all the times

280

we'd synced our devices for gaming. The second I felt cool air start to spread inside my suit, I sighed, staggering backwards. Without missing a beat, Jaden scooped me off my feet and began to run.

CHAPTER TWENTY-SIX

62 days to Augmentation Day

'You shouldn't be here.'

'You didn't think I'd leave her with you, did you?'

I stirred at the sound of Jaden's voice, everything rushing back. The party, the raid, our escape into the alley. Carl.

'Steady!'

A pair of strong hands held me down when I tried to get up. Jaden. His worried eyes were a few inches from mine.

'Drink this.' He lifted a bottle to my lips and I drank the lukewarm water greedily, letting my vision adjust to the room's low lighting.

'See, she's fine. You have to go.'

'Not without her.' Jaden turned to the speaker I now recognised as Rosita.

Her voice was husky, but she looked fine. She'd found time to change out of her party clothes. Judging from the black sofa I lay on, the armchair Rosita sat in, and the hideous blue gingham-print blinds drawn behind her, we were in a living room.

282

'What happened?' I asked, hearing the gravel in my voice. I hoped it was only a temporary after-effect of the acrid gas we'd inhaled.

'You don't remember? This one got it into his head to follow you,' Rosita explained.

'Which is why I was able to help,' Jaden countered. 'Good thing I hid in that alley after the raid team showed up. I didn't even realise there was a door there because the bins were blocking it.'

'Don't be so dramatic,' Rosita scoffed.

'Me, dramatic? You were the one blubbering.'

I turned to Rosita, unable to imagine her shedding a tear.

'I was upset about Carl.'

'Is he all right?' I was allowed to sit up this time, propping an equally ugly chequered cushion behind my back.

Rosita nodded, unable to put the rest into words. That was enough for me.

'Thank goodness.' I nodded back, reaching for the water bottle again. I frowned at Jaden. 'Those government officials were there to arrest me. You could get into trouble for helping. How were you even there?'

Jaden returned my frown. 'I told you I wasn't sure about this. I was worried, so I came to check on you.'

He'd been right, as he so often was. I should have trusted his apprehension instead of hoping I could do something normal, like attend a birthday party when everything in my life was clearly far from normal.

'This is serious, Jaden. You shouldn't get caught up in it any more than you have to.'

He smiled, pinching my cheeks gently. 'You know how you joke about having no friends and needing me to survive this wild, scary world? Turns out it's me who needs you. I would never have forgiven myself if I was at home gaming and this happened.'

'Jaden . . .' I stopped, not knowing how to respond.

'Do you two need the room?' Rosita cleared her throat, prompting Jaden to pull the cushion from behind me and toss it at her.

The flying object narrowly missed Manuel's head as he entered the room.

'How do you feel?' He smiled widely, approaching the sofa.

'Okay, I think.' I rubbed my stiff shoulders.

'That was quick thinking from you with the slider reset,' he said. 'And it's a good thing your friend was cautious enough to follow you to the pub.'

'Let's not forget he carried her like she weighed nothing.' Rosita winked at me.

Jaden shrugged. 'I finally got to put all the arm workouts I've been doing to use.'

I squeezed his hand tightly before steering the conversation to other critical issues.

'Who were those people?' I asked. 'That man wasn't dressed like he was in the Met.'

'Level Threes.'

When I continued to look lost, Rosita sighed and

added, 'Special Forces. This was probably the Freestakers Eradication Squad. Don't you know anything?'

'Wait, you mean that was a Special Forces guy you knocked out?' If I hadn't seen it for myself, I would have found it hard to believe. I was also a little ashamed for not knowing more about the world they had to navigate when I had so boldly entered it.

'He was hurting Carl,' she snapped. 'I obviously wouldn't have thrown in that last blow if I had time to think about it.'

Fleeing arrest was one thing; assaulting an officer was a felony nobody would want added to their record.

'That's enough, Rosita,' Manuel cautioned.

'She's right though, something feels off,' Rosita went on, disregarding her dad's warning. 'Why would they send FES officers to raid the place like that if the warrant was just for the two of you?'

'It did feel like they were trying to make a point,' Manuel agreed.

'You think it was a scare tactic?' They could easily have arrested us quietly in our homes. There was no need to gas the room or try to knock anyone out.

'It's possible. Perhaps they were hoping there would be other Freestakers there. Some less cautious factions have been known to meet under the cover of celebrations. From what I've gathered, everyone else was rounded up. They'll let them go if they have no proof anything untoward was taking place. The room's footage will show this.'

'That same footage will show the assault,' I realised. 'Maybe they went for Carl to provoke a reaction.'

Manuel shook his head. 'I suspect he was collateral damage. But if that was FES, the fact they are involved in a hacking case, even if it was of the mayor's system, suggests they have more to go on. If we are truly compromised, we can't risk returning home. We will head to a different safe house until we know more.'

We?

'By we, you mean your family, right?' Jaden looked at me as he addressed Manuel. 'Because Akaego is going back with me.'

'She's meant to be under arrest. How do you think that's going to work?' Manuel barked. 'She turns herself in and they slap her on the wrist?' Then he sighed. 'We don't have time. The FES team won't go door to door without a search warrant, but they'll get one if they suspect we haven't left the area. We have one shot. The streets will be rammed once Camden Market shuts in under an hour. Carl will be better rested by then. We should be able to make it to the station, but we have to split up if they are looking for a family.'

'What about my family?' I finally spoke up on the issue now I was past all the shock from earlier. 'I have to let them know what's happened. Dad will be in the same situation since he's the one who sent you the file.'

I wasn't going to disappear into the night without my parents. I didn't want to think of the possibility Dad could have been taken into custody straight from work.

286

And Mum would be frantic with worry. The market closed at nine, which meant I should have been home already.

'Your father will know what to do,' Manuel said firmly. 'He'll follow protocol.'

'What does that even mean?' I raised my hands in protest. 'You don't know whether he's already been arrested or not?' Not knowing felt way worse.

'I'm not sure, but I know his priority will be to keep you safe. That's why you must leave with us. Your mother has no involvement with any of this. They may question her, but they don't have enough proof to detain her.'

'I can't leave Mum wondering what could have happened.' If the raid was ongoing, it probably wouldn't be reported on the news until it was officially over. Mum would have no clue what was going on. 'Maybe Jaden can go to my house. Tell her I'm okay.'

'And what reason would he have to show up so late at night when you're not there?' Rosita offered, not unsympathetic. The desperation in my voice was hard to ignore.

'We're wasting time,' Manuel snapped. 'We must get to safety.'

'You know what?' Jaden stood, towering over Manuel, who would sense his presence even if he couldn't see him. 'I haven't once heard Akaego say she's okay to go with you. Shouldn't this be her decision?'

'Your friend is right,' Manuel said, surprising us all.

'We can't make you come with us, but you have to start thinking differently and long-term. The only person who can protect your mother now is your father, not you.'

That was the irony of all this. Dad's dream of protecting us from this type of danger was quickly evaporating.

All because I thought I could do it all.

'I'll go with you.'

'Akaego—'

I stood and held Jaden's hand. 'It'll be okay, Jaden. Go home and keep safe. If they know we're friends, they may already be looking for you. Think of your family.'

I could see he wanted to argue, but I had a point. Following me to a pub was one thing. Was he willing to get his parents in trouble because of me? Not a chance. That was why I had to play that card. He had done too much for me already.

'Promise me you'll reach out when you're safe. And don't say maybe. Find a way. Promise.'

I smiled, grateful he wasn't dragging this out. 'I promise.'

He drew me in for a hug that lasted for so long, Rosita and Manuel had slipped away by the time we pulled apart. Manuel had gone to let Ana know what had been decided, and without my slider, Rosita found me a clean device to programme my borrowed suit. Jaden had been foresighted enough to set his co-ordinates to show he was at home even before he left it. Hopefully, that was all the cover he'd needed.

I saw Carl leaning against his mother in the hallway as we were about to leave. He still looked a little off, but he managed a cheery smile. His helmet mostly covered the bandage that was wrapped around his head. Thankfully, someone had found him a suit that almost fit.

'Sorry, Akaego, but a kick-ass scar might actually trump your video as the best birthday present ever.'

I was glad his sense of humour hadn't suffered.

'Nah, you said mine was the most original, not the best. I'm still winning on that front.'

'Thank you for what you did back there,' Ana said, her voice breaking. 'Without those suits, we didn't stand a chance.'

I smiled, praying I would never have to be in a situation like that again. I wasn't sure I would always be able to make that kind of snap call.

Our exit schedule was set. Ana and Carl. Rosita and Jaden. Me and Manuel. I wanted to stay with Jaden for as long as I could, but I knew Manuel thought I would be swayed to carry on home with him if that happened.

His prediction about the crowd was spot on. In the darkness, we disappeared amongst the noisy swarm of bodies heading to Chalk Farm station. Ana and Carl were designated the shorter walk to Camden Town station. Rosita and Jaden would catch a train a minute behind so Rosita would know if they ran into any trouble. Manuel stayed close enough to use my body as his guide while I whispered coming obstructions into his ear.

'You're doing the right thing,' Manuel said when I glanced at Jaden's receding back.

I wanted to believe him, but my gut didn't feel sure. No matter what happened from this moment on, I knew nothing in my life would ever be the same again.

CHAPTER TWENTY-SEVEN

61 days to Augmentation Day

'This is unreal.'

Running my finger along the broad leaf of a romaine lettuce, I resisted the urge to separate it from the head emerging from the raised bed. Rows of lettuce-filled planters stretched out before me. More than enough to keep plenty of bellies full for weeks. Not on their own, obviously. They would be helped by the leeks, potatoes, tomatoes, turnips, beans, squashes and dozens of other fruits and veg in this room and the last one we'd walked through.

'This is powered from the grid?' I turned to Rosita, unsure how an illegal greenhouse could be operating so efficiently off a system that was trying to shut it down. Same as with the emergency rooms, she'd told me that Freestakers channelled their credits to secret accounts to be able to set up these sorts of places, but stealing power was different.

'Some of it.' She nodded with such pride, I'd have

thought she was the one who came up with the idea. 'Even though most cities are self-sufficient with their energy production, top-ups are still needed from wind and hydro plants in the outlands.'

'So you guys siphon energy that would be lost in transmission.'

'They won't know where it's gone because it would never have been accounted for at the point of use. We always make sure to switch to our own generated solar power when we can. Staying constantly connected to the system is riskier.'

When she'd told me about the greenhouses that day in Clapham, she'd implied they were totally off-grid, which clearly wasn't always the case. I could see why they had to tap into it. Solar panels were most effective from spring to autumn, less so in the winter months. They also had to be careful the panels couldn't be spotted by drones or ground patrols, so positioning and numbers varied from site to site.

The space we stood in was a good example of where things worked well. Located in what used to be the basement car park of a clinical laboratory building, the only light the plants received was from specialised overhead lamps, but this didn't seem to have done them any harm. I had been a little surprised when Rosita led me here. I guess she was confident I wasn't going to start belting out tunes.

'If you listen to the news, you'd think this place was an actual wasteland,' I said as we left the sealed space and took the stairs back to the much warmer ground floor.

'It kind of works in our favour.' She smiled. 'Half-burnt-down, abandoned urban spaces aren't exactly places anyone searches thoroughly. And our food trucks don't hang around long enough to be noticed when they come to be loaded up for community distributions.'

We'd arrived at what used to be Milton Keynes just before midnight. Despite the worries plaguing me, I could hardly keep my eyes open. Thinking we would be heading to another house in London, I'd been surprised when our group reunited near a refuse-sorting depot in Enfield after our successful crowd-mingling escape from Camden.

We were bundled into the passenger cabin of an autonomous truck headed to an anaerobic digestion plant in Bletchley, one of the few functioning facilities left in the area. It was a tight squeeze for five of us, and not particularly comfort controlled since the truck was supposed to be empty. Fortunately, the night air cooled the further away we got from the city.

When the truck pulled up outside a church, a scheduled engine cooling stop Manuel said wouldn't be seen as suspicious, we'd hopped off and walked to the repurposed laboratory nearby. Rosita had said factions didn't communicate to protect themselves, yet from the seamless way we moved from place to place, there had to be some chatter going on in the background.

'Thanks for that.' I turned to her when we returned to the windowless observation room we had been allocated to share.

The Freestakers had chosen this building because it already contained a few internally sealed spaces even before external airlocks were introduced. Which meant that from the outside, with a door or two strategically left open and externally facing room lights turned off, it always appeared vacant. The only extra insulation they'd had to do was in the basement. The plants produced enough clean oxygen to pump into the lab spaces.

I had spent most of the morning lying in a sleeping bag and staring at the white-lit ceiling as I gnawed at the skin around my fingernails, trying to come up with a way to fix the mess I'd put us in. If I hadn't downloaded a shadowing app that failed to cloak my file-copying activity like it was supposed to, we would all be safely in our homes, not out here wondering if FES would descend on us.

But as much as I wanted to focus on a plan that would somehow convince the authorities the whole hacking thing had been a prank or a mistake, I couldn't. Rosita's suggestion to tour the facility was the breather I needed.

'Later, I'll take you to the micro hydropower plant we're setting up by Furzton Lake. It's dry most of the year, but Aoife thinks there'll be enough water in autumn to power a cyclical system she's been working on. It's a bit of a walk, but there are spots to stop at.'

Aoife was one of five full-time non-stats living there. They were all engineers or agriculturalists of some form; a Londoner and a Mancunian, with the other members of the team being undocumented immigrants from Ireland and a tiny island I'd never heard of in the North Atlantic Ocean which had been swallowed up by the rising water.

'I bet Carl would love to tag along,' I said, thinking of how excited he had been when we arrived last night.

Like me, this was his first time at one of the isolated facilities. He had been a trooper throughout the journey, not complaining once. But the effort had taken its toll. Ana was paying close attention to a slight fever he'd developed. I wasn't sure how good they were for medical supplies, and I prayed it would break soon.

Rosita exaggerated a grimace. 'In that case, brace yourself for a million questions about every single thing we come across.'

Although she made it sound like this was an adventure we'd chosen, it was clear why Dad dreaded the idea of us living in the middle of nowhere. There was a reason why most Freestakers waged their anti-establishment campaign from within the same society they claimed stifled their freedom of choice.

I struggled to see how anyone could live out here without the many luxuries I'd never thought twice about before. Pubs, restaurants, clubs, arcades, concert halls, and even the rare but possible trip to a gig in a lusciously green biodome. When you threw in free public transport within cities, the system really looked like it was a winner.

'Nice bracelet.' Rosita reached across and touched the green stones circling my wrist.

I had changed out of my top and towel-dried my braids to get rid of the stink of whatever chemical had been in the gas at the pub, but the one thing I'd put back on was the bracelet. It was almost funny how I'd so easily lost my slider, yet the clasp holding the beads together stayed intact.

I really should have taken it off. Holding on to a memento of Joon was torturous. Every time I caught a glimpse of a shade of green, he filled my thoughts. Since it was a school day, he would either be in class or walking the halls with his friends. I wondered if he noticed I was gone.

I wondered if anyone would notice.

Someone tapped on the door.

'Can we have a word?' Manuel asked when I opened it to find him on the other side.

Following him a few doors down, I couldn't stop the thundering in my chest. If he had good news, I had a feeling he would have blurted it out without pulling me aside. The room we entered was kitted out differently from our sleeping space, with desks and chairs in rows.

'What's that?' I asked, walking to a black metal box with knobs on its side and a short cord attached to what looked like an oblong microphone.

'An analogue two-way radio,' Manuel replied, taking a chair next to it. 'These aren't completely safe, but radio frequencies are tricky to triangulate if we keep our communication brief and sporadic. And the channel we're transmitting on has to be known.'

I pictured the walkie-talkies in Jaden's bedroom. What I would have given to know what channel I could reach him on.

'There were three raids across London last night.'

Three? That sounded excessive.

'But that's not what troubles me,' Manuel went on, absent-mindedly tugging at his beard. 'There's been no word on the Camden incident. It's like it never happened.'

'That can't be good.' Publicising raids was similar to taking a victory lap for the government. Even if they weren't successful, news about them assured people efforts were being made to curb rebel action.

'Yes and no. We know it was a targeted arrest, not a raid. If they had to let everyone go, they may not want to make it known a kid's party was stormed.'

That made sense, except we both knew it probably wasn't that straightforward.

'It's possible so many raids were staged in one night to cover the one they were really interested in. Even if someone talks about the pub, there are concrete stories for the public to latch on to.'

'Have you heard from my father?'

There was no point stalling any longer. We could speculate all day about the government's intentions, but my priorities were different. I hated not having my slider to try reaching out myself. I'd checked the one I was given to activate my suit and noticed it had no wireless connection. Sly glances at Rosita's device earlier on had also confirmed she had no service. A blocker was probably installed in the building to prevent accidental exposure of our position if we pinged something out. But that didn't mean there wasn't a loophole.

Manuel stood and walked to the other side of the room. 'He made it out of the biodome before they could detain him. He knows you're safe.'

I let relief wash over me for a second. 'But?' I sounded him out, sensing his hesitation.

'We haven't received any indication of how he's going to play this.'

Now that made no sense. There was no way Dad was still deciding, especially knowing how paranoid he'd been lately. And he would never just wait around while Mum was left alone at home.

'You said there's a protocol to follow. That means he has options. What are they?'

Manuel's sigh indicated even more of a reluctance to share this with me.

'That's all I get?'

'Give it time, Akaego. Trust me, you being here is not a bad thing.'

298

That was easy for him to say. He had his entire family safely under the same roof.

'If we don't hear from him by the end of the day, I'd like to go back,' I declared with some finality in my voice.

'That's not a—'

'You said it was my decision to come here, so it must work the other way too, right?'

Manuel opened his mouth to keep protesting, then decided against it. 'We'll review this again tonight,' he agreed, his tone far from convincing.

When I got back to our room, Rosita wasn't there, which was perfect because I had no intention of sitting around waiting for the day to end. I would leave this place tonight if Dad didn't get in touch. If I couldn't use their radio, I'd find another way to make contact with the outside world.

Grabbing the slider I'd been given, I made my way to the loos and locked myself inside the furthest cubicle. My choice of location wasn't just for privacy. I'd worked out it was the closest I could get to the server without being in the same room. Remotely monitoring all that plant life in the basement meant there had to be a link to the equipment that automatically lit and watered them. A connection implied a signal existed, probably cloaked, but still in use.

I got to work, swiping and tapping at the screen. I knew the risk I was taking, the exposure that could happen if I tried to break through the blocker. All I needed was a few minutes. Hopefully, that wouldn't be long enough to be noticed.

I nearly burst into tears when a very weak bar flashed at the side of the slider after what felt like the longest half hour of my life. Thirty minutes where my heart sat in my throat, my body freezing whenever I heard the slightest sound outside, certain Manuel had caught on to what I was doing and sent the others to find me.

I took a deep breath before downloading the Roulette app. Two messages chimed immediately as I signed in.

J-2-da-d: Akaego, your parents have been
arrested.

I heard a high-pitched gasp and realised it came from me. When Jaden had downloaded the app a week ago, saying it might come in handy, I'd joked that he only wanted to feel included. I never thought I'd be so grateful he had.

Except gratitude wasn't the emotion that flooded my senses now, as I prayed my eyes were playing tricks on me. However irrational it may have seemed, I'd wanted to believe Dad had swooped in to whisk Mum away in the nick of time.

But I was wrong.

My quivering finger was about to break the connection when I had another thought. What if it wasn't Jaden? Joon had seen me use the app. He could have told his mother there was a chance I would communicate with it.

The timestamp showed the message was sent just after eleven last night. If it was Jaden, wouldn't he have reached out again if he hadn't heard from me in over twelve hours?

a-k-go: Proposal 29 – save parents.

The response came seconds later.

J-2-da-d: Keep count. Proposal 30!
J-2-da-d: I'm glad you're okay, but stay where
you are!

My sob broke through for two reasons. Only Jaden could correct my intentional error so quickly. The second, more crucial reason for my tears was what made me race out of the cubicle.

'You lied to me.'

Aoife was with Manuel when I waved the slider at them, and she grabbed the device off me, squinting at it. I was no longer connected to the network, but the messages clearly showed I'd been on it.

'How did you even—'

'Does it matter?' I sniffed loudly, tears and snot flowing freely.

'It does if it compromises everything we're doing here,' she snapped, moving to a big screen to check if the blocker was back in place.

'I'm sorry if my parents are not as important as your plants, but I had to know if they were safe.'

Manuel's continued silence was the confirmation I needed.

'Why didn't you tell me?'

'Your father asked me not to,' he replied calmly.

Wait, what?

'He spoke to you in custody?'

Manuel's head shook slightly. 'You wanted to know what his options were.' He counted off his fingers. 'Sit tight and wait it out, pack up and run, or surrender. He chose what he thought would keep you safe.'

'No!' My own head shake was vehement.

'I've known your father a long time. We may not always see eye to eye, but he won't want you back in London. He wants you safe.'

'No,' I repeated, refusing to accept the logic I knew was probably true. 'I have to go back for them.'

'I can't let you do that.'

'You have to let her go, Dad.'

We turned to the door where Rosita stood. Her expression was sympathetic.

'She'll flip if she stays here waiting. I would.'

I had never wanted to hug another living being more.

'This is different,' Manuel insisted with a solid frown. 'I can't deliver a Deathsim to the mayor in good conscience. I'm sorry, the answer is no. The risk is too high for all of us.'

'So all that talk about this being my decision was a lie.' I spat the words out. 'I'm being held hostage as much as they are.'

'I'm sorry,' he repeated, and I could tell that was final. 'We will monitor the situation, and I'll let you know if there are any other developments. In the meantime, get some rest. You'll need it if we have to act soon.'

Kicking a desk angrily, I stormed out. I didn't believe for a second that he'd let me in on anything he heard. Not after he lied so easily to my face. Rosita followed. As much as she'd tried to help me, all I wanted to do was turn and yell at her. I fell on to my sleeping bag and screamed into the quilted shell.

I wasn't sure how long she let me cry for, but when Rosita came to pull me up against her chest, I let her. Anger ravaged my entire being, but the simple gesture of compassion worked like a balm.

'This is all my fault.' I wiped my nose messily on my sleeve, getting a hold of myself. 'If I hadn't grown those plants at school, no one would even have known I was a Mechsim. And then I went and downloaded that file after Dad warned me to lie low. Oh Lord, and hanging out with Joon when I knew better. Literally everything I did led to this moment.'

'All you've done is try to protect everyone.' Rosita crossed her arms. 'None of this is your fault. And you actually pulled off the whole rebel thing pretty well for a newbie. You're definitely not as reckless as I was when I started.'

I stared at her for a moment. I had only loosely considered myself a rebel, but not in the way Rosita was. After everything I'd done, I guess I sort of was neck-deep in it now. Or maybe I was a rebel sympathiser. The thought didn't frighten me as much as I'd have imagined.

'I don't think you're reckless,' I said. 'You're super badass. Like someone we'll be reading about in the future.'

She rolled her eyes, but she couldn't stop a smile from touching her lips. 'I'm not gonna lie though, I can't blame you for the Joon bit. That boy is foooine.'

I wasn't sure if that was her attempt at cheering me up, but it got a laugh out of me. We sat in silence for a few calming minutes.

When I spoke again, my voice dropped as I glanced at the door. 'You wouldn't sit and wait if you were in my shoes, would you?'

She frowned and shook her head. 'If he's being honest, Dad wouldn't expect me to.'

This was the scariest decision I'd ever made, but it was time for me to step up. Maybe some of Rosita's courage had rubbed off on me after all the time I'd spent with her.

'If I want to go back to London, can you help?' I asked, shuffling up to my knees.

Rosita's face lit up.

'Come on, I wouldn't be such a badass if I didn't know how to break out of here and get you some wheels.' She quirked her brow. 'Are you really down?'

She didn't need to ask twice.

CHAPTER TWENTY-EIGHT

61 days to Augmentation Day

The heavens knew what a dump of a day it was, opening up in full force right after Rosita waved goodbye to me. But not even a hurricane would have deterred me from my mission. I had an ability the mayor needed. There had to be some bargaining power in that.

Leaving the facility had been ridiculously easy. We'd just walked out. Their security concerns were more about avoiding discovery and invasion, not escape. Because who would want to flee the sanctuary?

'Don't worry, my slider will let me back in,' Rosita explained when I asked how she would return.

She had been to the facility enough times to have her access programmed into the system. The other good thing about this was that she knew the schedule for trucks heading back to the Enfield depot. We'd timed it so we only had to wait a couple of minutes before one slowed down outside the church. The only way to hack the truck's navigator was from the inside, so I hopped in and used a code Rosita gave me, setting the truck to stop just before it reached the depot.

'It'll be a little warm in the cabin,' she said, 'but the rain will help. Good luck.'

She wasn't expecting the quick hug I gave her.

'Thank you,' I whispered against her cheek.

Neither of us brought up the world of trouble she would be in when she went back. Or the fact that if I got arrested, I might never see her again. If her family couldn't return to London, she was heading towards an uncertain future. Settling into the cabin, I prayed they would all be okay.

I could tell the roads were flooded from the splashing sounds the truck's wheels made as it raced towards the city. The water level rose past my ankles when I got out at my stop in a quiet street of abandoned houses. Despite this, the sun was doing its best behind the dark clouds to counter the chill of the rain, and the inside of my suit was drenched with sweat by the time I finally staggered into Enfield station.

'Mum? Dad?' I called out after the airlock let me into the hallway at home, praying with all my might that Jaden and Manuel had been given wrong intel. The silence hit hard.

There were no signs of a struggle. In fact, everything had been carefully put away. The most numbing sign was Clifford's absence, along with that of his bed, litter tray and automated food dispenser. If this was any other situation, my next stop should have been a police station, but what would I say? Hi, I'm a rebel sympathiser and I think you have my parents in custody. If Special Forces were involved, there was only one way I was going to see Mum and Dad.

When I arrived at the western airlock at Regent's Park, my suit dripping from the rain that wouldn't let up, the guards carried out a customary security body scan and let me in without question. My stomach plummeted. They probably knew my face by now, but this wasn't a scheduled visit. Realising I was expected was the first truly frightening confirmation that this was no mistake.

I was right where the mayor wanted.

As we shot past the winding road that led to the mayor's house, I let out a grateful sigh. If Joon was home from school, I didn't think I could face him if we'd turned that way. The cart stopped outside a pair of magnificent black and gilded-iron gates closing off what looked like a large, circular garden. Darren stood outside. He didn't smile as he asked me to go in alone.

A heady scent of roses hit me even before I stepped through.

'Glorious, isn't it?'

Mayor Bernard stood on the other side with a smile so radiant, I nearly returned it.

'I don't imagine you've ever been here. Not a lot of people have.' She turned and walked towards a cluster of rose bushes, forcing me to follow.

When we stopped in the middle of the multi-coloured full blooms, I prayed their strong fragrance masked the stale sweat wafting off me. It shouldn't have mattered, but seeing her in her honey-yellow top and white trousers, I knew I looked a sight. I still wore the oversized black top I'd changed into over my filthy jeans, and I'd lost my scrunchie somewhere along the way, leaving my braids hanging loosely over my face.

'This is Queen Mary's Gardens. Named after the wife of King George the Fifth.' She touched a white petal. 'I thought it fitting that we meet here. She was initially engaged to his brother before he died suddenly of influenza. Their shared trauma helped them grow closer. I've always found her a fine example of putting duty before past concerns.'

If she was telling this story to put me at ease, it wasn't working.

'Don't look so frightened. Come closer.'

I obeyed. I was willing to play this however she wanted until I knew Mum and Dad were safe.

'Are they okay? My parents.'

Her frown was amused. 'Why wouldn't they be?'

'You had them arrested.'

'I didn't, actually. Your father shared stolen classified information with suspected members of a rebel group. His arrest is of his own making. Your mother was brought in for questioning after you ran off from your group's gathering—'

'You mean, my friend's birthday party.' If we were being recorded, to protect Rosita and her family, I had to make it clear I had no idea what she was implying.

309

She chuckled. 'Your father showed up and, how should I put this, made it clear he was willing to bargain.'

Without knowing exactly what Dad had said or done, I could get him into bigger trouble by revealing something I shouldn't. I pushed my braids out of my face, stalling for time. The mayor's eyes followed my wrist.

'I know Joon is fond of you,' she continued, staring at the bracelet, 'but he understands why these people need to be snuffed out for good. When he finds out you stole files from me and shared them with Freestakers, he'll come to his senses.'

Did this mean she wasn't aware Joon knew of my actions at the reception? Did she even know I was involved? It no longer mattered though. If his mother had ulterior motives, we had no future.

'Even if what he believes about his father's death is based on a lie?' I asked, realising this could be my chance to find out if she knew what happened at Crintex all those years ago.

Her brow rose. 'Don't tell me you actually believe the rebels had nothing to do with it.' She didn't pretend to be clueless. She knew there was no way I had a recording device on me after I was thoroughly searched at the entrance.

'So the news wasn't falsified to make it look like their side had fewer casualties from the explosion?'

The mayor snorted, her irritation clear. 'I regret how my predecessors handled the release of information,

310

but it is not something I will apologise for. Would you think Freestakers were any less culpable if I told you the protesters' presence that day indirectly caused the blast?'

Her tone was so certain, my confidence faltered. 'How do you mean?'

'Like the media reported, there really were only a handful of protesters because they had to take it in turns standing in the heat. Their so-called peaceful demonstration escalated when a guard got a little rough and pushed an elderly woman to the ground. Once the scuffle started, the others rushed over from the Tube station where they had been cooling off.'

She paused, and I sensed she was unsure if she should go on.

'They stormed the building?' I prompted.

She nodded. 'As more guards came out to assist, they used the opportunity to push their way in, perhaps thinking they could wreak more havoc and make their voices heard. Or maybe they thought they could obtain footage of something underhand. We'll never know. Yes, their initial intention that day may not have been to cause harm, but the disruption set off the chain of events that caused the explosion. Isn't that enough to lay the blame on them?'

I processed silently. If this was true, I could see why she held Freestakers accountable. She would have been a grieving wife whose only concern was that her son had lost his father for no good reason.

But none of that justified the continued violent raids. The destruction of viable communities who wanted nothing of the system that gave them none of the choices they craved. The deportation of perfectly capable immigrants simply to preserve the norm.

'You still think what we do is excessive.'

I frowned, surprised she'd read my mind so perfectly.

'London just about runs on a working population of four million. We can't maintain our society if enough people don't contribute in a measurable way or if they try to live off the hard work of others. We had that before, and it was not sustainable.'

I already agreed with all this, so I waited for more.

'Your father must have told you what was planned for him. How Stevens hoped to use his ability to ravage hidden rebel resources. That's what you're struggling with, isn't it?'

There it was. I could have convinced myself she'd never actually read the EE-code document even though it was on her system, but this was finally confirmation she knew about Deathsims.

'Isn't that what you do now anyway?' I was growing impatient. 'I've seen footage of recently destroyed greenhouses. You can't pretend you're not complicit.'

Her soft smile gave me no comfort. 'That's why you must have figured out by now you're not needed for that.'

I wasn't? I rubbed my temple, confusion sending a

throbbing pain through my skull. Could Dad have been mistaken all along? But if it was all paranoia, why had she lied about the roses? Why pretend Mechsims didn't have a potentially damaging side when I asked? Why tell someone to alter my test results?

'My remit only stretches as far as London's bio-boroughs, but every leader before me has included anti-rebel promises in their manifestos. Do you think voters care what happens to a few rebels as long as they have food on their plates and extra credits to spend on things that give them pleasure?'

'I assume you'll eventually tell me what you want from me?'

Her smile widened at my snark. 'Like Queen Mary, we don't always end up where we thought we'd be at the start of our journeys. I planned on approaching you after receiving your test results, but I'm glad I waited. It was good for you to see for yourself that your new friends have little to offer society except mindless dissent that leads only to loss.'

I shut my eyes as I recalled all the times I thought I'd cleverly snuck around with Jaden, Rosita and Carl. Someone must have been watching us the whole time.

'After I discovered your family's genetic mutation in my father's files, I realised Stevens had been thinking too small.'

'Wait, we have a mutation?' My eyes flew open.

'You know less than a thousand Mechsims have

been discovered worldwide since testing began forty years ago. And amongst the few we've found on our small island, your father is the only one who exhibited the Deathsim trait. It can't be a coincidence his daughter is the only other person with the same ability.'

I figured Deathsims were rare, but I hadn't considered Dad and I could be the only ones.

'The odd thing is we've found nothing distinctive in his blood or yours. Your frequencies aren't even identical. Do you see where I'm going with this?'

My nod was slow, but I understood. 'You want to study us.'

'Yes, but you are too ingrained in society to suddenly disappear with no questions.' She said this casually, like she regretted not having that option. 'Once you are Augmented, your father will be offered a position outside London, and you will both be transported to a private facility. Imagine what we will be able to accomplish if we finally understand what triggers your unique trait. If we can alter other Mechsims to—'

My gasp of horror cut her off. 'Why would you want to create more of something with so much potential for destruction?'

All I could think about was how quickly the rose bush had died – and that was with my ability unenhanced. We should have been discussing finding a way to slow down the process, not replicate it. Augmentation was a definite no.

She looked surprised. 'It will be harnessed for more

than warfare. Our economy isn't as self-sufficient as everyone is led to believe. Borders and airspace need shoring up against external threats. Don't be misled into thinking we rely on communal work to fund that. If we are able to develop an enhancement to accelerate growth as quickly as you can, but one that stops short of destruction, struggling governments would pay a fortune for just one hybrid.'

I didn't like the idea of becoming a test subject, but in a way, what she wanted to accomplish with the studies was what I wanted as well. To help society with my voice, without the burden of devastation tied to it. The problem was that making Mechsims a commodity was no less worrying than weaponising us. We should be sharing our technology with poorer countries, not exploiting them.

'What of those who just want Deathsims?' I asked, because that was Dad's crisis of conscience. 'Once you figure out why we're like this, what stops anyone from developing Deathsim armies with the technology?'

She waved this off. 'That's for our scientists to work out. My contacts in the Ministry of Agriculture have already buried your real test results. No one outside the research group will know the source. And there will be many other benefits for you. For one thing, you will be upgraded to Level Three. Your family will receive round-the-clock protection.'

It sounded like she had everything worked out, but there was a pretty big sticking point.

'But how can I trust you'll follow through when the study alone could take years?'

'Don't worry about that. A chancellor gets three five-year terms. There's plenty of time to put everything in place.'

I should have known that was her plan. After being mayor for so long, chancellor was the logical career progression for someone as ambitious as her. If she wanted to run for that position, as she'd pointed out, her manifesto would require an airtight promise on national security. She'd need something that would knock everyone out of the race.

But there was no way of telling if her plans were for the best interest of the country or just for her own political advancement. And what happened if she lost? Would the hybrid programme end? Who stood to profit from the funds she'd have received from all those countries if she actually cracked our genetic code?

'I need some time to think.'

I had to stall until I could speak to Dad. Although she made it sound like Freestakers were no longer the target, the mayor hadn't explicitly taken using Deathsims as a weapon against them off the table. Would she be satisfied with plant studies alone? The document mentioned the potential effect on pain receptors for animals. Would she want to explore this? The thought of using any of this data on human subjects was sickening.

And what about Mum? She was probably still reeling from being locked up for no reason. She had her

316

job, her friends. I couldn't ask her to push all that aside and disappear into an underground facility.

'Dear child –' the mayor frowned – 'I must not have made it clear. Your Freestaker friends face multiple criminal charges. You handed me what I needed to make this non-negotiable the moment you stole that file. Their warrants can be dropped, and their names can be taken off the official watch list, but if you don't comply, I can't guarantee their anonymity stays that way. And let's not forget about your friend Jaden.'

A chill ran through me. I had deluded myself into thinking our conversation had been a proposal. *This* was the reason Dad didn't want me back in London. Because there was nothing to bargain with. It wasn't like I could take this story to anyone else without exposing myself. And even if I tried, it'd be the word of a suspected rebel against that of a high-ranking official.

'You can't do this.' My voice rose as the reality of the situation sank in.

'But I can, and I am. I knew you'd need some convincing, so I brought along someone to ease things along.'

I turned when she motioned to someone behind me.

'Mum?'

I was so relieved to see my mother, I didn't stop to think. I raced towards her, throwing myself into her outstretched arms and holding her tight. It was hard to believe it was only twenty-four hours since I'd said goodbye to her. It felt like a lifetime had gone by.

'I'll leave you to catch up.' I barely heard the mayor through my sobs before she walked away.

Mum's trembling hands wiped my drenched cheeks, and I frantically looked her over to check she hadn't been hurt.

'Gbaghara m, ada m,' she cried quietly, holding my face in her hands.

I couldn't understand why she was asking for forgiveness when it was my lies and actions that had brought her to this place. It was me who had failed her and Dad.

'She promised me you would be safe. I didn't realise your father would be detained indefinitely. That wasn't part of the deal.' Her head shook, her words a ramble.

'Mum, what are you saying?'

'If I had known they were all lies, I would never have agreed to help. I would never put you and your father in danger, ada m.'

'Mum, I don't understand. You were working with the mayor?' Even as I said the words, I questioned myself. Maybe I hadn't heard right.

Her silence shattered me. I took a step back, forcing her hands to fall from my face.

'Akaego, I had no choice. I left Nigeria just before things got better there, and I arrived at Newport with no papers, almost nothing to my name.'

She was making no sense, but I listened because I didn't know what else to do.

Mum brushed off her tears with the back of her

hands. 'I was detained at a centre for months. When I was offered a job by FES in exchange for permanent residence, I didn't think twice about accepting it. All they asked was that I befriend and shadow a rebel suspect. It was your father.'

I staggered, doubling over and gasping for air. I wanted her to stop speaking; I couldn't get the words out. She couldn't possibly be saying she was with Dad as part of a mission. That my entire existence was based on a lie she'd been pulling off for years.

'I never had anything valuable to report, and his threat level was eventually reduced. Somewhere along the line, we fell in love. I was given permission to marry him on the grounds that I would inform them of any notable activity. All these years, I felt guilty about keeping the truth from your father, but I justified my past actions with the fact that he still never trusted me enough to let me in on that part of his life.'

Her words swam in my head. This couldn't be real. Mum kept going.

'I heard nothing from FES for years, but we received extra credits every now and then, so I knew I was still on their payroll. It was only after your Mechsim ability was discovered that I was told to provide daily reports. They said it was a formality because of your father's past ties. I didn't realise what both of you could do until today.'

It was almost funny how I'd spent so much time worrying about Joon, when it was me who had ratted on myself, innocently telling Mum every time I met up with Rosita and Carl. She must have reported them that same day she came home and found us in her study.

No. She must have contacted them all those months ago when the note showed up in our delivery receptacle.

When Mum pulled me up, I was too numb to react, letting her hold me as she repeated her apology over and over again, wondering what would happen now everything I'd held as good and true was washing away as quickly as the salty tears flowing down our cheeks.

CHAPTER TWENTY-NINE

60 days to Augmentation Day

A laugh.

A cuss.

Two.

An excited squeal.

Something banged against a metal surface.

I walked through the crowd, not quite seeing anything, my focus solely on putting one foot in front of the other. All I had to do was get through my first class, and then the next.

'Sorry,' someone called out after they slammed into my shoulder.

I envied their innocence. The fact that they could go about their business, only thinking about where they were meeting their friends at the weekend, what they might be eating for dinner.

Nothing felt real. Not when everything I thought I'd known in life was a lie. Not when the one person I thought would always have my back was the one who had stabbed it. The one who had betrayed Dad.

The mayor had commanded I show up at school to

give the impression of normality until Augmentation Day, but I didn't deserve to be there, acting like my whole world wasn't collapsing around me. The only reason I was here was for my friends. If I didn't act like I was going along with the mayor's plan, what would the consequences be for them? As it was, I doubted any of them would ever want anything to do with me.

It was almost laughable to realise I possessed an ability with the potential to do so much good or devastate entire communities, yet I had never felt so powerless in all my life.

I ignored a vibration in my pocket. It wasn't the first time that morning. I should have shut my slider off, but knowing someone was trying to reach me made me feel a little bit connected to the world. The device had been handed to me as Mum and I left the garden. I hadn't switched it on until after midnight though, and only because sleep refused to find me.

There had been a dozen messages from Mum, from before the raid and after. I'd deleted them all. One was from Dad at around ten on the night of the raid. I'd saved it without listening. I wanted the next time I heard his voice to be in person, whenever they let me visit him at the holding centre.

There was nothing from Jaden, probably because he knew I'd lost my slider, but surprisingly, I had a missed call from Joon.

'Akaego.'

I looked up to see Joon, almost like I'd materialised

him with my thoughts. It was inevitable I would see him at some point. I should have turned and walked away, but I was frozen to the spot. He took a step forward, and I saw relief in his eyes when I didn't move. It was only when he grabbed my shoulders and pulled me against his chest that my brain unstuck.

My eyes widened as his arms dropped to wrap around my waist, yet I didn't try to break free.

'I thought something was wrong when you didn't show up at school yesterday. I was afraid you had been—'

He stopped himself and hugged me tighter. That was all my body needed to react. The concern in his voice. Suddenly it didn't matter that we'd agreed to keep our distance. He cared too much not to show how he felt when I was potentially in danger. I knew he could see the same feeling in my eyes. My arms reached up and crossed themselves against his back.

The hug was unexpected, but when Joon dropped his head and kissed me right there in front of everyone, my mind actually full-on exploded. Or maybe it was my heart pounding so loudly that I could feel it in my head.

Time must have stopped. I couldn't tell how long his lips stayed on mine. All I knew was that when he drew away, it was like he'd pulled all the air in my body along with him. I opened my eyes and stared up at him, not quite sure what just happened.

The look on his face was uncertain.

'Sorry, I—'

I leaned in and pressed my lips to his again. If he thought this had been a mistake, I needed a little bit more of the squishy feeling in my gut before the taste of his lips was taken away forever.

This time, when he pulled back, the light in his eyes was unmistakable.

'That was . . .' He paused, his lips hovering close to mine, his breath tickling my skin.

This was ridiculous. Dad was locked up, Mum was an FES sleeper agent, my friends were in danger and I was going to be poked and prodded by Joon's mother for profit, yet I felt giddy just standing there with him.

'Way too early in the day for this, you guys, way too early.'

The yelled reproach snapped us back to where we stood. In a corridor at school, surrounded by dozens of amused and confused faces.

Thankfully, the bell for first period went, and everyone began making their way into classrooms. Joon put a hand out to me, and I took it. We ended up in the gym because no one ever had PE as their first period.

Settling on one of the lower benches, I was reminded of the day I'd seen Rosita there. Her schoolmates would arrive later that afternoon, but unlike me, she didn't have the luxury of easily slotting back into her life.

'Are you okay?' Joon asked, still holding my hand.

I nodded, struggling to decide what to reveal. The fact that he didn't take my absence from school as a sick day or something less sinister said a lot about where his mind was at. But how exactly did anyone tell a boy they liked that his mother was the villain in their story?

I couldn't look at him. 'I don't know how to tell you what's going on, or if I should, but we can't do that again.' If his mother found out, would she see it as a violation of the unwritten terms she had set out for my future?

'Oh.'

The disappointment in his voice gave me the courage to meet his gaze.

'It's not that I don't want to. It's just, with everything going on, it's too confusing.'

'This has to do with my mother, doesn't it?'

I wasn't going to deny it. 'Remember what my friend said about Crintex? She didn't quite get it right, but she wasn't far off.'

If I gave him nothing more, he had to know his hatred of Freestakers was misguided. It wasn't fair for him to hold such bitterness in his heart based on a lie.

Joon frowned. 'And Mum confirmed this?' When I nodded, he went on. 'But what does that have to do with you? Why do I have a terrible feeling she's pulling you into something you have no choice in?'

It sounded like he knew his mother well.

'How much do you want to hear? I don't want to force anything on you that will make you see her differently. She's your mum.'

He hesitated for a moment before squeezing my hand. 'I've always known she doesn't always colour within the lines, but her decisions never affected anyone in my life directly. Not anyone I cared about.' He rubbed the back of his neck with his other hand. 'Saying it out loud, I can hear how selfish that sounds. The truth is, if I have to see you every day for the next two months, even if we have to pretend we don't like each other, not knowing why will eat away at me.'

And so I told him. I kept details loose and omitted names. I didn't mention the disruptor. That was one thing the mayor hadn't raised. Even if Dad couldn't work on it in detention, I couldn't give Joon extra info which could accidentally slip out.

Joon sat back when I stopped speaking. 'That's a hell of a lot to take in.'

'I'm sorry.' I was upset with Mum, but what she did paled in comparison to the mayor's plans.

I'd expected him to be angry – at me, at his mum, at the irrationality of it all. Instead, Joon let go of my hand and leaned against his knees, burying his face in his palms. His deflation was unnerving.

'I'm finding it hard to believe Mum would go this far,' he said, looking over at me after a stretch of silence. 'This is just . . .'

I could understand why he struggled with the idea. If Mum hadn't confessed directly to me, I would have laughed if anyone suggested she was capable of maintaining such a prolonged cover.

'I don't gain anything by making something this ridiculous up.'

'I'm not saying you're lying.' Joon's hands rose defensively. 'It's just, Dad wouldn't want any of this done in his name. I don't remember him much, but my halmeoni always talks about how social-minded he was. The researchers at Crintex recruited him from Korea to help create better building materials before the immigration restrictions kicked in. This isn't the legacy he would have wanted.'

I chose not to state the obvious. His mum's vendetta might have started because of the Crintex tragedy, but she'd moved on to other politically motivated schemes. The public would always see the deaths as her fuel, and she would no doubt use it in speeches to rally support.

'What happens now?'

'She wins.' I cringed, saying the words out loud for the first time. 'I'm not going to make a choice that could endanger my family and friends.'

I thought I'd feel less shame admitting it, but the ball knotting away in my chest tightened. Because this meant I was going back to being the sidekick in my own story. I was accepting I was never going to be worthy of badass status.

I was giving up.

'Hey, shouldn't you two be in class?'

If Joon had a response to my declaration of defeat, I never got to hear it. Mrs Rendell was standing at the gym doors, arms crossed, glaring.

'We'll finish this later, okay?' Joon whispered, squeezing my hand one last time before we parted ways. 'Don't disappear on me.'

He knew me better than I thought. Unfortunately, that didn't mean I wasn't going to disappoint him. I couldn't let the mayor find out we'd been talking, so I went back to my old tricks, sitting at the front of classes so I could dash off and hide after, skipping lunch, and running out of school with the first batch of kids let into the airlock.

The most difficult part was keeping that glorious kiss out of my mind, knowing I might cave if I let myself think about it. I even put my slider on silent so I wouldn't be tempted to answer if he called.

The Tube journey home felt a million miles long. I knew Mum would be waiting with another round of apologies. A part of me understood she'd acted out of desperation all those years ago, and her recent actions were based on a sense of duty and ignorance. That didn't stop the other part of me from hating the fact Dad was sitting in a box because of her lies.

'Your friend is here.' She stood by the living-room door when I walked in.

I had started heading for my room without a word, but I quickly changed direction. It could only be one person.

'Jaden,' I cried, flinging myself at him with so much force, we nearly fell over.

'Whoa,' he laughed, steadying the both of us before hugging me. 'I'm glad you're all right. I was losing it when I didn't hear back. Why didn't you answer my messages?'

'I'm sorry, I couldn't bear the—'

'Carl's in hospital,' he interrupted, his tone serious.

'What?'

Carl had been running a fever when I left, but he'd been okay.

'He had—' Jaden stopped and glanced at the door where Mum stood watching us.

Taking his hand, I walked past her, leading him to my bedroom, where I shut the door. There was no way Mum would bring up our usual open-door rule.

'Sorry, I wasn't sure how much she knows,' Jaden said.

I had forgotten he wasn't aware of Mum's contribution to our current position.

'What happened?'

'Turns out Carl had a severe concussion. They must have been really worried because they came back to the city so he can get medical attention. Rosita reached out to me this morning. She said they couldn't deal with his condition at one of their secret emergency units, whatever that is.'

I pushed down a tiny wave of curiosity at the thought of Rosita contacting him. To be fair, even if she'd tried to call me, I had been ignoring my slider.

I sank on to my bed. 'This is all my fault.'

'How can you say that? It's not like you knocked him over.'

'I should never have said yes when he asked for

my help. Mum wouldn't have known any of you were involved if I hadn't brought them home.'

'She knows?' Jaden sat beside me with a frown.

My tongue felt like lead as I told him how the mayor had kept tabs on us. How Mum and I were only allowed home because they thought we'd stay in line with Dad in custody as insurance until Augmentation Day.

When I was done, Jaden placed a hand on my shoulder.

'There's one other thing.' My voice cracked a little, but it was better to just spit everything out now I had the courage. 'I told Joon what's happening.'

'Akaego!'

'He has a right to know.'

Jaden huffed. 'How can you be sure he's not going to run off to his mother and—'

'Tell her that he knows the truth? We lose nothing by him being clued up. If anything, he's the one who lost his mother today. At least the idea of her.' I tried not to look at the door.

'Aunty had no choice. I know that's not what you think now, but your mum loves you. I mean, anyone can see that.'

I blinked back tears, knowing he was right.

'So what do we do now?' he asked.

'How do you mean?' I turned to him again.

'Plan B. Or C. You're not giving up, are you? Not after everything your dad did to make sure you didn't get trapped in the same position as him.'

My brows pushed together. It had been easy to tell Joon the mayor had won. But seeing the expectation in Jaden's eyes made me wonder if I was letting all of us down by doing nothing. The mayor had lied to me from the start. She was lying to her son about his dad's death by letting him believe Freestakers deliberately caused the explosion. She'd forced Mum to spy on us. Could I really trust her to leave my friends and family alone if I went along with everything she said?

The problem was, I couldn't blatantly disregard her warnings. The reason Carl and his family probably weren't being picked up from hospital as we spoke was because I wasn't running. It felt like I had nothing to offer to protect the people I cared about. But I wasn't okay sitting back and watching as she destroyed my life while someone like her became chancellor.

Something flashed in Jaden's eyes, and he smiled a little too widely. 'I can literally see your wheels turning.'

'We need something tangible,' I said slowly, not wanting to be over-buoyed by his enthusiasm. 'Incriminating documents or a recording of her threatening us. The file we have only proves she knew about Deathsims. She's had everything wrapped up from the start.'

'If we figure out how to give you the upper hand,' Jaden said, unfazed, 'then maybe we can take that power away from her.'

'You're forgetting she has your fate in her hands.' I knew Jaden was an eternal optimist, but there was

331

no point pretending things weren't as dire as they seemed.

Jaden waved this away. 'Her long-term plan is tied to nobody knowing what you can do, right? She needs you to lie low until she makes you and your dad disappear, but she's also using your fear of exposure to hold you hostage.'

I frowned, thinking. 'What if we blow all that up? If the public sees how dangerous Deathsims can be, there'll be no way they'll endorse her creating more. The good of one won't really be benefiting all. They can't backtrack on that if everyone knows.'

It sounded counter-intuitive, but being exposed as a Deathsim was more Dad's fear than mine. If I really wanted my idea of health parks to come true, people would eventually have to know my abilities surpassed that of other Mechsims. We'd need to get a muffler of some sort working, but I would still clearly be different.

'Eh, I wasn't thinking that grand a scale,' Jaden admitted. 'Doesn't that mean you'll be putting a target on your back? If anyone else has the same idea as her, they could also make you disappear.'

'Not if we sell the right narrative,' I said with more confidence now the idea was taking root. 'Get me upgraded to Level Three for the right reasons and have the protection that comes with it.'

'Okay, I'm just not seeing how that's possible.'

'Being part of the Augmentation Day Pageant was Mrs Miguel's idea,' I went on, my mind working fast. 'It'll look suspicious if the mayor stops me attending.

I'm guessing she won't have me switch on the enhancer because it would destroy the plants I project on to. My frequency strength on its own could be enough if I use it on plants with really short lifespans. Or maybe they plan on saying there's an issue with my implant.'

When I thought Dad's disruptor could be activated before the pageant, I had been bracing myself for everyone's disappointment at me losing my Mechsim ability. I had been worrying about the loss I would feel. This was a different dynamic.

Jaden gasped. 'Wait, you're thinking we do this at the pageant?'

I nodded. 'Can you think of a better nationally broadcasted live platform?'

The event would be held in an open space in the very green Hyde Park Biodome. I knew how much damage I could do in a space like that. Only a few seconds had ripened the tomatoes and bloomed the marigold at my evaluation with the enhancement simulator. But if I held back like I'd done that day and directed my voice to the display, keeping it brief, it could produce enough damning progression during the length of the broadcast.

Jaden grinned again.

'It's not airtight, but I don't think she'll expect it. You said your dad will be allowed to attend the pageant to make it look like there's nothing wrong, so you'll know he's safe. The best part is you'll play along for the next few months, and then, bam!'

This was, without a doubt, the scariest thing I'd considered so far, yet I felt like it wasn't totally outrageous because I had him on this journey with me.

'So you think it isn't completely unreasonable?'

'We'll work on it,' he said with conviction, 'but we have to find out exactly what protection Level Threes get.'

Seeing as the mayor had offered me the upgrade, I pulled out my slider to see if I could find anything on their supposed elevated security. Jaden caught sight of my screen.

'You like him a lot, huh?' he asked, seeing the missed calls from Joon alongside his own calls from earlier.

'Yes,' I sighed, staring at his name for a second too long before clearing the call log. 'But none of that matters any more.'

We spent the next half hour searching for details on Level Threes and finding hardly anything before deciding it would be better to come back to it later. Jaden hadn't told his parents he'd be home late. After I saw him out, I noticed Mum hovering by the kitchen door.

'I fried some plantain,' she said, her voice as subdued as it'd been since yesterday.

Seeing her standing there, looking so small and uncertain, it occurred to me that our access to the pricey fruit was probably a perk we were able to afford with her FES credits. Mum had no luxuries of her own, and she never asked for anything. There was no doubt she gave up all she had for us.

Jaden wasn't wrong when he said she loved me more than anything else. And I knew she loved Dad. Although she'd hidden so many facts about her life, I knew where her heart lay. She was still the person who'd held me at night when I cried, confused by the pain of my first period cramps. The person who took time off work to come to school with me on my first day at the Academy of Music because she sensed how nervous I was, even after I insisted I was too old for her to accompany me.

I offered her a small smile, then nodded and followed her into the kitchen. We had a long way to go, but we would eat, and then we would talk.

CHAPTER THIRTY

51 days to Augmentation Day

'I know what you're going to say.'

'That I hate seeing you here like this?'

'That I should eat all the beans I'm given to keep my strength up.'

I hadn't expected to smile at all, yet I heard myself laugh. We always nagged Dad about his loathing of pulses, and those were probably the main protein source on the detention centre's menu. His sunken cheeks made me certain we were right to worry. I hoped the guards would pass on the food-filled care package I'd brought for him.

Dad leaned towards the glass screen between us. 'Your mother didn't mean to hurt us, you must know that.'

Mum and I had talked a lot about her choices over the past week. I wasn't sure if I would have made the same decisions, but my actions during the last couple of months proved we could never know how we would react in any situation until we were in it.

'Did you know? About any of it?'

'I had my suspicions.' He sat back, the metal chair scraping against the concrete floor. 'Not about her recent actions. Back when we started dating, I sensed a disconnect, like she was hiding something, but I loved her too much to hold it against her.'

He glanced at the blinking light of the camera behind him. 'Over the years, I was always conscious of what I felt back then. Maybe that's why I never shared anything about you-know-what with her. Why I wouldn't let her bear the burden of your discovery.'

It stung to think there'd been this lack of trust between them, even with all the love they shared. Mum had visited Dad twice so far, but she never told me what they discussed.

'I thought they wouldn't let you come,' Dad continued, voicing the surprise I'd expressed when Mum confirmed my name had been added to his visitor list.

As much as we suspected it was the mayor playing her cards, I wasn't going to sniff at the opportunity. Dad's colleagues had been told he was being temporarily transferred to an out-of-town biodome for some highly confidential work. It would make the permanent relocation cover all the more believable after Augmentation Day.

'I'm sorry I couldn't stay out of London.'

He smiled. 'You're stubborn. That's why I asked Manuel to hide it from you. When I was sure you were safe, I hoped to get them to spare your mother if I turned myself in. I didn't stop to think I was playing right into their hands.'

We both looked at the floor.

'I guess you know what's been planned for us,' I said. 'You just have to sit tight until Augmentation Day. It won't be long now.'

I couldn't tell him what I was working on with Jaden. Even if the cameras weren't there, Dad would be livid if he discovered I wanted the world to see me for who I was. The one thing I wished we could talk about was the disruptor. It was my shot at having another choice. I'd looked everywhere at home and finally accepted it must be at his workplace.

'Two minutes,' a voice blared over the intercom.

I couldn't believe fifteen minutes had gone by. It felt like I'd just arrived. Placing an open palm on the divider, I sniffed to prevent a sob.

'I love you, Daddy.' I smiled weakly. 'We're going to be okay.'

I must not have held my emotions in well enough because his smile was watery when he positioned his hand over mine. 'I love you too, Ego. I need you to know I'm never going to stop fighting.' Then, leaning forward once again, he added quietly, 'Give Clifford a hug for me.'

I had expected something more covert from his dropped voice, but I nodded. 'I will.'

Dad wasn't done. 'Hold him to your chest, and rub that spot below his collar, just the way he likes.

338

You know he loves it best when you're in your mother's study.'

I was about to ask more about this mysterious spot Clifford liked so much when it hit me. It was a coded message.

The only way I got home without exploding with curiosity was by distracting myself with thoughts of the last couple of weeks. So much had happened. Joon had found me the day after our kiss.

'I don't expect you to trust me, but I want to make things right,' he'd said. 'I won't be able to help your father, but if you need credits to get you and your mother far away, I'll find a way to transfer mine to you. I'll give you everything I can access.'

'You know your mum's probably having us watched,' I reasoned.

'So what?' He puffed his chest out defiantly. 'If she cared what I thought, she wouldn't do this to my friend. She wouldn't try to control everything like she always does.'

I'd sensed resentment before, but he wasn't hiding it this time. Even so, I couldn't ask him to act against his mum. If I was going to blow up his lifestyle and put his existence under a microscope, it was only fair I did it without his help.

'Thank you, Joon,' I said, resisting the urge to reach up and ease out his furrowed brow. 'I'd be putting my friends in danger if I ran. Besides, I don't think we'll ever be able to gather enough credits to fund that big an escape. And I could never leave Dad.'

He must have known that would be my response because he didn't argue.

My afternoon outing that Friday had been more daunting. The trauma centre at St Mary's Hospital in Paddington. Rosita nearly popped an artery when she saw me hovering outside the room.

'Should you be here?' She scanned the corridor as if she expected a squad to emerge.

'I'm here to see my friend,' I said, pulling her in for a hug.

She stiffened. When her weight finally sagged against my body, it was my turn to have a shoulder cried upon.

'How's he doing?' I asked after she composed herself.

'Better. He had a seizure. I've never seen Dad so frightened, and Mum was in pieces. There was no way we were going to wait it out.'

She glanced back at the room where I assumed her parents sat with Carl.

'Does the mayor know about him?' she asked then.

'I don't think so.' I was glad I'd never mentioned Carl to the mayor, and I prayed she had no clue he could be a Mechsim.

Rosita's nod wasn't firm.

'So this is it? We just let her get away with whatever she has planned?' she asked with the same indignant tone as Jaden.

There was no way of her knowing the details of our agreement. But she'd probably worked out some sort of deal had been made.

'All this time, I couldn't picture how this would end,' I admitted, 'but I hoped Carl would achieve his wish at least. I have to leave after Augmentation Day, but he can continue working on what we started, with your help.'

If our plan didn't work, I didn't want to give her hope. After watching footage from the last time a Mechsim appeared at a pageant, I realised one big problem we faced. A microphone was hooked up to the boy's lapel as he belted out his frequency. To keep the destruction focused, we were going to have to figure that part out.

I didn't stay long after that. In the end, the coward in me couldn't deal with seeing Carl. I felt too guilty.

At home, I found Clifford curled on a cushion, purring lightly. The day after my return, Mum had brought him back from her friend's house where he'd been stashed for her fake arrest. It seemed a shame to wake him when he looked so content, but I couldn't contain myself.

Avoiding his bared claws at being woken suddenly, I felt along the edge of his collar. I tried not to let disappointment take over when I found nothing. I must have missed something in what Dad said, so I thought back to his exact words.

The spot below his collar.

Did that mean it was under his skin? And if it was, how the hell was I supposed to find whatever it was without cutting him open?

Mum's study.

Holding on to the now lively tabby, I raced to her study and looked around. There had to be something here to help me figure out what Dad meant, since Clifford never showed interest in the room. Once my eyes settled on Mum's monocle, I tilted my head. It was programmed to respond only to her retina, yet I couldn't think of anything else I should pick up. Slipping it over my left eye, I switched on the device and gasped.

A welcome message asked if I wanted to access the last information saved under my profile. When my shaky voice said yes, the monocle responded, and I knew this was no accident. Dad must have covered all grounds in the event that he was taken in. I couldn't help smiling at his beautiful, paranoid mind.

Lifting Clifford, I unclipped his collar. Dad had a chip installed on him ages ago. It wasn't like we thought it'd actually happen, but if our adventurous cat ever managed to escape into the heat, Dad said it would help us find him quickly.

A series of texts rolled out in front of me when I focused on the area at the back of his neck. Mostly numbers and tagged words, nothing that made any sense – until I got to a graph and commanded the auto-scroll to pause. I had seen that pattern before.

Ten minutes later, I logged on to Roulette.

a-k-go: How would you feel if I said I think we
could have a plan B to our plan B?

Three long minutes later, I got my response.

J-2-da-d: I'll be right over!

CHAPTER THIRTY-ONE

7 days to Augmentation Day

'Okay, which one of you sadists said this wouldn't hurt?'

'If you sue, I'll back you up.'

I lay with my eyes closed, wondering if they'd mind if I chipped in as I tried to ignore the throbbing in the left side of my neck. They weren't wrong.

It was surgery day, and the procedure ached a lot more than we'd been told it would. It used to be called Augmentation Day in the early days because it was when we actually became enhanced, but after having more than a few teething problems, the process was adapted to allow a week between surgery and the graduation pageant. The slowly subsiding pain I felt where a flat disc had been inserted under my skin proved someone had made the right call.

It was a pain I could endure. For me, the true challenge was yet to come. The ball of anxiety in my chest at the thought of meeting Jaden and Rosita later on to work on a failsafe for my enhancement chip almost numbed the pain of the surgery. Almost.

I opened my eyes and scanned the room. Estrella

sat across from me with a massive bandage around her neck. I would have chuckled if I didn't know I looked as ridiculous as she did. Our year had been split into surgical groups based on our talents, so Joon was with the limb-enhancement batch.

Estrella must have felt my gaze because she looked up and waved. She'd been decent to me in general, but I couldn't help having my guard up with anyone in their group. Despite that, I thought it was a shame a band like Sky Sailors wasn't representing our school on Augmentation Day. They would have created an amazing vibe, but our school always went safe, like with the operatic ensembles who were performing 'Nessun Dorma' yet again.

There would also be my performance this year. The thought sent a shudder through me. But I had made my decision.

I smiled politely before turning to my side and shutting my eyes again. I needed every restful minute of the next couple of hours we had left in monitored confinement.

The moment the doors opened, I was the first out. Mum expected me home to ride out the effects of the sedative, but the clock was ticking. We only had days to make sure plan B was a real option now my implant was in place. When I arrived at the karaoke bar and slipped into a padded booth, a stifled snort greeted me.

'What part of this do you find the most amusing?'

The sound had morphed into a full-blown guffaw.

345

'Come on, you have to admit you both look like you fell off a bullet train,' Rosita said, wiping her eyes.

Jaden eyed me from across the table. 'Tell me I don't look as crappy as she does?'

'You look worse.' I stuck my tongue out at him, wincing with the effort.

I wasn't kidding. He'd received his enhancement, and because his disc was placed at the top left of his skull, most of his head was wrapped in a bandage. He also looked quite tipsy. The position of his implant probably meant he was more drugged up than me. I was glad at least one of us was sober.

Bringing Rosita on board had been Jaden's idea. With everything her family had gone through, I was reluctant to pull her back in, but he'd pointed out that creating a failsafe meant we would be messing with a device that was remotely connected to my brain and vocal cords. We had both seen how nifty Rosita was with tech.

'You had an engineer and a surgeon working on this before,' he'd reasoned. 'We haven't even graduated secondary school. Three heads are definitely going to be better than two. If we split the research, we may just have a chance.'

'You're sure it's okay to be here like this?' she'd asked when we finally met up for the first time. 'I'm pretty sure we're being watched.'

'We're hiding in plain sight, baby, hiding in plain sight,' Jaden sang to a made-up tune before ducking to avoid Rosita's smack.

I hadn't been sure either, but Jaden's logic was that anyone tailing us wouldn't think we'd be rash enough to move forward with such a bold plan. As long as we didn't do anything obvious in public, we were just friends spending time together.

'Seriously though,' Rosita said now, getting herself under control after kicking off again when Jaden and I both itched at our bandages, 'are you guys okay?'

We nodded. I should have clarified that I was only okay with the physical pain. I had been looking forward to getting Augmented for years, but that joy was tainted with the knowledge I'd gained over the past few months. If we did this right, maybe this day could still be one I could look back on with a sense of pride.

'They said the connection will be up and running within six hours of the surgery.'

'That should be right about now.' Rosita pulled out a small silver box from her pocket and held it below the table, out of sight of any cameras.

I was expected to give at least a thirty-second full vocal blast at the pageant. The point of the failsafe was to activate a timer to shut off my enhancer halfway through, even if sound continued to come out of my mouth. The tech we'd been working on used the principles of Dad's research I'd found on Clifford's chip, just tweaked, which meant it had to be tested against my frequency, like he'd done. That was why we'd booked a semi-private space this time. Somewhere I could make strange sounds without question.

Rosita's face clouded over about a minute after I pushed down on the sore spot on the side of my neck.

'What?'

'It shows you're being amplified, but there's something else being picked up.'

She slid the frequency counter across to Jaden, who also frowned at the screen.

'Bloody hell, they really don't want you belting out any killer tunes that day. Looks like your enhancer's in safe mode.'

I snatched the device off him and scanned it. This was not good. There was no way we would be able to expose the mayor if we couldn't even access the enhancer.

'Wait, does this mean they know what we're planning?'

Wide eyes stared at each other as we contemplated the alarming possibility of Rosita's words.

'I don't know, but I'm not willing to stop now based on a what-if,' I said.

The more I thought about it, the more I realised this wasn't just about our present dilemma. If the Deathsim trait was genetic, if I had kids of my own, they could also be targeted. I couldn't fail where Dad had because of a fear that could end up being nothing.

'I'd understand if you guys want to back out,' I carried on. 'If things don't work out as planned on the day, I can swear you had nothing to do with it. My fate is sealed either way.'

348

'Can we bypass it?' Jaden confirmed his position with a slight squeeze of my shoulder.

'I'm not sure,' Rosita admitted. 'We may be able to reverse the polarity temporarily by overriding the signal shutting it out, but the only way I can think of is by using the device to do the opposite of what we intended.'

I didn't like the sound of that. 'That means we lose our failsafe.'

She nodded. 'I'm sorry, Akaego, we can't have both.'

I hated to think we'd be going back to full Deathsim mode. She was right though. We couldn't use the device we'd been working on for two functions.

'Do you still think an earring is the best medium? It'll be moving around a lot, and I'm less convinced now we'll be turning it into an on switch.'

Since we no longer had access to Dad's and Manuel's expertise, I couldn't wear a collar or swallow a capsule. The plan had been to rig up an accessory and position it close enough to my enhancer to interfere with its signal. This was well outside the software-programming realms Jaden and I were used to. Rosita was the one who shone in that area.

We'd ruled out a brooch as I wasn't the type to wear one, and a necklace needed a pendant large enough to mask a chip. I had volunteered a pair of Mum's oversized adire-fabric-wrapped earrings with a flat surface area.

'I can't think of anything else. A hair clip, maybe?

But the earring would be better since it'll be almost perfectly in line with the disc,' Jaden replied.

As the only one with access to a kitted-out engineering skills lab, he had been working on the chip at school.

'There's just one other thing,' Rosita said, her tone of voice causing me to frown. 'If we're going to effectively turn the earring into an anode, we're going to need a bit more tantalum than we've got at the moment. to reduce the risk of a short circuit.'

Jaden and I cringed in unison. Enhancement discs were coated in tantalum because of its corrosion resistance and biocompatibility when used for implants. It was also great for frequency tuning. We had been able to cobble together some of the metal by breaking into Jaden's old devices, but there was no way we would access anything as big as the size Rosita was suggesting we needed to temporarily swap the enhancer to a cathode.

'Any idea where we can get one?' I dared to ask.

'You're not going to like it.' Rosita's voice dipped even more.

Now she really had me worried.

'Joon?'

Jaden and I said this at the same time with a matching tone of incredulity.

'There's a massive old coin collection hanging in one of those entertainment rooms at their place. I noticed it at the reception,' she explained.

I was still lost. 'What does this have to do with anything?'

Rosita's eye-roll suggested I was being slow. 'I'm pretty sure some countries had special issues of tantalum coins. If we find out which and he can nick one, we'll be sorted.'

I shook my head. 'I don't want him involved.' It wouldn't be fair to ask for his help when we were trying to expose his mother.

'Come on, you won't have to tell him what it's for. Just say it's your going-away present or something. We're not even sure the right coin will be there.'

'We'll be asking him to steal. The coins probably belong to the government,' I countered lamely.

'I can't believe I'm agreeing with Rosita on this,' Jaden piped up, 'but we don't have much time. It's worth checking.'

Hearing him side with her was the sign I needed that we really had no other option.

'That's settled then.' Rosita didn't wait for my response. 'You ask him today, and Jaden and I will work on a reversal strategy for the chip.'

'I'll bring the walkie-talkies next time we meet,' Jaden reminded her, moving on. The plan was for them to use the devices to communicate on Augmentation Day. Jaden was going to gut the bulky cases and move the analogue tech into something that wouldn't be obvious when they were searched at the entrance. 'Has your pass cleared?'

Even though the pageant was open to everyone to attend, our worry was that Rosita would be rejected if she was already on some form of watch list.

'Yes.' She beamed at the good news before wrinkling her nose. 'But I have to bring Carl.'

Jaden and I exchanged a glance.

'Are you sure that's a good idea?'

'You know how he is. You would think the concussion would have slowed him down.' She mumbled that last bit under her breath. 'Which reminds me, I have to get back soon.'

There wasn't much left to discuss, so we pretended to go a couple of rounds on the karaoke machine, in case someone watched the room's recording and wondered why we hadn't done any singing. I also used the time to send Joon a meetup request since theft wasn't the sort of thing that could be asked via unencrypted text.

'Are you all right?' Joon rushed over to me when I entered the walk-through patisserie he'd suggested. 'Did your procedure go okay?'

I nodded, looking down at the bandages around his wrists and suppressing the urge to ask him the same question. Although we didn't talk much lately, I felt the weight of his gaze on me in classes. Sometimes I wished he would walk up to me and kiss me like he'd done that day of my return.

'Can I ask a favour?' I dived straight in when we joined the food dispenser queue.

'Anything.'

After I rattled off my request in as low a voice as possible, he frowned.

'Do I even want to know what this is about?'

'Probably not.' Definitely not.

He sighed. 'And you're sure you know what you're doing?'

The truth was, I had no clue if any of it would work. When Jaden pointed out that I risked losing my ability altogether if we were even remotely off with our calculations, I full-on hyperventilated. All I could offer Joon now was a nod.

'Kazakhstan?'

'Yes,' I said, confirming the coin we thought was most likely to be in the collection. 'It'll be one of the special issues. I promise, this will be the last thing I ask of you.'

His pained expression was clearly about that last part. 'Okay, if it's there, I'll bring it to school tomorrow.' He reached into the receptacle we'd stopped at and pulled out two blueberry muffins. 'Your favourite, right?'

The warmth I'd been ignoring in my belly suddenly expanded until it filled my chest.

'Thank you.' This was the reason I couldn't spend time with him. He made it all the harder to let him go.

'Just keep safe,' he said, touching my cheek lightly before he walked away.

CHAPTER THIRTY-TWO

Augmentation Day
Hyde Park Biodome, London

'As always, I would like to thank our hosts at Hyde Park for staging this spectacular display of the remarkable talents our nation has to offer.'

Roaring applause.

Breathe.

'Of course, we wouldn't have anything to celebrate if it wasn't for the hard work our wonderful students put in over the years to get to this stage,' the mayor continued, smiling into the lens of the drone hovering at her eyeline.

More thunderous applause.

Just keep breathing.

'Are you all right up there, Akaego?' A voice crackled in my ear.

Rosita.

I squinted at the sea of faces in the tiered seats in front of me, although I knew she wasn't amongst them. With the interjected commentary she'd been giving from her hiding place ever since I stepped on to the podium with the other performers, I'd wondered if she'd forgotten I was looped into the channel Jaden set their walkie-talkies to. But she was most definitely referring to me this time.

'Scratch your chin if that's a yes.'

I obeyed, having no way of relaying my worries to her through the one-way earpiece hidden underneath my braids. We'd decided against giving me a mic because there could be a clash when I had one fixed to my lapel for my display later on.

My concern about having my voice blasted across the park had been eased when I found out at a dress rehearsal a couple of weeks ago that the mic would only pick up sounds for the home broadcast. The organisers weren't rash enough to risk a Mechsim's stray frequency causing the park's long-standing plant life to grow out of sync.

'Maybe she's just tired of hearing you go on.' Jaden's voice came through hushed as he was near his classmates. 'You know she can't ask you to shut up.'

I tried not to smile.

'Sod off, Jaden,' Rosita snapped.

'I can't, you'll miss me too much.'

I felt myself relax a little. Whether he intended it to or not, his wisecrack did the trick.

The truth was, Jaden was way off about the reason for my concern. Clips of past pageants we'd found showed performers, a bit of grassy backdrop and the odd shot of audience members. Now, from my vantage point onstage, it was impossible to count the number of trees surrounding the area we'd been designated.

Great, big, mature trees covered in beautiful foliage.

The mayor must have been certain my enhancer wouldn't work if I tried to use it. Knowing what we planned, even if my mic wouldn't be set up to affect them, the sheer scale of the greenery made me uneasy.

As if she knew I had her on my mind, Mayor Bernard turned to our group with a smile. I'd missed what she'd said, but she was gesturing towards Joon, who should have been with the rest of our graduating year on the larger podium to the left of ours.

Like all of us students, he was cloaked in a heavy black robe with a tasselled flat-top cap. It did nothing to hide the vibrant candy red of his shirt beneath it. He had also dyed his hair the same shade, just in case we somehow missed the shirt. He didn't look pleased about being assigned a spot beside his mother. Every now and then, I caught him glancing my way, but his gaze didn't linger.

The mayor stepped away from the lectern, letting a stout, salt-and-pepper-haired woman in a cream jumpsuit take her place, and I stiffened.

'Maybe we should grab her attention now and get this over with,' Rosita said as Chancellor McKenzie began her much less gushy speech.

I don't know why I'd imagined she'd be sitting at home on a day like this. The fact that this soft-spoken, powerful force would witness my ability first-hand was what we wanted, yet I found myself wringing my hands under my robe. I had no idea who might have ties to the mayor, but surely one higher up had to be clean. I just wished we knew who. I couldn't stop thinking what might happen if this didn't work. If their reaction would be to hide me away like the mayor intended. If their moral objectivity would be skewed towards her ideals.

I shifted my attention to the main crowd again. Most guests were enjoying the opportunity to bask in the radiance of the sun without suits, waving at family members on the graduation podium, or smiling wide at the airborne drone cameras transmitting the event to millions of homes across the country.

I wasn't surprised to spot Dad and Mum upfront in the second row. Freshly shaven and in a white collared shirt and black trousers, no one would have guessed Dad had been escorted directly from the detention centre. But even from that distance, I could tell he'd lost more weight.

The only thing that warmed my heart was seeing Mum's hand intertwined tightly with his. Her visits seemed to have repaired some of the damage between them. Dad's free hand rested firmly over theirs.

When I turned my head to the right, the anxiety on Mrs Miguel's face was clear, from where she and Mr Ericsson sat amongst a group of academic staff. The cover story we'd been given was that a minor glitch with my enhancer meant it couldn't be tested. Despite multiple assurances the issue would be fixed in time for my display, my ambitious head teacher wouldn't be sitting still until I actually pressed down on my neck.

'Hey, what are those?' Jaden asked.

'The poles?'

I looked up as subtly as I could on Rosita's direction. I hadn't noticed the dark grey metal rods hovering high above the stage. Now I did, it was impossible to miss the orange flashes that lit up the bottom of each pole in a rhythmic pulse.

'I'm not sure,' Rosita went on. 'Probably decorative like all the other frilly nonsense they've decked this place out with.'

There was a pause before she spoke again.

'Wait, Carl thinks they could be blockers. Makes sense after our little act at the reception.' She chuckled slightly.

I glanced up once more. We'd considered the security measures in a crowded scene like this, but we'd discounted electromagnetic signal blockers. The rods looked nothing like any blockers I'd seen. Those were usually white shiny metal panels. Besides, they wouldn't install anything that could affect the enhancers we were expected to use for our displays.

'Should we be worried about flash bombs?' Jaden said the words I couldn't voice.

'We've heard nothing at our end. Doesn't mean there isn't a solo set-up like what we're planning. Let's just hope we get this done in time.'

On cue, applause marked the end of the chancellor's speech when she reminded us of the importance of each individual's actions. As she returned to her seat, I could see why she'd been elected as the head representative for all the devolved municipalities. Like Mayor Bernard, the chancellor had a quiet but strong countenance that resonated even when she was silent. I really hoped that was where their similarities ended.

Our group was swiftly ushered offstage to make space for the showcase. Other than the performing arts, there weren't a lot of skills worthy of fanfare, but the organisers always gave random acts a go. Besides my well-advertised appearance, the current buzz was about some chemists paired with an oboist to put on a display that resembled a magic trick.

I was scheduled as fourth out of ten, sandwiched between a Liverpudlian ballet troupe and the excited chemists who still couldn't believe they were allowed to participate. I almost felt sorry the world would never get to see their act.

'Are you nervous?' a pimple-faced boy with a Geordie accent asked as we watched the show from the sidelines.

My hand unconsciously shot to the bulge behind my left earring. Joon had done well with his search, taking the covert nature of his mission very seriously and slyly passing his find to me in the packed corridor at school without a word. Jaden bonded the chip he'd adapted to the stubby tantalum coin and then to the wide face of my earring, which we'd covered again with the stiff adire fabric.

359

'A little,' I lied, not wanting to let on how petrified I was.

'I'm absolutely bricking it,' he laughed uneasily. 'You music people get to perform all the time, but we're usually stuck in a lab.'

I smiled politely. There was no point in correcting his misconception about me.

'And now we are going to be treated to something truly special,' Mayor Bernard announced with relish. 'Something we've not had the privilege of witnessing at these pageants for a few years. From my very own city's Academy of Music, please welcome Akaego Eke to the stage.'

I froze. We had been waiting months for this moment, yet it felt too soon. I would have given anything to turn and flee, but I knew this wasn't just about me. This wasn't even about my family and friends any more. If the mayor got away with using my ability, there was no telling what other secret pot she would stick her fingers in. No knowing if she would try to explore the effects on humans.

'Be a badass,' I said out loud, receiving a puzzled smile from the chemist boy before I placed my foot on the first step and power-walked my way up.

The audience applauded, and my confidence wavered. I felt totally exposed. Without the others, all eyes had nowhere else to focus but on me. We'd been allowed to remove our robes for the performance, and I was wearing another of Mum's outfits, a bright green

360

and yellow adire jumpsuit she said showed the essence of my life-giving ability. An ability she chose not to see as destructive despite all the evidence. Something I still wanted to believe was true.

I risked a glance at my parents. The distress on Dad's face was painfully obvious. Mum was wincing from how tightly he held on to her. That was the push I needed. I had to end this as quickly as possible.

For everyone to get the best view, the organisers always created a green wall instead of a flower bed. At two metres high and just as wide, it was the most stunning arrangement I'd ever seen, dotted with a colourful array of flower buds. Daisies, primroses, asters, marigolds, lilies, and a host of wild flowers I couldn't easily identify. They would definitely make an impression when in full bloom. It was a shame they'd have to die so soon.

Silence descended when I turned my back on the audience. Clearing my throat, I took a step closer to the wall, hoping to reduce the surface area my voice would hit directly. It was probably a good thing I couldn't see his face because Mr Ericsson would be frowning. He had been nearly as frantic as Mrs Miguel when he learnt my enhancer was set to safe mode. My odd positioning would do little to ease his concerns.

'Good luck,' Rosita and Jaden chorused. They had been quiet for a while, and I suspected the nerves were kicking in for them too.

Struck by a sudden burst of self-assurance, I turned

to face the mayor so she could see the moment the blue light flashed. So she could remember the moment her plan was quashed, even if she hadn't realised it yet. Her eyes narrowed with slight curiosity, but her smile didn't shift.

I pressed down on my neck.

Nothing prepared me for the spasms that shot down my neck, forcing my head to jerk upwards. Mr Ericsson never mentioned any side effects of this nature. The simulator had been painless on testing day. I'd felt fine when we tested the polarity-reversing chip two days ago and Rosita's device had shown we'd succeeded in activating the enhancer.

So what the hell was happening?

'What are you doing?' Rosita hissed. 'You have fifteen seconds before the chip shuts off.'

I had stopped, transfixed by the metal rods above my head. The lights at their bases no longer pulsed orange; instead, they flashed with a bright red intensity that would probably hurt my eyes if I carried on staring at them. But Rosita was right. I didn't have time to wonder what any of this was about.

Without holding back, I let my voice flow out at the right frequency and started a silent countdown. I was three seconds in when loud gasps of delight hit me from behind before almost instantly plunging into sharp inhales of horror. I'd known what to expect, yet like everyone else, I was stunned by what played out before me.

One second, the buds were opening with a beautiful flourish, reaching towards the sound of my voice like it was the elixir of life. The next, they recoiled like they'd been stung, drooping as they began to wilt. Some smaller flowers were already beginning to fall off the rapidly browning stems which held them to the wall.

'It's happening too fast.' Jaden's voice echoed the alarm I felt.

From the trajectory we'd worked out based on the progress I'd made at my last few training sessions, they weren't supposed to start dying for another few minutes.

'I think you'd better stop.' Rosita sounded equally anxious.

She didn't have to tell me twice. Fifteen seconds were already up, and with the damage I'd done, I had no intention of letting any more sound out. But when I tried to shut off my voice, I couldn't.

I literally couldn't stop the low-pitched sound pouring out of me.

It was like something had hijacked my body, forcing my jaw to slacken and my vocal cords to stay open. The scariest part was that with my head still angled upwards, I could see leaves on the trees at the back of the stage slowly starting to brown. The sound was being projected further away than we'd imagined.

My hand shot to my neck, and I pressed hard on the enhancer.

Nothing happened.

'You need to shut it down!' Jaden yelled.

Couldn't he see I was trying?

The gasps behind me escalated to screams, but I didn't dare turn, afraid the focus would shift and spread the damage I was inflicting on the trees in my line of sight. An announcer was asking people to stay in their seats. One of the trees in the direct path of my voice had already withered so much, it leaned dangerously towards another equally parched tree.

'Akaego, stop.' This unexpected voice came from right beside me.

Joon.

Something was obviously wrong, and he was the first to reach me from his nearby stage seating. I shook my head, unsure of how to tell him I was stuck. I knew Mum and Dad would also be trying to get to me, but I wasn't sure if they would have an easy path from the stalls.

'Get away from her, Joon!' I heard the mayor's panicked appeal from the side. 'We have to get to safety.'

Joon didn't move.

'It's going to be okay,' he said to me, despite having no way of ensuring this.

A loud snapping sound shifted our attention back to the trees as the leaning lime gave up trying to hold its own weight, crashing into the one next to it and causing that also to fall over. I dropped to my knees, hot tears stinging my eyes.

Why couldn't I stop this?

'What the hell is happening? How is she doing that?' Jaden said in my ear, addressing Rosita.

'I don't know,' she replied wildly, 'but we have to stop her or there'll be nothing left to save.'

Thank goodness! If anyone was going to figure out a way to help, it would be them.

'And how exactly do we do that?' Jaden asked. He sounded slightly breathless, like he was running.

'We have to break the sync.'

Wait, that didn't sound right. If they tried to sever the link the enhancer had with my brain, things could get even more out of control. When we jacked the implant up with the chip, we must have messed with something that controlled my neurological abilities. We'd already established this was territory we were even less sure of.

'No, it's too soon, it could kill her,' Jaden said.

If I could hug him, I would have. But now he'd put a greater fear in my mind. I hadn't considered death. Mine or anyone else's. We weren't there yet, were we?

Just then, an armed guard appeared in front of me and gripped my shoulders, shaking my body fiercely.

'No!' Joon jumped up and prised the man's hands off. 'Can't you see she has no control over this? We need to figure out what's going on.' He turned to me with so much worry in his eyes, I felt my tears start to flow.

Two more guards had come up to us, but someone must have asked them to stand down because they nodded and waited.

Although she couldn't possibly have heard Joon, Rosita was the only one not having any of this wait-and-see mentality. 'Would you rather she brings it all down?' she asked Jaden. 'We have to try.'

I could see why she thought that way, but there was no way I was letting things go that far.

Almost as if the universe was laughing at my optimism, another tree fell heavily in the distance. All I could think was that millions of people were watching this at home. We had wanted them to see the destructive potential of a Deathsim, but not like this. Dad's ability was never enhanced for any of us to have known what to expect, so what if this really was what we were?

Monsters.

As if he'd read my mind, Joon knelt with me. 'I'm going to cover your mouth,' he said gently. 'Is that okay?'

Why hadn't I thought of that? Even if we didn't block out all the sound, maybe we could reduce the effect of what was being emitted. When I nodded, he placed a shaky palm over my open mouth. The effect was instant, muffling my voice to a steady hum. I knew it didn't solve the problem, seeing as a simple hum in a skills lab was what started my Mechsim journey, but maybe it would buy us time.

'Are you still there?' Rosita asked Jaden in my ear. I could also tell now that she was on the move.

'I'm thinking.'

'While you take your time doing that, I'll just go ahead and start programming the disconnection.'

'Wait!' Jaden shrieked.

'We don't have time for this.'

'Okay, fine!' he barked. 'Do it. Just promise me one thing.'

'What?'

'If she has to die, make it quick.'

What the actual—

'Don't be ridiculous!' Rosita's shrill yell nearly pierced my eardrum. 'Of course I'm not going to let my friend die.'

Over the last few weeks, I had been the only one to refer to what we shared as a friendship. It was funny how hearing that word even in that critical moment filled my heart.

'Akaego!'

I looked up to see Mum and Dad had made it to the stage. There was a small cut on Dad's left cheek, and Mum's blouse was ripped at the sleeve.

'Is it the disruptor?' Dad asked, kneeling beside Joon, only briefly glancing at the position of his hand. 'Where did you try to hide it?'

He had the disruptor part wrong, but he reminded me of the effect the earring could still be having on the enhancer. We'd programmed it to switch off after fifteen seconds, but it may have done the opposite and amplified my frequency to a point where I couldn't access it.

I yanked at my left ear, only registering a slight twinge of pain as my skin split to release the metal stud. My heart sank when I heard it clatter to the floor and watched Dad stamp on it but still found I had no control of any muscles connected to my vocal area. Even with Joon covering my mouth, each breath I took was becoming progressively more laboured as my nostrils struggled to compensate for the air leaving my body.

'We could try a sedative,' Mum suggested, her eyes red with tears. 'There must be a medic with shots we can give her. She can't possibly go on if she's asleep.'

Before I had time to consider this, Rosita's voice came through again.

'Akaego, I don't know if you can still hear me, but Carl stopped me from breaking the connection,' she said. 'He has an idea. Something about destructive interference. Please hang on, we're nearly there.'

Destructive interference?

Of course! Carl was truly brilliant and remembered what I'd said in Mum's study. Even if we didn't share the same frequency, there was a chance a head-on clash with a similar enough growth-stimulating frequency could create a distortive effect that would break this loop. The only problem was, as far as I was aware, he hadn't found his frequency.

I signalled to everyone surrounding me to wait, but I didn't have to. Carl suddenly ran up behind Dad. It was impossible to miss the new jagged scar on his forehead. Despite that, other than being out of breath, he was the only one who didn't appear completely freaked out.

I pushed Joon's hand away and indicated for them to let Carl through.

368

'He knows what he's doing,' I heard an equally breathy Rosita explain from the side, even though she must have had no idea if it was true.

Carl crouched where Dad had been and held my hands. 'It's okay,' he said quietly, offering me a small smile. 'I've been practising. I'm going to smash this.'

I squeezed his hands back tightly, hoping he could see my gratitude through my tears. If he succeeded, everyone would know what he was, yet he was willing to sacrifice his future and his liberty to save this park from falling apart.

Standing and stepping back until he was about a metre away, Carl tilted his head downwards to compensate for my kneeling position. We had no way of knowing if it was a direct path, but we didn't have time to work that out. The sound he released came out shaky and much higher pitched than mine. He cut it off quickly.

'What is he doing?' Jaden asked behind me and received no reply except a shush from Rosita.

Carl squared his shoulder and tried again, this time letting out a steadier sound at a different pitch.

'It's not working,' Dad snapped. 'We need that sedative now.'

'I have one more,' Carl stopped and yelled with a head shake. He didn't wait for permission before hitting me with a third blast.

The instant his voice reached mine, I felt a sharp throbbing in my aching throat, like a pulsing wave trying to force itself down my open mouth. Carl was on to something, but I could tell the intensity wasn't enough. I needed a more direct hit.

Staggering to a crouching position that brought me level with him, I gripped Carl's shoulders, pulling him closer, praying he would understand the signal I gave him with my watery eyes. This wasn't just about frequencies; the power of his output had to be close enough to trip mine, and he wasn't giving it his all. He looked confused until I pressed down on his shoulders, then pressed down again, harder. His eyes lit up. With a nod, he also held my shoulders, pushed his face closer to mine and yelled his frequency at the top of his voice.

It felt like my throat would explode as the sound he emitted hit me with full force. But the sensation lasted only a moment. The tension I didn't realise I was holding in my shoulders eased as the area surrounding my enhancer tingled. The numbness that followed was such a sharp contrast to the strain my body had been feeling, my eyes widened.

Triumph registered on Carl's face as he noticed my reaction before he gave one final powerful push, his body trembling with the force he put into it.

And then there was silence.

For a second, I couldn't tell if I was imagining it. I was too afraid to turn towards my family and friends, in case I was the only one who had stopped hearing the awful sound. The catastrophic effect on the trees ahead of me was ongoing as they continued to fall.

It was only when Mum pulled me into her arms that I knew something really had changed.

Carl had done it. We'd done it.

I shut my eyes, feeling Mum's tears mingle with mine, letting my body rock with the violent sobs that ravaged hers just before I let exhaustion take over as I slipped into the warm bliss of unconsciousness.

CHAPTER THIRTY-THREE

Augmentation Day

'I think she's waking up.'

'Thank you, Daddy Lord, Jehovah Sabaoth!'

Turning my head in the direction of the drawn-out exclamation that could only have come from my mother, I opened my eyes and blinked. Sure enough, her face was pushed close to mine, red-tinged eyes and all.

'Ifeatu, give the girl some space.' Dad pulled her back.

'Ada m.' Mum smiled widely, smacking Dad's hand away before she sat on the edge of the bed I lay on and placed the back of her hand on my forehead. 'How do you feel? Are you comfortable?'

My throat was too hoarse for speech, but I nodded, attempting to sit up. With its stark white walls and strong smell of disinfectant, the small room must be part of a health facility. I felt a little dizzy, though I was relieved to note I wasn't hooked up to any of the machines beside me.

'Take it easy.' Dad came closer. 'Ifeatu, bring her something to drink.'

'What happened?' I managed to get the words out before Mum returned from the dispenser with a warm cup of water.

'Where do you want us to start?' she asked.

'Are we under arrest?'

I wasn't cuffed to the bed, and I could see nothing binding Mum and Dad, but that didn't mean we weren't confined to the room. Or that we weren't in some heavily guarded black site.

'That's a little bit complicated at the moment,' Dad admitted with a faint grimace. 'Let's just say we are currently negotiating on where we go from here. But for now, we are not anyone's prisoners.'

I let out a sigh of relief.

'You chose your friends well,' Mum added with her unwavering smile. 'A lot of this has been courtesy of their efforts.'

I shot her a quizzical look. 'My friends?'

She nodded. 'They are outside. I'm sure they'll prefer to tell you some of what's happened.'

'You need to be checked out by a doctor first.' Dad pressed a call button by my bed. 'Your neuroscans showed no adverse residual effects from the seizure, but you're going to be monitored for a bit longer just to make sure.'

A seizure? Was that what it had been? When I thought of the word, I imagined something entirely different; something with more devastating effects. Uncontrollable jerking limbs, loss of consciousness.

That sort of thing. But now I thought about it, I'd experienced spasms and a loss of control of my vocal area. Maybe it had been a seizure after all.

'Yours was triggered by photosensitivity,' Dad explained, seeing the question on my face. 'Do you remember looking up at the start of your display? There were some poles above you.'

He must be talking about the blinking red lights at the base of the rods. But how could something so simple have set off such a powerful reaction? Something had caused my head to tilt upwards even before the lights did whatever it was they'd done to my brain.

A doctor came in to examine me. She let Mum and Dad stay, so they used the time to explain.

Carl had been right about the rods being blockers. What we hadn't realised was that they were based on a new design adapted to target specific signals the authorities associated with flash bombs. That way they could be installed at events like the pageant without affecting everyone's enhancements.

As it turned out, we'd set up my booster to be on one of those blacklisted signals, so the second I hit my enhancer, the blockers latched on, throwing everything out of sync. When I looked up, the combined effect of the flashing red lights had well and truly messed me up.

'You were lucky,' the doctor said after checking my eye movement. 'The blockers were still on, but by distorting your frequency, your brain was tricked into shutting out the signal. We're going to run further tests and simulations to understand how this was possible.'

'And now we know it was a seizure, a sedative could have worked,' Mum offered. 'I pray we never need to test that theory.'

Although I was glad we knew what caused the issue, I hated thinking we'd brought this on ourselves. If we had known even just a fraction more, we might have avoided all that destruction.

'You can't blame yourself,' Dad said after the doctor left, picking up on my thoughts. 'I wish you'd been able to tell me what you kids were planning. I admit I would never have gone along with it, but I wouldn't have been able to stop you, so I could have steered you towards the right documentation.'

'Your father is right,' Mum agreed. 'And none of this would have been necessary if the mayor hadn't threatened us. The blame lies with her.'

'What terms are we negotiating?' I asked since she'd brought up the mayor. I couldn't imagine Bernard would be happy to let things go so easily.

Dad's expression turned to one of hope for the first time. 'The chancellor has agreed to launch an investigation into the way the discovery of your ability was handled. One of your teachers sent a query to the Ministry of Agriculture after your test because he didn't think your results matched what we'd witnessed.'

Mr Ericsson? I frowned. He only said he thought the Ministry's report could have contained more details in it when I asked about my results, but he must have been digging in the background. I took back every moment I had cursed under my breath at my tutor's fastidiousness.

'There's a case to be made that you should never have been allowed to be enhanced in the first place. If they're able to recover your original results, it'll be clear there was a cover-up.'

'But how does this provide us with protection? The mayor can say she had nothing to do with it. And everyone saw me . . .'

I broke off, unable to allow myself to think about the plant life I'd killed. All I'd seen was the damage to trees at my eye level; there would have been so much more low-lying vegetation destroyed. And with the scrambling sounds I'd heard behind me, I had no idea if people were seriously injured. I doubted my parents would tell me if that was the case.

'We'll let your friends in. Like your mum said, they'd love to share this part with you. And I'm sure they're eager to see you're okay.'

Jaden, Rosita and Carl rushed in. Jaden reached down and flung his long arms around me.

'I was so worried,' he sighed against my cheek. 'I kept thinking I'd done something wrong with the chip. I kept thinking we should never have tried to do anything.'

'No, Jaden,' I sniffed, wiping at tears I hadn't been able to stop from falling, 'we had to do something. It didn't quite go to plan, but if it wasn't for your help, Dad and I would be on our way to some unknown facility right now, not here with you lot.'

'I thought maybe I'd killed you with that last shout,' Carl joked, despite the anxiety on his face. 'Your mum had to keep showing me you were breathing.'

'Oh, Carl!' I cried, reaching for his hand. 'I don't even know how to start thanking you.'

He grinned. 'It was all because of you though. I wouldn't have found my frequency if you hadn't shared all those techniques.'

'I can't believe I'm saying this –' Rosita smiled too, ruffling Carl's hair – 'but I'm glad this one got it into his silly head to get you to train him. And I'm glad you helped him.'

Mum liked to say that everything happened for a reason. Without Carl's intervention, we could have been telling a very different story.

'Thank you for not giving up on me,' I said to Rosita, gripping her hands. 'And for trusting in Carl's ability at that moment. I'm not sure I'd have been so confident.'

'You haven't even heard the best part.' Rosita smiled.

'Right after you passed out, Rosita had a genius idea,' Jaden explained. 'You know how she likes to work super fast.'

'Hey, how many times do I have to tell you I was not going to kill her?' Rosita huffed at him before turning to me again. 'This was inspired by you, actually. I remembered how you doubted the footage I showed you that first time, and that was because I wasn't telling the story in the most convincing way.'

I couldn't understand where she was going with this until she brought out her slider and pulled up a video-sharing site.

'Is that—'

'Milton Keynes, yes,' Rosita said as I watched myself walk around the artificially lit greenhouse with her, touching plants as I went along.

Without audio, the expression on my face was one of confusion at the impressive achievement the Freestakers had pulled off in the unlicenced underground facility. The next few clips were also familiar to me, although not ones I featured in. Masked agents wiping out greenhouses in dozens of similar undocumented sites, each one stamped with a date and location. The footage ended with a short clip from earlier in the day.

Seeing an aerial view of myself standing on the almost deserted stage, the dried-out green wall in front of me, and a massive expanse of dead trees further away, I couldn't help the shudder that ran through me. The caption running below the video read 'Monster or Pawn?' and appeared to have been posted by an account called TruthBeTold.

I frowned, unsure how this was supposed to have helped. It all looked pretty damning.

'Keep reading,' she assured me.

When I did, I understood. In the description, the author asked whether my ability could be used by the authorities to destroy unsanctioned yet perfectly viable food supplies to stop Freestakers from thriving despite mass shortages around the world. The view count was over ten million and the video had only been up for a few hours. The likes were almost the same number, and there were just under a million comments. I only had to read a few to see why Rosita was so confident.

'That's only one site,' Carl added proudly. 'The video was uploaded to eight, and they've all got similar stats.'

'You obviously weren't going to destroy any of our greenhouses, but I figured we'd play the government's own game and get people to discuss things they wouldn't have taken seriously without the authenticity of the live broadcast,' Rosita said, alluding to how the incident at Crintex had been cunningly used to rack up fear against Freestakers. 'Just seeing your face in the Milton Keynes video was enough to get tongues wagging.'

'People are already signing petitions asking for an investigation into your situation and the food destructions,' Jaden chipped in. 'There are stories from migrants who were deported back to their countries sharing their experiences about what they'd seen here.'

'I can't believe this is happening.' I shook my head in disbelief.

Rosita had been right. Most people might not agree with Freestakers, but they would never ignore irrational loss once they saw it. The trick was finding the right way to sway public sentiments.

'That's all we've ever asked for.' Rosita looked a little teary. 'A fair chance for our cause to be considered without us only being seen as flash-bomb-wielding anarchists.'

'But everyone now knows what you are.' I was referring to Rosita being exposed as a rebel because her face was visible in the video, but I also meant Carl's ability. What did this mean for them?

'What we all are.' Dad spoke up from where he stood near the door and approached the bed. 'I can't pretend we're not all in this together. I became a rebel the moment I chose to defy Stevens.'

He glanced at Mum and she gave him a sad smile.

'That was why I asked to speak to Chancellor McKenzie directly. She's conceded to some form of protection. Whatever I negotiate for us, I negotiate for them.' He pointed at the others.

I could see where this was going now. 'You came to an agreement because the video doesn't just show the mayor in a bad light. Most of those sites were nationwide and she wouldn't have had that much reach.'

'McKenzie may not be complicit in trying to revamp the Deathsim project, but she's not innocent either.'

'It turns out the mayor was already under some suspicion for abuse of power.' Mum took over with a note of victory in her voice. 'We don't know the details, but it looks like she's not going to hold her position for much longer.'

My thoughts rushed to Joon. So far, I'd successfully pushed him to the back of my mind. I wanted to ask if they knew how he was. He couldn't be in the best position with his mother after the way he'd helped me. The rest of us walked into this with our eyes open, but he had been dragged into this mess.

'I told the chancellor about the disruptor,' Dad revealed. 'Once I get it up and running, you will no longer be a threat.'

'But what if I don't want that?'

All eyes turned to me. It wasn't the first time Dad had heard me voice this, but he still looked shocked. After what had happened at the pageant, he must have thought this was now settled.

'What are you saying, ada m?' Mum drew closer. 'You can't possibly want to remain a source of destruction.'

'No, of course not, but look what Daddy achieved by himself with limited resources.' I turned to him again. 'With the best minds working on it, we have to be able to come up with something that lets me keep the best part of what I can do. This time, we will be doing it in the public eye.'

'You're saying you don't mind being studied?' Dad looked so perplexed, it was almost comical. After trying for years to find a kill switch for the Deathsim ability, I had not only exposed his secret to the world,

I was suggesting we work on it with a government he didn't trust.

'We have to try. If not, what's the point of this gift? What's the point of having all these advancements in technology if we can't actually push ourselves? We can't keep living in fear.'

'You really think that's possible?'

'We have to try,' I repeated more quietly.

The room was silent for much too long before Dad let out a sigh. 'It's your voice, Ego, and you're a young woman. It is not my place to tell you what to do with it. I'll be no better than the government if I try to force you.'

Hearing the sincerity in his voice, a weight lifted from my shoulders. All this time I had been trying not to disappoint him and Mum, and it had eaten away at me. Knowing the choice of using my voice was mine was one thing, but he hadn't exactly acted or sounded like he believed that until now.

'Actually, Uncle El,' Jaden said, 'Akaego was hoping to show off her ability as an asset. She has some amazing visions for the future.' He smiled.

'Ooooh, I have ideas.' Carl raised his hand like he was in class, receiving a unified groan from Rosita, Jaden and me before we all burst out laughing. He crossed his arms and pushed out his lower lip. 'Okay, I'll save them for later. Or just keep them to myself.'

'I'm sure you have great things to share.' Mum put an arm around his shoulders. 'But perhaps we should let Akaego rest.'

Their parents had been waiting with them, but no one would be going home just yet. Since we had been exposed as Freestakers and sympathisers, the chancellor had agreed to house our three families securely until things died down. There were victims of the Crintex incident who would be all too happy to take out some of their long-held grievances on us.

After they left, Mum turned to me and whispered. 'You have one other guest.'

'I do?'

'Your mother insisted we let him wait.' Dad didn't pretend he hadn't heard us.

I didn't want to let my heart hope.

'Eloka, let the girl decide. You saw what he did for her. It's only fair we let him say goodbye.'

That was Mum's not-very-subtle way of telling me what this had to be. A necessary end to something which had barely begun.

When Joon entered the room in his ridiculous bright red shirt, it took all the will I had to stop myself from standing. Silly, I know, but I'd come to realise my body had a mind of its own when it came to him. It probably also helped that Dad refused to leave the room, choosing to loiter by the door while Mum went for a loo break.

'Hey,' Joon said, glancing nervously at Dad.

'Hey,' I replied sheepishly, rearranging my loose braids even though I'd moved them to one side just before he came in.

'It's so good to see you smiling.'

My grin widened at his words. I had been pretty stone-faced at school over the last few weeks. Then I remembered why that was.

'I'm sorry, Joon, I shouldn't have—'

'I keep thinking maybe I should have asked what that coin was for,' he interrupted. 'But I don't think I would have stopped you even if I knew the details. Not when you were literally fighting for your life.'

'Is your mum okay?'

'You're really asking that?' He looked genuinely perturbed.

'All right then, are *you* okay?'

He shrugged. 'Other than the fact I may have to apply for a one-way trip to Daejeon to live with my halmeoni.'

'Really?' I couldn't keep the alarm out of my voice.

'Dad never applied for naturalisation here, and he had me registered at birth in Korea, which means I have dual citizenship. If Mum gets charged and convicted, moving there is on the cards. I was never close to Mum's family. Not that they'll want to take me in after, you know.'

'I'm so sorry, Joon.' Because of me, his whole life had been upended, yet he was here checking on me.

'You have to stop apologising.' He tried easing the conversation with a smile which came out as a wince. 'Besides, I have other options. Dad has a cousin in Aberdeen who may not hate the idea of taking in a teenage boy. And since I only have nineteen months until I'm eighteen, there's always temporary state guardianship.'

He was avoiding the main issue, but I could see why he wouldn't want to discuss the fact that we were where we were because of his mother.

'Can I at least say I'm sorry for messing up graduation?'

He let out what sounded like a genuine laugh. 'I think you did us all a favour. No one wanted to see those chemists shake their beakers to weird sounds from an oboe.'

When I laughed in return, I could see how happy it made him.

'I guess now I know you're okay, I'd better get home. Face the music and all. Mum's been calling every five minutes.'

'Hey, are you going to tell me how you knew I was lying all those times?' I asked, not wanting our parting words to be about his mother. 'What's my tell?'

Joon looked puzzled before his face cleared up. 'How about you ask me again next time we see each other?'

Those were the most beautiful words I'd heard in my entire life.

'Promise?'

'I promise.'

Turning slyly to look Dad's way, I wondered if Joon was thinking the same thing as me. That I wanted him to kiss me so badly it hurt. But he must have liked the idea of his neck being left on his shoulders, so he let his index finger lightly trace the back of my hand, sending tingles all the way to my toes. And then, without a word, he turned and walked away.

'Are you okay, Ego?' Dad asked softly, coming to my bedside.

I nodded, putting on the bravest smile I could muster. But when I spoke, my words couldn't live up to the act.

'No, Daddy, I think my heart is actually going to break.'

I'd known we probably wouldn't be able to see each other, but not being in the same city as Joon felt so final. If he went off to live with his grandmother in South Korea or his uncle in Scotland, this could really be the last time I'd ever see him. Like, ever, ever.

Sitting on the bed, Dad pulled my head against his shoulder and let me weep.

CHAPTER THIRTY-FOUR

206 days after Augmentation Day

'You realise how ridiculous this is, don't you?' I yelled at Jaden over the impossibly fast electronic sound assaulting our eardrums.

'You have to feel it, Akaego, feel it, feel it, feel it,' he yelled back, except his words were synced to the lyrics blasting at us from dozens of speakers positioned around the arena.

I laughed when he threw in a leg movement that somehow managed to send his entire body into a roll, making him lean dangerously close to the hefty man in front of him.

'Nah, I'm with you on this one, he's the only one feeling Broxxie,' Rosita cackled from his other side. 'Next concert, I'm picking.'

That stopped Jaden in his tracks. 'Eh, please, none of that Bohemian nonsense you listen to. This here is authentic music. I'll even allow Akaego to choose before I let you drag us through that living hell.'

They began bickering like they always did, only stopping when Jaden pulled Rosita in for a kiss.

'Ew! How many times do I have to tell you—'

'No PDA,' Jaden finished for her. 'But nobody is watching.'

'Oi, when did I become nobody?' I poked Jaden in his side, receiving a playful but painful jab back.

It had been super weird seeing them hold hands for the first time three months ago, but Jaden told me they'd decided to see if their squabbling friendship actually meant something more. What was even stranger was hearing Rosita giggle at the odd corny thing Jaden said when she forgot I was there. I shouldn't have been surprised things would turn out this way when they continued texting each other daily after what everyone now referred to as the Armageddon Day Pageant.

'I swear if you don't cut it out, I'll take this collar off and bring the whole place down.' Even as I joked, I cringed at the thought that people would still believe my voice could cause that scale of destruction.

Maybe not in a venue like this, which had no visible plant life, but I'd been banned from entering large event spaces without about half a dozen safeguards in place. One being the grey metal band around my neck. It didn't matter that my enhancer was deactivated most of the time, only coming on for test sessions I had with Professor Aiko at the Ministry of Agriculture's headquarters in Kew Gardens Biodome. No one was willing to risk another unexpected interference with new or unknown tech.

I hated having to deal with the extra precautionary

measures, even though they were what gave me my freedom, but today was different. There was no way I'd miss Jaden's birthday celebration just because I didn't like the alarmed look people gave me when they realised I was that girl with the killing voice. Especially not after he'd saved enough credits to buy three tickets for this.

'I should have just left you lot at home and brought Carl.' Jaden sighed before squealing with joy when Broxxie launched into an identical-sounding song that only his true fans could differentiate.

Even after all these months, I found it hard to believe what Dad had negotiated for Carl. The whole world saw him use his frequency, so I'd assumed his fate as a Level Two was sealed. Yet, somehow, Dad got the chancellor to agree the choice of his future was his. With all the concessions McKenzie made to the Freestakers, I sometimes wondered if Carl would still end up going up a level. Because now, even if he helped the rebels with his ability like he'd wanted, it would no longer be illegal.

At least for a while.

After multiple petitions were delivered to the government, we were currently in the second month of a five-year parley during which non-stat Freestakers would be allowed to grow their own food without the threat of destruction because they didn't have licences. No one knew what the end agreement would be since the government still held on to hopes the rebels could be convinced to reintegrate, but there had been no kidnappings or bombs reported in these past months, and the prospect of this being a forever thing actually felt real.

My slider buzzed. Rosita caught me glancing at the screen.

'Is it time?' she mouthed, sliding her head behind Jaden's back.

I nodded, feeling the pressure in my chest start to build like it always did when these moments came.

Rosita squeezed my hand before nudging her head in the direction of the door. Jaden was so into the song, I don't think he noticed me slip away. He'd know where I was headed though.

He always knew.

'Hey.'

I turned the moment I stepped into the much quieter, much cooler concourse.

'You've missed the whole thing.'

'I'm sure the birthday boy is enjoying it enough for all of us.' Joon flashed me an easy grin as he lifted himself off the wall and walked towards me.

One day, my heart would stop pounding when he looked at me that way. It had to, right? It wasn't possible that I would always feel this giddy because I knew he'd sat on a train for nearly four hundred miles to see me.

'You just want me to say I wanted you with me for the whole evening.' I pouted playfully when he stopped inches away from me.

He'd cut his hair since I last saw him, which made

390

his facial rings stand out more. I didn't mind the look at all. I just wished I got to see it more often.

'I had to see Mum,' he said quietly.

After Mayor Bernard went on trial and was convicted for siphoning funds from a handful of departments to fund her secret Deathsim hybrid project, the only crime the government got to stick in the end, Joon came down from his music college in Aberdeen once a month to visit her. It cost a small fortune, so it was a good thing he had plenty of credits saved up under his father's name.

People thought his mother's three-year sentence was light, given what she could have carried on doing if the Armageddon Day Pageant hadn't happened, but I reckoned manual labour at a food-growing biodome for even one day was punishment enough for someone like her. The humiliation alone probably kept her up at night.

'How are things with your parents?' Joon asked.

I shrugged because I was never sure how to talk about them after all that happened. It felt weird knowing Mum and Dad managed to keep so much from me and each other for so long. I had a feeling we would never quite get back to where we'd been before, but Dad's behaviour hadn't changed too much. With Mum, it sometimes felt like the things she did these days were an apology for her betrayal, and I still wasn't sure how to deal with it all.

'How long are you here for?' I asked instead, knowing his Dad's cousin never let him stay the night.

'Midnight train. I should at least buy the birthday boy a drink first. How about you?'

'Mum said it was okay to be back by eleven. Plenty of time.'

I'd suspected Mum knew I'd been seeing Joon for a few months. It was pretty hard to hide my dopey smiles whenever he sent a song he'd written for me. I hadn't realised how much of a hopeless romantic she was because, in spite of who he was, I think she warmed to him after finding out how he'd protected me all along. At least I hoped it was that and not her guilty conscience.

I only knew for certain she was on to us after I was playing one of Joon's songs with my name in the lyrics quite loudly. She'd rushed in to get me to turn it down so Dad wouldn't hear. We both knew he would need a lot more convincing. But as Mum liked to say, patience is a virtue.

I had all the hope in the world.

As intense as the year had been, it was good that things played out the way they had. If I hadn't found out I was a Mechsim and moved to the Academy of Music, I would have stayed the same, relying on Jaden's protection, and not giving room for the life-changing friendships I'd formed with Rosita and Carl. I would have continued to be pulled in different directions by what I thought were my parents' desires and my devotion to a system I was raised to believe was always right. I would never have used my voice in the way that mattered the most, to speak up for myself. I would still have been the sidekick in my own story.

And I would never have come to this moment here with this stunning boy who looked at me like I was the only one in the room.

'Want to get out of here for a little while?'

'Not before I do this,' I said, reaching up and placing my lips on his for the briefest of touches.

'Is that all I get?' He stepped back, touching his lips in mock shock.

'Well, I've been thinking of starting a no PDA policy like Rosita, so—'

He pulled me in before I could go on, and I let him kiss me deeply, just like I knew he would.

ACKNOWLEDGEMENTS

I have to start by thanking the Imagined Futures Prize judges who saw promise in my winning entry – Jamie Bamber, Laura Dodd, and Duncan Bell, with Faber's Leah Thaxton, Natasha Brown, and Vicki Cheung. Most especially to Natasha for carrying on with *Augmented* as my editor with the fantastic Jenny Glencross. Your developmental edits transformed Akaego's story in ways I never imagined. Also, thanks to Jessica White, for your clear copyediting, and Susila Baybars, for your keen eye with the proofread. Dani, my authenticity reader, thank you for catching the things I'd never have clocked. And to Jack Bartram, for all your additional support.

Manzi Jackson's cover art brought Akaego to life in the most stunning way with Emma Eldridge from Faber's design team. Thank you to the amazing Bethany Carter and Carmella Lowkis in publicity and marketing. A massive shout out to Simi Toor and Emma Golay for all that you did, and to Ama Badu and the rest of the crew at Faber who made this book a reality (I see you sales, rights, accounts and production teams).

Nicki Marshall and Catherine Coe, I can't thank you enough for choosing me to be part of the All Stories mentorship programme. Nicki, I said I wanted to get the first draft written for the competition in under three months and you didn't say it was impossible. Thanks for believing in me.

I wouldn't be the writer I am without the constant care and enthusiasm of my family. Double shout out to my sister, Nesochi, who alpha reads everything I write before anyone knows it exists, and who listens to me go on and on about how many words I've written (or not written) each day. Props to my mum for beta reading the first draft and calling to make sure I eat well and rest between my writing schedules. Dad, Okechukwu, Chioma, Dana, Ekechi, thank you for being patient with me and always keeping it real. Matthew, Noel, EJ, thank you for showing interest and asking if the book's finished. It certainly is now! Serena, Naomi and Mariah, thank you for always blowing kisses and keeping me smiling. I know you'll read this one day when you're grown.

To my closest friends and cheerleaders who've tirelessly read my stories over the years and were very excited about this one even before all the buzz, Dumebi Ogboli, Nnenna Okarter, Chizoba Onyiuke, Frances Cobley. It's really happening!

Thank you Nazima Pathan and Lucy Hương Nguyễn for being insightful first readers for the opening chapters. I also received helpful first chapter comments from my awesome Megaphone Community critique group. Thank you Kirsty Capes, my HarperCollins

Author Academy mentor, for your early reading and reassurance. To the many brilliant and encouraging writer pals I've made over the years (so many WhatsApp groups, haha), especially my 2024/2025 debut friends, we're in this together!

To Joni Tyler, my incredibly generous boss who lets me be flexible with work and inspires me with lunchtime concerts, exhibitions, and London walking route suggestions. I couldn't ask for a better team leader and supporter.

John Baker, my agent, thanks for sending me that message during that Black Girl Writers' workshop that kick-started our relationship. Here's to future contract signings . . . movie deal? TV series?

And last but in absolutely no way least, all glory to God for bringing these wonderful people and opportunities into my life.

PS: Dear reader, I didn't forget about you. Thank you too.